Praise for *The Poet*

"An absolute keeper . . . There are books I review and love and can't wait to put into the hands of friends who I think will love them, too. Then there's a subset of books I love that will never leave this house, because I want them nearby—to dip into, reread and feel comforted by . . . *The Poet's House* is the newest addition to that subset of books that's staying put. It's a closely observed, droll coming-of-age story about an insecure young woman drawn into a shimmering clique of poets; it's also a wise story about the corrosive power of shame and the primal fear of sounding stupid, unsophisticated and sentimental . . . Thompson's charged depiction of Carla's unfocused yearning to be more . . . powers this story and makes it so emotionally resonant."

—Maureen Corrigan, NPR's *Fresh Air*

"A coming-of-age novel, a novel of manners (Jane Austen, make some room on that big bench, dear), a page-turning narrative with laugh-out-loud scenes, and ultimately a hopeful, affirming book about how words can stir the mystery in us, help us find ourselves, and maybe even make us, however reluctantly, bigger versions of ourselves. *The Poet's House* is a book I'll be recommending to my friends who are readers and even to those who are not, but who will, to be sure, fall in love with Carla, with her discoveries, and with that master storyteller Jean Thompson."

—Julia Alvarez, author of *Afterlife*

"Wry, canny, and delectable . . . As a tribute to the soul-saving value of art, a cri de coeur for women striving to make authentic lives, and a pipeline of guidance from the elders to the emerging, *The Poet's House* offers many rooms, infinitely worth the tour."

—*San Francisco Chronicle*

"Charming . . . Part of the fun of *The Poet's House* is in its small details and memorable descriptions, but the biggest pleasures are Carla's evolution, the many well-drawn characters and subtle pokes at the competitiveness of the literary world."

—*BookPage*

"There's no doubting and no escaping the joyful, hopeful spirit that inhabits *The Poet's House*—the spirit of poetry that by the end of this charming novel Carla so clearly embodies—and the irrepressible Jean Thompson so smartly imparts."

—Ellen Akins, *The Washington Post*

"Ever insightful, imaginative, compassionate, and funny, Thompson is a virtuoso of thorny interactions between wholly realized characters rife with contradictions. And she is so in her element, bringing this richly dimensional book-anchored mise-en-scène to life with lacerating wit and rueful tenderness while adeptly interleaving a poet's long, covert battle against sexism and regret with the verdant tale of a young woman taking root in an unexpectedly sustaining realm."   —*Booklist* (starred review)

"Beautifully rendered with wry wit, unusual charm, and poignant insights."   —*The Christian Science Monitor*

"Jean Thompson is a national treasure. She's the kind of writer who can make you laugh and cry at the same time, a consummate prose stylist whose work is full of insight and wisdom and a deadly keen eye for the foibles and self-deceptions of her characters. *The Poet's House* is yet another indelible masterpiece in her oeuvre."　　　　　—Dan Chaon, author of *Sleepwalk*

"A literary charmer . . . Amusing and true to life."
　　　　　—*Minneapolis Star Tribune*

"Jean Thompson makes hanging out with poets look like even more of a good time than one suspects, in real life, it might be. *The Poet's House* is terrific company: funny, poignant, and full of realistically quirky and original characters. A thoroughly enjoyable read."

　　—Julie Schumacher, author of *The Shakespeare Requirement*

"The brilliantly rendered mise-en-scène of quarrelsome, ego-ridden yet touchingly fragile poets and the literary entrepreneurs who circle around them makes a vivid backdrop for this classic coming-of-age tale. More thoughtful, elegantly written fiction in the classic realist tradition by the gifted Thompson."
　　　　　—*Kirkus Reviews* (starred review)

"Thompson's talents for immersive storytelling and sharp characters are on brilliant display, particularly in her portrayal of Carla's longing for something greater, and of Viridian's conflicted feelings about Mathias's work. The author's fans will savor this."
　　　　　—*Publishers Weekly*

"Surprising plot twists, including a mystery involving valuable missing poems, take Carla to an upscale San Francisco neighborhood and a deep-woods writers' retreat, all populated with a cast of diverse, quirky characters . . . The story is enhanced with dialogue ranging from laugh-out-loud funny to lines of poetry . . . Readers will long recall these women fondly." —*Shelf Awareness*

the
POET'S
HOUSE

ALSO BY JEAN THOMPSON

Novels

My Wisdom

The Woman Driver

Wide Blue Yonder

City Boy

The Year We Left Home

The Humanity Project

She Poured Out Her Heart

A Cloud in the Shape of a Girl

Short Stories

The Gasoline Wars

Little Face and Other Stories

Who Do You Love

Throw Like a Girl

Do Not Deny Me

The Witch: and Other Tales Re-told

the
POET'S
HOUSE

a novel

Jean Thompson

ALGONQUIN BOOKS OF CHAPEL HILL 2023

Published by
ALGONQUIN BOOKS OF CHAPEL HILL
Post Office Box 2225
Chapel Hill, North Carolina 27515-2225

an imprint of Workman Publishing Co., Inc.
a subsidiary of Hachette Book Group, Inc.
1290 Avenue of the Americas
New York, New York 10104

© 2022 by Jean Thompson. All rights reserved. First paperback edition, Algonquin Books of Chapel Hill, July 2023. Originally published in hardcover by Algonquin Books of Chapel Hill in July 2022.

Hachette Book Group supports the right to free expression and the value of copyright. The purpose of copyright is to encourage writers and artists to produce the creative works that enrich our culture. The scanning, uploading, and distribution of this book without permission is a theft of the author's intellectual property. If you would like permission to use material from the book (other than for review purposes), please contact permissions@hbgusa.com. Thank you for your support of the author's rights.

Printed in the United States of America.
Design by Steve Godwin.

The publisher is not responsible for websites (or their content) that are not owned by the publisher.

This is a work of fiction. While, as in all fiction, the literary perceptions and insights are based on experience, all names, characters, places, and incidents either are products of the author's imagination or are used fictitiously.

LIBRARY OF CONGRESS CATALOGING-IN-PUBLICATION DATA
Names: Thompson, Jean, [date]– author.
Title: The poet's house : a novel / Jean Thompson.
Description: First Edition. | Chapel Hill, North Carolina : Algonquin Books of Chapel Hill, 2022. | Summary: "A contemporary story about the insular world of writers, centering on a notable female poet and the young woman to whom she reveals her long-guarded secret about a famous manuscript"—Provided by publisher.
Identifiers: LCCN 2022003016 | ISBN 9781643751566 (hardcover) | ISBN 9781643753003 (ebook)
Subjects: LCGFT: Novels.
Classification: LCC PS3570.H625 P64 2022 | DDC 813/.54—dc23
LC record available at https://lccn.loc.gov/2022003016

ISBN 978-1-64375-392-8 (PB)

10 9 8 7 6 5 4 3 2 1
First Paperback Edition

". . . and thus cruelty, envy, revenge, avarice, and the passions purely evil, have never formed any portion of the popular imputations of the lives of poets."

—PERCY BYSSHE SHELLEY, "A Defence of Poetry"

"What you seek is seeking you."

—RUMI

the
POET'S
HOUSE

POET

Before I met Viridian, I didn't know any poets, any real poets. "Real" meaning other people agreed that you were a poet, and published your poems in books and magazines, and made a fuss over you. Was she a famous poet? What did that even mean? What was a poet anyway? Was that a trick question? I didn't even know what to ask.

Viridian hadn't ever been on television, which is usually what *famous* means in America. Neither she nor any of her circle would have expected such a thing. Every so often a poet might be singled out and elevated by reading at a presidential inaugural, or the dedication of a monument, but that wasn't exactly steady work. People said that books of all sorts were losing ground to videos and podcasts and blogs. The whole enterprise of poetry had been pushed into a kind of outer orbit, unseen but still capable of exerting a gravitational pull, a slow shaping of thought and language that people call culture.

Of course, the poets themselves kept track of their prizes and awards and who had the hot hand. They gossiped and nursed

intricate grudges among themselves. They harbored secret hopes
of literary immortality, of their poems bursting into bloom a hundred years or more from now, like fireweed. And who was to say
it wouldn't happen for them?

But these were all things I came to understand later. At the
beginning, she was just Mrs. Boone, and I was there to put in
some plantings she wanted.

What did I know about poets? Nothing, or maybe less. None
of my schooling had exactly set my soul on fire when it came to
literature. Poets wore berets and drank too much—this at least
was often true—they lived in Paris or New York or they were
already dead, they wrote about going down to the sea again, to
the lonely sea and the sky, or else they wrote in scrambled words
and sentences that an ordinary person couldn't follow, although
they were no end impressed with themselves. I'd gotten along just
fine so far without poetry.

I was so perfectly ignorant, an irresistible blank slate. No wonder everyone took it upon themselves to try and mold and educate me.

My boss, Rick, was going to meet me at Mrs. Boone's house
so he could introduce us, as Mrs. Boone did not want people
just showing up. "Even girls," Rick said, one more of his helpful
remarks. He thought he deserved all kinds of credit for hiring me
in the first place.

I had to be in San Rafael to drop off a part for an irrigation
system, so it was no problem to head out west to Fairfax, where
Mrs. Boone lived. It was May and the sky was already blue and

hot, even early in the day. I hoped I could get the job knocked out before the air really started to cook. Northern California is supposed to have this perfect climate (in between mudslides, forest fires, and earthquakes), but a dry heat is still heat. It could get really hot in Fairfax, where the hills kept the cooler ocean air from piling in. Thirsty deer came down from the higher ground and munched the roses and vegetable gardens into stubs.

I reached the little downtown, with its yoga studio and coffee shops and ice-cream shop and brew pubs and natural food grocery. Fairfax used to have a doped-up, pleasure-seeking hippie vibe, and there was still an air of that left, even as the price of real estate had soared. More shiny new restaurants had opened, more of the old, haphazard houses had been torn down. The vibe was now more like expensive mindfulness. Green Party candidates won elections here; they actually ran things. Nationally owned chain stores were banned, as were pesticides, plastic bags, and Styrofoam. Fairfax was an official nuclear-free zone, for God's sake. Like nukes were some pressing local threat.

I lived in Petaluma, which was less than an hour away but was all box stores and fast food. It was fine with me. It felt more like the real world.

I took a couple of wrong turns off Bolinas Avenue through the flat and sunny parts of town, before I got the GPS on my phone to stop squawking at me and I headed uphill. The road climbed and curved along a canyon, and on its outer edge people had built homes into the hillside below. They parked on pads built out along the roadway and walked down to their front doors.

Mrs. Boone's house was on the opposite side, on the hill itself, at the end of a steep lane. A gate in the board fence stood open. I nudged the truck through the gate and pulled over to one side of a wide, brick-paved courtyard. Rick wasn't here yet, so I stayed behind the wheel to wait for him.

The house was brown-shingled and sprawling, two stories, and it looked like it had been here awhile without much updating. Parts of it seemed to have been built out as additions. One wing ran back to connect with a barnlike garage, while another made up a kind of breezeway with a screened porch at its end. For a hillside house, there was a good amount of sun. The courtyard had a center island planted with agapanthus, it looked like, along with poppies and succulents and lavender. Someone had made an effort at plantings around the house foundation. There were overgrown rosemary bushes, daylilies, Mexican sage, plumbago, and a section where trailing nasturtiums fought with foxtails.

Through the big windows of the breezeway, I saw a flat space of sunny lawn, with deer fencing all around. It enclosed a square of vegetable garden, a few fruit trees, and a great many weedy, terraced beds. Beyond that, redwoods and ferns and the green tangle of woods. The gardens had the look of the house itself, things thrown together and improvised over time.

Rick arrived ten minutes later. His big Ramcharger truck came close to knocking the gate off its hinges. I rolled my eyes at him to make sure he knew I'd noticed. He took off his baseball cap and ran a hand over his black hair to slick it in place. He was always convinced that his sweaty charms impressed the lady clients.

"Oh Ricky," I said. "Hold me tight."

"You're weird, Sawyer."

"Why thank you."

He shook his head. "Nice attitude." His real name was Ricardo, but he thought he'd get more business if he sounded white.

Rick rang the bell, which sounded somewhere deep inside the house. "Any special instructions?" I asked while we waited.

"Try not to screw up."

I might have said something smartass back at him, but the door opened and Mrs. Boone, I guessed it was her, stepped out onto the front porch. She had long gray-and-silver hair brushed straight back from her forehead and standing out like a lion's mane. She was barefoot. She wore loose white linen pants and a blue knee-length top with wide, drooping sleeves. I saw older women wearing clothes like these in Marin, equal parts yoga practice and Star Wars costuming. I wondered how old she was. Sixty? Seventy? Then I found myself asking another question: whether she had been, or was perhaps still, beautiful.

All this in a moment, only as long as it took Rick to say hello and tell her we had everything she'd ordered. "This is Carla, she'll be doing your work today."

I don't remember Mrs. Boone saying much—hello, probably—looking me over while I tried to appear obliging, capable, harmless. She had a wide forehead, and her blue eyes were wide-set also, and there was something about her eyebrows that made you think of birds, the wings of birds, although not until later when you tried to recall what in her face had struck you.

And what would anyone have seen in me? I was tall, a full head taller than Rick, which was why I got away with giving him shit. I wasn't one bit big or muscled, but I could lift my share of loads. My hair was tied up in a knot under my canvas hat. I wore shorts and work boots and my skin was red-brown from sun and full of different half-healed scrapes and bites. At least before I started working this morning, I had been clean.

Mrs. Boone went back inside, and Rick and I unloaded the nursery stock from his truck. There were rhododendrons and hop bush and guara, some dwarf cypress, and salvia and shasta daisies. These were all meant to go in the back of the property, in the terraced beds. Rick went over the plan with me, gave me a little more grief, and drove off.

I'd been working for Rick for almost a year now. It wasn't my dream job, though I couldn't have said what was. After graduation I took some courses at Santa Rosa JC, but I have one of those brains that doesn't process words on a page very well, and I hated composition classes and anything else that was reading-heavy. I was considered "intelligent" (which was something that seemed to be used against me), but also an underachiever. And although the brain wiring was beyond my control, everyone seemed exasperated with me. They believed I was not trying hard enough, not applying myself. My mom kept telling me to go into a medical field, like taking X-rays or working in a lab, but those jobs just screamed boredom. At least, working for Rick, I was outside every day, seeing actual results, things growing. I didn't have to dress up or put anything on my face except sunscreen.

I lived with my boyfriend, Aaron. On weekends, we went out to listen to music, or maybe we'd take his dog, Batman, to the beaches or go camping. We were good together. I figured that one of these days we'd get married, and life would fall into place for us without a lot of special effort, the way it happened when you loved each other. We were lucky to have found each other and we knew it.

But from time to time, I was overcome by a sadness or strangeness, a feeling of too much feeling, if that makes sense, of standing just outside of something desirable and urgent and important. And then I had to get a grip and tell myself, as my mother surely would have, that I must not have enough real things to worry about.

I had a lot of nursery stock to get in the ground for Mrs. Boone. I started off well enough. I had a load of mulch in the bed of my truck, and I shoveled a wheelbarrow full of it and walked it out to the backyard. The edges of the bed with patchy shade, where the rhododendrons would go, were easy enough. The soil in the sunnier portions was hard and compacted. Some kind of deep-rooted shrubs had died there, and I had to dig them out. It was a chore and a half and slowed me way down.

And then came the heat, right on cue. Even in the shade, the air was breathless and unmoving. The house behind me was quiet. In the woods, a sudden bird squawked and then went silent. I had a big thermos of water and a jar of Gatorade. I kept pouring fluids into my mouth and it tells you something about heat and sweat that I only had to pee once in about six hours. I found a wooded part of the lot that was out of sight from the house and, also very important, didn't have any poison oak.

The dwarf cypresses about killed me, as they had the biggest root balls. I watered them in right away, a slow soaking. I needed a break, not just for rest but from my own frustration. It was past three o'clock now, and although I'd saved some of the smaller and easier plants for last, by the time I got everything planted, watered, and mulched, it would be a longer day than I'd figured.

Behind me I heard the door to the screened porch open and I jumped. I heard Mrs. Boone say, "Here's some iced tea for you," but by the time I turned around the door had swung shut again. I saw her head of silver hair as she walked back to the house through the breezeway.

"Thank you," I said, though I doubt if she heard me. I hadn't planned on stopping, but I didn't want to seem impolite.

I opened the door to the porch. The screens were covered over with trumpet vine and the dimness inside made me blink. A ceiling fan turned overhead, and a big electric box fan whirred cool air across the floor. The tea tasted good. I have to say, it all felt pretty good.

There was a wicker couch and chair with some upholstered cushions, and a little table where she'd set out the tea, a whole pitcher of it: hibiscus, which I liked, with a separate tall glass of ice cubes. There was also a plate of small sandwiches, cream cheese and brown bread. I hadn't eaten any lunch. I sat in the path of the whispering electric fan and scarfed it all down.

I should have eaten standing up. Because of course between the food and the dimness and the cool breeze, I closed my eyes and fell asleep. I woke all of a sudden, knowing exactly what had happened and that I'd made trouble for myself. The light outside was sloping into late afternoon. The sweat had dried on me and I felt unwell.

Back outside, I calculated what I might get done before the
light failed, which up here on a hill was likely to be early. I'd water
and mulch everything I'd already put in the ground and clean up
so that everything was tidy and looking good. There was no way
I could avoid coming back tomorrow. Rick would have to be told
something, but I hadn't yet figured out what.

I texted Aaron to tell him to get home early enough to feed
and walk Batman. Then I got to work watering, raking, sweeping
up after myself. I spread the mulch around and dumped an extra
wheelbarrow-load of it on a tarp to one side. I set the unplanted
items together in a place where they'd be out of the morning sun.

When I was done, I carried the iced tea and the empty plate
up to the back door of the house. It stood open. I knocked, then
called. "Mrs. Boone?"

There was no answer. I took a step inside, to a pantry area with
a kitchen beyond. I walked in just far enough to put the pitcher,
glass, and plate next to the sink. I was nervous about being there
and anxious to get back outside. I couldn't tell much about the
room; it was big and dark and there were layers of smells within
it, of cooking but also of something dense and muddy, spices or
incense, maybe.

"Mrs. Boone? I'm sorry, I didn't quite get finished but I'll be
back first thing tomorrow if that's all right. It won't take me real
long."

No answer.

I wasn't quite awake yet, and I had a moment of true weirdness, as if everyone in the world had disappeared while I slept.
Like Rip Van Winkle, but nuttier.

I backed out of there, got in my truck and headed out, stopping to close the gate after myself. I went down the canyon road, careful on the turns. When I reached downtown Fairfax there was still daylight in the sky, but I decided to go all the way to 101 rather than take the back roads to Petaluma and dodge the deer, who liked to practice jumping in front of headlights right about now.

I texted Aaron that I was on my way, and he texted back, COOL, NO RUSH, BE CAREFUL

Of course the traffic was a slog and slowed me down. It wasn't entirely unwelcome to have a little time to myself, a chance to shake off the peculiarness—if that was a word—of waking up alone in a strange house and come back to myself again.

By the time I parked next to Aaron's car and opened the front door, I was good and tired in a way I hadn't been when I left. Batman thumped his tail from his bed in the corner. Aaron had heard me pull up and already had a Sierra Nevada in a holder for me.

"You're the best," I said, reaching for it, but he held it above him until I kissed him. He was tall, like me, so we were always knocking our heads into the cupboards.

"I need a shower," I said. "And then I want to eat a lot of whatever is in the oven."

"Enchiladas. Chicken with green chiles. Hurry up, I'm hungry."

Maybe this day was turning out well after all. I stooped to pet Batman. He was an eight-year-old German shepherd, getting gray around his muzzle. He was Aaron's dog, at least to start with. I was still getting used to the idea of things that were his, things that might now be ours. We'd been living together almost a year now. A year seemed like an important marker.

The shower felt good, it melted the soreness right out of me. I knew I'd struggle to stay awake after dinner. It was hard to be good company during the week. Aaron had an office job, in the IT department of a banking headquarters in Santa Rosa. Computers. Smart guy, or at least, smarter than me.

"Hard day in the field?" Aaron asked me as we ate. He had a shaved head and a dark moustache and beard that he kept trimmed short, and people sometimes mistook him for a biker if he wasn't cleaned up for work, and maybe even then. He was so not like a biker. He was a total sweetie.

"It shouldn't have been that hard, but it stretched out longer than I wanted." I wasn't going to talk about falling asleep, literally, on the job. It was embarrassing. "I have to go back tomorrow and finish up. Ricky will be unhappy. How was work for you?"

"Good. Nothing broke down. Nobody threw anything." We never spent much time talking about work. We didn't really intersect there, and there were more interesting things to talk about, like what to do on the weekend, or the people we knew, or what movie we wanted to watch, or, though we didn't say it in so many words, how lucky we were to have each other.

After we ate, I went out to water my fruit trees, apricot and plum, and the two olive trees I was nursing along. I checked the soil moisture in the rest of the plantings. The landlord had let me do over the yard with ornamental grasses and other low-water perennials. I was trying to make it into something people would notice, something that showed what I could do with my materials.

Before bedtime, which came pretty early, Aaron and I took
Batman for a walk. The pavement was still hot under our feet, but
the air had cooled way down. Our neighborhood was between 101
and another main road and was an unfancy mix of mobile homes
and small bungalows like ours. It had ragged bits of open space
along the roadways and in between developments so you didn't
feel closed in or on top of somebody else. I thought it was a fine
place to live. I had just turned twenty-one and it was my first real
place after moving out from my mom's.

I was dragging as I walked. "Sorry," I said, trying not to yawn
so hard I fell over.

"You figure out what you're going to tell Rick?"

"Yeah, my truck has an oil leak. It's not so hard to believe."
Mrs. Boone was being charged by the job, not the hours. It
wouldn't make any difference to her.

"It'd be great if you could be your own boss," Aaron said, in
that casual way he had of sneaking up on a suggestion. He didn't
fool me for a minute.

"Then I'd have to work harder."

"You wouldn't have to. You'd be a better manager than him."

"He's not so bad at it." I had a perverse urge to defend Rick.

"Or you could run a nursery. A greenhouse. You wouldn't have
to drive all over the Bay. I'm just saying, there are possibilities. If
you want to stay in this line of work."

"It's okay for now," I said. I appreciated that Aaron was looking out for me. But I didn't want to feel like a problem everybody
had to solve. You could get tired of all the encouragement.

The earliest we were supposed to show up at a client's house was eight a.m., and I was going to push that a little with Mrs. Boone, so as to head off the wrath of Rick. I was out of the house way before seven, while Aaron was still sleeping. I took the back roads this time. They were prettier, you just had to not be in too much of a hurry, especially since there was still fog in the valleys and along the reservoir, and not much out here except cattle if, say, your truck sprang an actual oil leak and you needed help. Aaron had a point about all the driving I did for work.

I went over White's Hill and on into Fairfax and found Mrs. Boone's road without too much trouble. When I reached her gate it was shut, and I had one of those oh shit moments when I saw all my cleverness coming apart, and I'd have to call Rick and tell him how I screwed up so he could call Mrs. Boone to give me access. But the gate wasn't latched from the inside, and so I opened it and pulled up in the same spot as yesterday and closed the gate behind me.

My plan was to sneak around to the back, ninja quiet, get the rest of the plantings in, water, etc., then ease my way out again. I was careful with the tools so as not to drop or bang anything together, even though from what I could tell of the house, I wasn't close to any bedroom windows.

I started in and worked as fast as I could. In my mind I was already done and on my way to the job in Corte Madera where Rick was probably even now using my name as a swear word. Then a man walked around the edge of the house, the same way I'd come. He stopped short on seeing me, held up one finger of one hand, and I think the word I'm looking for is *declaimed*:

I heard an old religious man
But yesternight declare
That he had found a text to prove
That only God, my dear,
Could love you for yourself alone
And not your yellow hair

He stopped and gave me an expectant look. I mean, WTF. "My hair's not yellow," I said, just to be saying something. I'd left my hat in the truck. Mistake.

He shrugged this off. "It's close enough." He was about fifty, I guessed, with a fleshy, sagging face, a high forehead, and long, droopy hair. He had one of those big chests and big bellies supported on skinny legs. I've had to deal with obnoxious men before, who hasn't? A couple of times on the job, and once I had to use the electric hedge clipper to get a guy to back off.

I had to make up my mind about this character in the spaces between words, since there were at least a couple of ways things could go wrong. Just to buy more time, I said, "Are you Mr. Boone?"

He seemed to think this was funny. "Ha! No such person!" He wore long, baggy shorts, a black T-shirt, and rope sandals. In Marin you could never tell if people were bums or billionaires.

"But you live here," I said, since it was easiest to keep talking. "With Mrs. Boone."

"Is that what she's calling herself now. I'm in residence. Is Viridian up yet?"

"Who?"

"Viridian. Like the pigment." I expect I had the same suspicious look on my face. "It's a color," he told me. "Green."

We were back to colors now. "I just got here," I said. "I haven't seen anybody." I started in digging again. I wasn't afraid of him by then, but a planting spade is a good thing to have in your hands just in case.

"You're the gardener, huh."

"I work for a landscaping company."

"That must be great. It's the closest you could come to being a plant yourself."

I looked up to see if he was making fun of me, but he had such a blissed-out, pleased expression on his face, and I remembered my mom saying you could never tell when somebody might be a little bit off, a little simple-minded, and you should treat them charitably.

"You mind if I do my exercises here? I won't get in your way."

"Go right ahead." I was all right as long as it wasn't naked yoga or something like that. I kept digging and didn't look up.

Whatever kind of exercise it was, it involved a lot of loud breathing and grunting, a lot of bending himself double and reaching this way and that. This went on for a while. Then he stopped and clutched at his knees and puffed out his cheeks. His face was bright pink. He didn't seem to be in very good shape. When he caught his breath again, he said, "So how do you like California?"

"Fine, I guess."

"I find it takes some getting used to. I mean, it's like walking around inside a giant piece of fruit, isn't it?"

Yeah, whatever. "I wouldn't know. I haven't lived anywhere else."

"A California native? Wow. I didn't think there were any of those."

"We were hunted almost to extinction for our pelts, but we're making a comeback."

I thought I'd stepped in it and was going to get myself run off the place, but after a moment he started laughing, or wheezing was more like it, anyway, he wasn't mad, and if I could get these last few plants in the ground, watered up, and covered over, I could make a break for it.

Then I heard him say, "Virdie, look what I found in your garden!"

Mrs. Boone was standing in the breezeway, looking through an open window at us. She came out through the screened porch, holding a coffee mug. The man said, "Look at her, she's perfect. She's like something out of a Thomas Hart Benton mural."

To me, Mrs. Boone said, "Is he distressing you?" I shook my head. I didn't trust myself to give any other answer. "Oscar?" Mrs. Boone said to the man. "Would you go get something from the house for me?"

"Sure." He braced himself again on his skinny knees and stood up straight. "What do you need?"

"Anything that's going to take you a long time to find."

He opened his mouth, closed it, then shrugged and went in through the screened porch. When he was out of sight, Mrs. Boone said, "I'm sorry. He shouldn't be pestering you."

"It's okay," I said. "I'm in the way. I should have finished up yesterday."

She was wearing a big gray sweater over some kind of long white dress or nightdress. I kept my eyes on the salvia I was tamping in, but I'd already noted the deep hinged lines around her mouth, the lines in her wide forehead. It was like a beautiful face carved in stone.

"Carla, is that right?"

"Yes ma'am."

"Would you like some coffee, Carla?" Her voice was husky, a little rough, maybe from sleep.

"No thank you. I really do have to get to my next job."

Mrs. Boone said, "It's my fault for letting you sleep. I should have woken you so you could finish. But you looked so tired."

It made me feel odd to learn that she'd come in and seen me asleep. I couldn't decide if it was no big deal, or a little creepy. "Honest," I said, "I just took too long. I'll get everything squared away for you and watered in. You'll want to water every day for at least a week. The cypress need more water than anything else. Early morning's best, it helps prevent wilting."

"I used to be able to take care of this whole yard myself. Not anymore."

"That's what we're here for," I said, making myself into a *we* and trying to sound as businesslike as I could. I didn't much like people watching me, looking me over, whether I was awake or asleep. I didn't like being an object of somebody's stupid comments. I got to work with a rake to spread the mulch around and when I looked up again, she had gone back inside.

When I was done with everything, I packed up and left without seeing either of them, nor did I expect to see them again, until of course I did.

MOM

My mom works hard. She'll tell you so herself. She runs the medical records department at Memorial in Santa Rosa. It's the reason she keeps after me to get a hospital job. She hears about the openings and she knows how to get things accomplished. If I worked at the same place, we could complain about all the people we didn't like, and she could check up on me five times a day. I'm not sure she thinks I could manage to get myself married off to a doctor, but maybe I could snag a pharmacist or a physical therapist.

No thanks. I love my mom, she's awesome, but she never lets up. Her latest big idea was that I should grow legal pot. She had it all figured out: the permits, the expenses, the marketing. I told her she should take it up herself.

It's not just me. My older sister is married with two super-cute kids and she's as settled down as it gets, nice house, loving hubby, etc. And she's still in line for plenty of mom-grief about how she could be doing it all different, or better. Of course, my mom dotes on those kids and she'd do anything for any of us except leave us in peace.

"Your skin is so dry, Carla," she told me. "Your face is going to look like a yard of corduroy if you don't use a better sunscreen."

"I'm thinking of the chicken salad. What are you going to get?" We were in line for lunch at Panera, so I was especially pleased to be having a conversation about my complexion flaws. People were going to be sneaking looks at me, thinking, Yup, yup.

"I thought I wanted soup but now I'm not sure." My mom pushed her sunglasses up on the top of her head so she could see the menu better. You had to let her throw one of her mom bombs, then she'd settle down and we might have a nice time.

We got our drinks and found a table and waited for the buzzer thing to go off. The place was crowded, and I sat with my feet and elbows pulled in so as not to trip anybody up. "I like your hair," I told her. "It looks kind of surfer girl." Or like, Surfer Mom Barbie, but I didn't say it.

"I guess that's a good thing. They put in more highlights." She patted her blonde hair with one hand. My mom takes care of herself. She gets facials and manicures and she's got the makeup thing down but exactly. I expect she's right about sunscreen. She dresses up for work because, she says, she's a supervisor and she'd better look like one. Today was a Saturday so she was wearing casual: pink denim jeans and a white linen top, white sandals. Her fingernails and toenails were pink, as was her lipstick. I always tell her she's way prettier than me, and she says that pretty was a long time ago.

She and my dad divorced when I was five. He lives in Phoenix and he's more or less a nonperson in our lives. Mom hasn't had a really serious boyfriend in all that time. When my sister and I were younger, she'd say she didn't want to upset us by bringing somebody around who might put on a dad act but then go away again after a couple of weeks. She doesn't have that excuse now, she could do what she wants, but I don't believe she's been out on a date for months. Years, even. She says it's too much trouble.

We settled in with our food. "Daniel has another ear infection," my mom said. Daniel is my sister's youngest. "It's that day care. The kids there are always sick."

I knew where this was headed. Something my sister was neglecting or screwing up. Anita and I don't get along all that famously, but we have a mutual defense pact: We don't let mom trash one of us to the other.

My mom took her turkey sandwich apart and set the top piece of bread aside. She'd been on a diet since 1989. "I wish they could keep him home. Find somebody to come in."

"Nobody can afford that, Mom."

"They could if they made it a priority. Netflix is not a priority."

Even I knew that the monthly Netflix bill wouldn't pay for one hour of childcare. If Aaron and I had kids, we'd move to a sealed biosphere. I said, "Day-care kids develop better immune systems, they're exposed to more germs."

"You read that somewhere and accepted it uncritically."

"It stands to reason."

"As long as nobody brings in tuberculosis."

I said, "Nobody has tuberculosis anymore. Seriously, what is it you're so afraid of happening, Mom? You're always pick, pick, picking at stuff, mostly little stuff nobody else worries about. Don't you get tired of it?"

"You mean you get tired of it." This wasn't the first time we'd had this conversation.

"When are you going to ease up?"

"When the world is a righteous and beautiful place. When the lion lies down with the lamb."

"Never mind."

"You think you can go through life being careless. You think there's nothing out there you can't talk your way out of or maybe just give it the finger. I know you, Miss Juvenile Delinquent."

"I was never a juvenile delinquent, come on."

"No, but you wanted to be."

So maybe she did know me. "What does any of this have to do with sunscreen?"

"You know what, bake yourself like a potato, I don't care. But women can't get away with things the way men can. That's the world we live in."

We always seemed to get back to this. How women had to fight with one hand tied behind their backs. How we would be held to unfair and unforgiving standards, how we had to play a rigged game. Didn't I watch the news? Didn't I see what might be visited on me? On any woman? Hadn't I been paying attention? Somehow, confusingly, this all filtered down to things like my failure to keep my eyebrows plucked.

You'd think, after all this, she'd be telling me to run the other way from men, all men. But no. Life was about finding a good man (while avoiding the many varieties of bad ones) and using strategy and guile to keep him home at night. It was not exactly a feminist message, as even I, from my one-half unit of study, could recognize. It was more like she saw it as a hopeless fight.

At least my mom liked Aaron, or said she did. "Just don't get pregnant," she was always telling me. And I never got tired of putting my hands over my ears when she talked about the pros and cons of different kinds of birth control.

We finished our food, and I cleared our trays and plates. My mom fixed her lipstick and we headed out to the parking lot. I asked her what she was doing tonight and she said she was going to catch up on some shows. "Come on out with us," I said, meaning it, but sorry as soon as I said it. "There's a zydeco band. Aaron can take turns dancing with us."

She shook her head. "I wouldn't do that to Aaron. He'd be mortified."

"No he wouldn't. He'd be up for it. He says I dance like a farmer."

She stopped to take her car keys out of her purse and looked at me a little sadly. "You know, sometimes we think things are going to last forever, and they just don't."

"Yeah, okay." I leaned in to give her a kiss on the cheek. I'd meant it as a joke. I wish I could live my life so that I didn't disappoint anyone.

Aaron and I headed out early that night to get something to eat before the band started. We were going to Rancho Nicasio, this little bar in the middle of nowhere. There was a dusty town square with a baseball diamond, a church, a flagpole, a one-room post office. It was like a stage set from an old western. Sometimes people rode horses there and tied them up at a hitching post, mostly for show. Real cowboys don't eat brunch.

We ordered burgers. We were both hungry and we scarfed everything down. Aaron didn't have the daintiest table manners sometimes but that's part of him being so goofy, a big kid in spite of his smarts. "You should get a cowboy hat," I told him. Some of the men in this place wore them, it being horse country. But then, they might have driven over from Berkeley for all I knew.

Aaron ran a hand over his shaved head. "You think? I can't imagine they fit right with no hair."

"Tie a bandana underneath."

"So what are you going to wear?"

"Prom dress with cowboy boots."

"Totally hot."

I started to fill out the details of our new looks, but instead I clamped my mouth shut and got busy with my plate of food. "What?" Aaron said.

I shook my head, a warning. It was no good. He'd seen me.

"Garden girl!" He was standing over our table, grinning down at me.

"Hello," I said. I wasn't on a job. I didn't have to be nice to him. Without looking up I could feel Aaron paying attention, trying on answers. "A jerk from work," I said, not making much effort to keep my voice down.

He was Oscar, I remembered. I don't think he heard me. The room was filling up and getting louder. The band was wandering around the stage and making their electric squawking noises as they tuned. Oscar was wearing a coat and tie, which was the only kind of getup that stood out here. His shirt was red and the tie was lavender with a sheen to it. The coat was black corduroy and he'd been wearing it long enough to bake permanent wrinkles into the elbows. His hair was pulled back in a little ponytail. Nice touch.

Nobody had invited him to sit down, but then, we hadn't told him not to. He pulled up a chair and stuck a hand in front of Aaron. "Oscar Branco."

Aaron had a look on his face like, what's an Oscar Branco? But he's polite. He shook hands and said his name. We were both wondering, Now what?

Oscar said, "So amazing that I'd see someone I know here!" I could have pointed out that he really didn't know me, but I was hoping that he'd go away if I ignored him. "I love this place! It's like, a mashup of American culture. Creole accordians! Suburban cowboys! Dispossessed Spanish and Native Americans!"

He had a way of admiring things, me included, that made you want to smack him.

"I wouldn't go around saying things like that," I said. "People think you're making fun of them."

Oscar leaned in, peering at me. His big loose face worked visibly at remembering. "Carol."

"Carla."

"Carla, I apologize. I talk too much. Everybody says so. How about I buy you both a round of your favorite beverage." He was already waving at the waitress. Aaron and I traded glances. We didn't want to party with the guy, but a drink is a drink.

"Thanks," Aaron said when the drinks came.

I was getting the same feeling as before, of being mad at somebody who couldn't help themselves, like a socially inept child. He was as annoying as hell, but here he was dressed up like he was going to a clown funeral, acting like we were now his good buddies. Clueless.

Aaron must have felt something similar, and because he was nicer than I was, he said, "You haven't been here before, huh?"

"Total virgin. I came with some people I met." He looked around the room, didn't seem to locate them. Aaron and I were drinking beer and Oscar had ordered a glass of white wine. Wine isn't what people usually drink when there's a band. It's not really frowned on. But it was one more thing about him. He said, "Virdie's having one of her workshops. I thought I'd better clear out."

"Virdie?" Aaron asked, still carrying water for both of us.

"The lady I was working for," I explained to him. "Mrs. Boone."

"Viridian," Oscar said. "Boone is an alias."

"An alias for what?" Aaron was still trying to puzzle it out.

"She's the poet," Oscar told us, and if that was supposed to clear everything up, it really didn't.

"Sorry, we don't speak poet," I said.

"Hah, well, who does these days." Oscar shrugged and stuck his nose in his drink. "More people should," he said. "They really should. They should especially know her. It's criminal that they don't. She's the goddamn real thing. The women poets all get put in the same basket. So she's not as angry as Sharon Olds, okay. Not as popularized as Mary Oliver. Blah blah blah."

Aaron and I looked at each other. I guess we'd disappointed him or hurt his feelings, but what were we supposed to say?—Oh, hey, we were just reciting poetry the other night.

"And Mathias. She'll never get out from under his shadow. Even now when he's long gone."

"Who was Mathias?" I asked. Oscar gave me a look that was half pity, half loathing.

"Mathias, oh, only the most famous, brilliant poet of his era."

"Well excuse me," I muttered. I really hadn't heard of him.

Oscar put his drink down. "'It is difficult to get the news from poems, yet men die miserably every day for lack of what is found there.' William Carlos Williams. He knew a thing or two about a thing or two." He nodded at us and picked up his drink again.

I guess I still hadn't learned my lesson. "So what does that mean," I persisted. "What are you supposed to find that you die miserably without."

"Poetry is breath and bread"—he leaned forward, snapped his fingers like a magic trick—"changed into words."

"So," Aaron was laboring over this. "I guess it's supposed to be super important. Like, the Force in *Star Wars*."

"Lord help me Jesus."

"Are you some kind of a poet?" I asked. "Did you write that one about yellow hair?"

"Some kind of a poet, yes. Did I write it, no. It's William Butler Yeats."

I said, "Maybe you need a middle name. Like the other poet guys." I'd had a couple of drinks and I didn't care what he thought of me. Poets were from some other planet. Though I'd liked

Mrs. Boone all right. At least she didn't go around throwing poems at people.

The band started up then and put an end to all the intellectual conversation. They had a hot fiddle player and a keyboardist who kept up with him. People got up to dance and then Aaron and I did, too. In spite of what I told my mom, the two of us were fine together on a dance floor. More than fine. Nothing showy, but we could turn loose. If anybody could find words for how it felt to be dancing right on the edge of the music, high and righteous and sweaty and sexy, now that was a poem I'd read.

The first song led right into a second and a third and after that we headed back to the table for a break. Oscar was gone, I didn't see him anywhere. I can't say we were too torn up about it. We saw some other people we knew and we had another drink with them. We danced some more. Rinse, repeat.

Shit happens, is pretty much my go-to explanation for the universe. Not fate, or God's plan, or everything happens for a reason. If we'd left the bar a little earlier, or stayed a little later? Who knows. Then we wouldn't have walked out when we did. Maybe shit happens for a reason.

Aaron saw me yawning and we got up to leave, even though the band was still cooking.

We came out the front door and into the lit space just beyond it, the covered porch that bordered the parking lot. The bouncer, Roy, was standing over someone seated on the ground. Roy was as tall as Aaron but jumbo sized, and I couldn't see around him.

Roy said, "Let's work on getting up. Count of three."

"The honor of a lady was at stake."

"Yeah, great, but you can't stay here. Either go home or we'll let the sheriff's department sort it out."

We stepped around Roy. Oscar was the shit that was happening. He held a white towel over his forehead and one eye. Blood was seeping through and he kept refolding the towel to try and stop it. "What happened to you?" I said.

"A contretemps. A *liason dangereuse.*"

Aaron and Roy and I looked at each other. I said, "I don't think he got brained. I think he's always like this." One sleeve of his jacket was torn loose at the shoulder, giving him the look of a coming-apart doll.

Roy said, "He took a swing at a guy and the other guy connected."

Aaron bent down and poked and prodded at the towel. Oscar mewled a little, but he let him.

"I'm thinking he's gonna need stitches over that eye."

I bent over him. "Oscar? Hey. Where are the people you came with?"

"He's a coward and a putrid piece of monkey meat."

Roy said, "I think his friend's the one who hit him."

I tried again. "Do you have insurance? Do you have your insurance card on you?"

He muttered something that sounded like "uninsurable." Finally, Roy said that one of the volunteer firemen was in the bar. He could get a medical kit from the fire station, clean Oscar up and probably keep him from bleeding all over our back seat. We were going to take him either home, home being Mrs. Boone's, or to Marin General, whatever the fireman thought advisable. I was so tired, in spite of all of Oscar's drama. I got the keys from Aaron and fell asleep in the passenger seat while I waited for the men to get everything settled.

I woke up when Aaron loaded Oscar into the back seat and started the car. "How is he?" I asked, trying to see behind me. There was an Oscar-shaped heap back there, making distressed noises. Whatever he'd been drinking smelled pretty bad by now.

"Hey man, keep your head elevated. Remember? Sit up. He'll live. We're taking him to Fairfax. You have to tell me where."

It was lucky I'd been to the house twice already, because driving around in those hills in darkness was confusing, and Oscar wouldn't be any help. His head hurt, and he didn't suffer in silence. "So where are you from?" I asked, to keep him from mooing and moaning and carrying on. I didn't want Aaron to get distracted while he was driving. It was too easy to end up in a ravine out here.

"Are either of you a lawyer? I intend to file a lawsuit. Personal injury."

"I hear you threw the first punch."

"Any gentleman would have done the same."

I could see Aaron's face in the green dashboard light. It was not a happy face. I knew he was sorry we'd gotten involved in this rescue mission, going miles out of our way for some silly man he didn't know and didn't want to. He was driving too fast, another sign of pissed-offedness. Nicasio Valley Road was a two-lane through empty ranchland, with the dark curling in over the headlight beams. It wouldn't have hurt him one bit to slow down.

I walked my fingers up Aaron's arm toward his shoulder, but he didn't look my way. Now it was turning into my fault, too, though I didn't see why. I couldn't remember exactly how we'd ended up driving Oscar. I didn't think it had been my idea or anyone else's. The situation had sort of evolved.

"Where you from?" I asked Oscar again. Really wanting to fill the space with a little normal conversation.

"Providence, Rhode Island." His voice was muffled. He was trying to get his coat off and his head was caught inside it.

"How interesting," I said, though it wasn't especially. "Rhode Island, the smallest state."

"It's been miniaturized and now fits in most home offices."

I thought that was pretty funny. Even later, after I found out it was something he said a lot, I still thought it was funny. I laughed. Aaron didn't.

"Do you miss it?" I asked, trying to keep my streak going.

"Haven't seen it for years."

Guess not. "Where have you lived instead?"

"London; Johannesburg; Houston; Ann Arbor; Durham, North Carolina; New York; Boulder; Buffalo. Some others. I forget."

"Why so much moving around?"

"Work."

I waited for him to say more, but he was slowing down, running out of words, finally. Maybe the night was catching up with him. "I didn't know poets worked. I mean, I didn't know there were poet jobs. Like in the classifieds."

Later I learned that there were nooks and crannies in the economic wall, places a poet might get a toehold and hang on. Things like fellowships, residencies, visiting jobs at colleges and universities. Temporary appointments of a few months or a year.

A poet could cobble together an itinerant life, as Oscar had, teaching at one school while applying to the next, subletting apartments, cajoling favors, getting hired at summer conferences, scoring maybe an award or two, and when none of this was going well, moving in with friends until the next gig came along, as he was currently doing, sleeping in the guest quarters above Viridian's garage.

There was no response from Oscar. I turned around and saw his head sagging into a corner of the seat. Eyes closed, mouth open. "Oscar?"

Aaron said, "Let him sleep."

"Aren't you supposed to stay awake if you have a head injury?"

"It's quieter this way."

We'd passed over White's Hill and were heading into Fairfax. "Turn here," I said. I wasn't going to start an argument by asking, Why are you in such a bad mood? He'd only tighten his jaw and say, Why did I think—meaning, he thought he'd be back home having sex by now, though this would not be said in so many words. Then I'd say something reasonable like, You didn't have to say we'd drive him home. But being right wouldn't help.

I guided him up the canyon road to Mrs. Boone's lane. The gate at the top was open and the courtyard was lit up, as was the house. Three cars were parked inside the gate. Aaron pulled up as close to the house as he could. "Oscar," I said. "This is your stop, buddy."

He stirred but didn't wake. Aaron suggested we put him in somebody else's back seat, but I ignored that. We got him out of the car, upright, and walking, sort of, with Aaron supporting him. I knocked on the front door, then rang the bell.

A woman I didn't know answered. She had impossibly black hair cut spiky short, and glasses made of clear pink plastic. Two aggressive fashion choices, I thought. She was staring at us and keeping the door mostly shut. "Hi," I said. "We gave him a ride."

Oscar opened his eyes then. "Christ," he said. "The hens are still here."

The door closed.

Now what. Could we leave him on the porch, even if they refused to accept delivery?

The door opened again. This time it was Mrs. Boone.

I was ready with another speech in case she didn't remember me.

"Carla?" she said. "What's this?"

"He was, ah . . ."

"Never mind. Is he all right? Can you get him inside?"

We could, barely. Aaron half-lifted, half-dragged him across the threshold and through the small entry, into the room beyond. Here in the brighter light, I could see how unlovely Oscar looked, his face splotchy and swollen, a butterfly bandage and stitches on the welt in his eyebrow. There was a lot for me to take in, including Viridian herself, who always eluded any quick first glance. As well as the room we stood in and the two or three other people in it. I was tired and a little drunk and I kept yawning and wondering how I'd gotten my head so far up my ass as to be here.

Viridian—I might as well call her that, it was her name—said, "He's getting too old for this."

Her voice, as before, husky, with a roughness that must have been age.

"I am not."

"Oh do be quiet, Oscar. Can you see my finger? Can you follow it?" She didn't seem all that worried, only grim, in a way that did not bode well for Oscar. She was wearing black pants and a loose white shirt.

Aaron said, "Where do you want him?" He was still propping up Oscar's not quite dead weight. Viridian said they should get him upstairs to bed.

I wasn't all that anxious to help tuck Oscar in. So I stayed behind while Aaron did the heavy work of bumping and laboring Oscar down a corridor, with Viridian following them.

The two women in the room with me, the one with the black hair and goofy glasses, and one with sandy hair and a dry little face, looked me over, sized me up as a temporary interloper, and spoke around and over me.

"I don't know why she puts up with it."

"She has the kindest heart."

"Too kind."

"He certainly takes advantage."

A third woman came in then, carrying a tray of ceramic mugs. "I'm making some matcha. It's sustaining."

"Oh I love matcha."

"White dragon matcha with pine pollen, reishi mushroom, and coconut cream."

"That sounds amazing."

"I'd wait until—"

"Of course."

"She should be more careful. You never know who—"

"Exactly."

They weren't bothering to whisper. It seemed that I was included in the contagion that was Oscar, another piece of riffraff for them to disapprove of. This third woman was, like the others, about my mom's age, that is, forty-something. She and the others had an artsy-funky look (earrings, ethnic print fabrics), which my mom would have described as "rich hippie." I thought of what Oscar had called them, the hens, and I decided I didn't like them any better than they liked me.

Trying to ignore them, I examined the room. Without being entirely crowded or untidy, it was full of a great many things: books on shelves and in piles, pictures in painted frames, candlesticks, pottery, an overgrown ficus, a chandelier made of pink crystals. There was a big sofa, brown velvet with a carved wood frame, sagging at one end. Some other, newer upholstered chairs and one of those lumpy leather ottomans that serve as coffee tables. A sheaf of typed papers was spread out there, and just as I noticed them, and bent closer, one of the hens came along and whisked them away, like I was about to blow my nose on them.

Aaron and Viridian came back then, minus Oscar. Viridian looked tired, but she was smiling, as if there was some humor to be found in the evening, and I guess there was. Aaron, too, looked as if his bad mood was gone. He inclined his head toward her so he could hear whatever it was Viridian was saying, some version of thank you, I imagine, and then she turned her head so that the smile included me.

It was a transporting thing, that smile, as it had probably been all her long life, and I felt its power to fix you where you stood (or sat, or fell); it lifted her beyond age, in a way that the other women present, with their more effortful looks, were not lifted. These women came toward her now, fretful and hovering, offering teacups, concern, questions, and although I still did not like them, I began to understand how they and others might want her attention and approval, wish to be a part of whatever she did, wherever she was. But I did not know if that had to do with love, or possession, or poetry, or all three.

Viridian spoke above them now, saying, Yes of course, and, In just a moment. She walked Aaron and me out the front door and we stood on the steps and she laughed and shook her head and we laughed, too. Beyond the yellow light from the house and the yard lamps, the woods were deep and dense, busy with all the animal life we couldn't see, things prowling, grazing, burrowing. She said, "I hope nobody else got hurt."

"I think he was the only casualty," Aaron said.

"He shouldn't drink. He's been told. At least he doesn't drive anymore."

At least he's good at getting other people to drive him, I thought but didn't say. I said, "I hope he'll be all right." I was mostly being polite.

"He'll be embarrassed in the morning. And feeling sorry for himself. This time tomorrow, I expect he'll be bragging about it. He's very proud of his bad boy credentials. He's so smitten with the notion of the misbehaving genius."

Viridian brought her hands together, indicating that we were done talking about Oscar for the moment, and I realized I was feeling exactly like the hen-women, wanting to be protective of her for expending good will on the likes of Oscar.

"Anyway," she said, "you'll have to come back some time, both of you. I'll have a garden party, we can admire all the beautiful flowers Carla planted. Would you come?"

"You bet," Aaron said, all enthusiasm, and I said, "Sure, we'd love to." She took a step back inside for a pen and paper and wrote down my cell phone number, though it was one of those times when everyone was riding on a tide of cresting good feeling, and I figured that when the tide receded, we'd just as likely never see her again.

We turned to start down the stairs. "You know what I'm going to tell him? Oscar?" Viridian said. "There's an active warrant out for his arrest."

She laughed and waved to us and went back inside and so maybe she wasn't Glinda the Good Witch, or at least, not entirely that.

WORK

That next week, Rick got on my case when he shouldn't have, and we both ended up sorry. At least I wanted to think that Rick was sorry, somewhere below that layer of macho assholeness he wore like a skin. I was sorry, then I was not sorry, and then sorry all over again. None of it had to happen.

It was all so stupid. I delivered the wrong order to a customer, something that was truly not my fault. Rick's mouth-breathing sister-in-law wrote up the tickets while she was glued to her phone screen. And she couldn't tell a cypress from a carrot. It wasn't the first time she'd made a mistake.

So I'd picked up a big blue yucca at the wholesaler. Blue yucca is a total pain to handle, since the leaves are spines and can slice you up. One of the crew guys, Ruben, was with me and the two of us wrestled the thing into the back of my truck and drove to the address in Novato. Rick had taken a picture of the site and staked it, so at least we got that part right. Ruben and I unloaded the yucca, trying to keep the swearing to a minimum. We half-rolled, half-walked it over to the planting site, then shoveled out a crater-sized hole, got the root ball out of its burlap wrapper—I'm making it sound too easy—and shimmied the yucca into the hole. Did I mention it was hot? It was hot.

We were just starting to fill in the dirt around the roots when an undersized old man wearing golf clothes, at least I hope they were golf clothes, came out of the house with his hands on his little hips and asked us what the hell we thought we were doing.

"We're from Greenworks," I said, speaking up since whenever there's any kind of a scene, Ruben starts shaking his head and saying *no hablo*. This from a guy who didn't learn any Spanish until the ninth grade. "This is the plant you ordered."

"Oh, is it now." He was wearing light blue shorts with long, light blue kneesocks to match, and a pink-and-blue plaid knit shirt. You felt embarrassed to look at him, like you'd interrupted him playing some private dress-up game. "Who said you could put that thing in my yard?"

Ruben and I looked at each other. Usually we got yelled at for not doing something. I tried again. "My boss said—"

"I'm talking to you. I ordered an oleander. That look like an oleander to you?" He was so little and scrawny and furious. It was like being scolded by a garden gnome. "Dig that back up and get me my oleander."

"Sir, I need to call my boss first." I got my phone out to signal I was done with him, but that didn't stop Fancy Pants, who was thrilled to catch somebody in a mistake and kept going on about what kind of idiot would think a cactus belonged in this yard, and didn't we know anything about plants, and I didn't bother

telling him that yucca wasn't a cactus, technically, but a flowering succulent. I left a message on Rick's voice mail and then sent
him a text in addition, something along the line of BEING HELD
HOSTAGE BY INSANE SENIOR CITIZEN HA HA SERIOUSLY THIS
GUY IN NOVATO IS PISSED AND WANTS TO TALK TO YOU.

Rick texted back: CAN'T YOU HANDLE IT?

NO, I informed him, then I walked away from the screeching
and went to sit in the truck. After a minute Ruben joined me.

"He went back in the house. He said he's going to call the
police."

"Good idea."

"Shouldn't we dig it back up?"

"This is a Rick problem. For all we know, the guy signed a
work order that said yucca, and now he's trying to get out of paying." I'd started the truck and was running the air conditioning.

I waited for Rick to call or text me back and when he didn't,
I figured he was on his way here. Fifteen minutes later he pulled
up in his Bossmobile, got out, and walked over to us. Through
the glass he said, "Open the goddamn window," and when I did,
"What the hell's going on here?"

"A dissatisfied customer."

"Why are you sitting in there?"

"He performed a citizen's arrest and told us not to move."

"Get out."

I shut off the ignition and Ruben and I got out and trailed
after him as he walked up to the glass patio doors and tapped.
The old man came out right away. "Mr. DeGroot, how are you
today?" Rick said, in his best bootlicking tone of voice.

"How do you think I am? I paid over one hundred dollars for an oleander, and these characters keep trying to tell me I want a yucca."

"That true?" Rick asked me.

"The ticket says yucca." I shrugged. The funny thing was, the yucca was perfect there. I hadn't argued or even offered an opinion, no matter what the old man said. But the yucca made for a good focal point, where an oleander wouldn't have the same presence. The drainage was suitable for yucca. And it went great with his outfit.

Rick was still on his "The customer is always right" kick. "Sir, I'm sorry my employees' response was unsatisfactory. I'm going to make sure you get that oleander. What color did you specify?" Rick took out his phone and started punching things in.

"White," the old man said. "So don't show up here with pink or red. I don't intend to waste any more time on this."

"Sir, we won't. We'll have that yucca out of here in two shakes. First, you two need to apologize to Mr. DeGroot."

"For what?"

"For arguing with him."

"You're kidding, right?" I genuinely didn't see that one coming. Ruben kept his head down, admiring some unusual rock formations around the patio. I didn't expect him to back me up, but he might have shaken his head or done something besides stand there like a beaten dog. "I didn't argue with him. You don't pay me enough to argue with people." All the while I'm distracted by the little old man's blue legs, dancing around, egging Rick on from the sidelines.

"Mr. DeGroot says you did." If it was a joke, Rick didn't look like he was in on it. "He has a complaint."

"Only one?"

"What's that, Sawyer?"

"How about we talk about who wrote up the wrong job ticket."

"Right now, we're talking about your attitude."

Oh were we. He didn't like me talking back to him. I was supposed to go along with his little performance, play stupid, take one for the team. Well, I wasn't in the mood. The yucca had given me a few good cuts, even through my clothes, and they stung, and the heat had turned up a few notches since we first got here. And Rick was a little too into the whole thing, kicking the girl around just to show he could, and now we were expected to get the damned yucca out of the ground, with the rude old man gloating.

I turned and walked back to the truck, removed a couple of tarps and a hose, property of Rick, and laid them on the ground. I saw Rick take a few steps toward me, then stop. I got in the truck and drove off. The rearview mirror showed the three of them standing around the yucca, like kids with a disappointing Christmas tree. I made a turn and didn't see them anymore.

Ruben was going to have to help Rick dig the yucca out again, and I felt a little bad about that but not much. It wasn't as if he'd demonstrated any actual worker solidarity.

I drove around for a while, got on the highway, then got off again. I didn't have anywhere to go. And I wouldn't have anywhere to go tomorrow or the next day or the day after that.

I suppose it was possible that Rick would call me to apologize. Or that I could show up for work tomorrow as usual and hash things out with him. But that was getting less likely by the second.

I wound up at home, two hours earlier than usual. Batman at least was happy to see me. I took a shower and dabbed antiseptic on the yucca scratches. I didn't know what to do with myself. I cranked up the air conditioning and lay down and fell asleep until I heard Aaron come home from work.

I knew all the sounds he made: greeting the dog, unloading his pockets, retrieving the mail. The refrigerator door opening as he surveyed the options. He turned the music on, as he always did. Everything was the same except me.

After a while he wandered back to the bedroom and sat on the edge of the mattress. "Hey Garden Girl." He'd been calling me that lately, like it was funny. He must have seen something in my face.

"What?"

"I walked off the job today." I told him everything that happened. I tried to keep it matter of fact and not sound like a weepy, blubbering female, though I did show him the places where the yucca had torn me up, and made him feel sorry for me. "You should have seen this old guy. If you sent a kid to school dressed like that, he'd get beat up."

I was waiting for Aaron to say how unfair it was, how wrong-headed Rick had been, maybe even make warlike noises about threatening Rick. Not that I expected that to happen; it wasn't Aaron's style. But it would have been thrilling, since Aaron could have squashed him like a bug, and damn it, weren't men supposed to fight for you? The honor of a lady was at stake, as Oscar would've said. Not that I wanted to be thinking about Oscar just then. But Aaron only sighed and looked all serious.

"You might want to think about patching things up with him."

"No way."

"I said, think about it."

"He was a total prick. It's not the only job in the world."

"Yeah, but it's the only one you have."

"Had," I corrected.

"So, there's nothing you can even pretend to apologize for? Did you have that look on your face? The one that says, 'I am talking to the biggest jackass in creation'?"

"I don't do that." Although maybe I did. "Anyway, I don't know how I looked, there weren't any mirrors, and what does that have to do with Rick reaming me out? Don't tell me you'd apologize."

"There's times at work I've had to suck it up and do exactly that."

"How about he apologizes to me," I said. "Sorry, but I'm not sorry."

We were both quiet then. He didn't mention money. We were going to have to talk about it sooner rather than later. I didn't bring home any big paycheck, but we used every bit of it. We could let a few things slide for a while, we could put a few more things on a card. But not many, and not for long. I said, "Don't tell my mom. I'll tell her, but not right away. I don't want to end up wearing scrubs and carpooling to work with her."

"Don't bite my head off, but would that be the worst thing you could do?"

I didn't trust myself to say anything. Now I wasn't just losing a job—or more accurately, walking away from it—I might be herded into one I'd loathe.

When I didn't answer, Aaron said, "All right, don't work at the hospital. Fine. Figure out what you want to do instead. Seems like we're always talking about what you want to do and what you don't. Here's your chance to sort it all out."

"One door closes, another opens," I said, meaning to be sarcastic, but Aaron nodded, like, finally I was getting it. "Could you hold off on the helpful suggestions?"

"I was just trying to be—"

"Because you sound like you think something's wrong with me."

"Helpful. It's called involvement. Never mind." He got up and went into the kitchen and I heard him giving Batman his supper and talking to him in an endearing tone of voice.

Later we started talking again, and I ended up feeling better about things. I reminded myself that nothing at work was Aaron's fault, he was on my side, and that he did want me to be happy, if I could just come around to thinking of myself as a happy person.

We decided that I should take another whack at college classes, either at Santa Rosa JC or College of Marin. I'd focus on business and computers this time, things that other people were always taking, practical, vocational classes that would keep my mom off my case. I'd be attempting to educate and better myself, and who could argue with that? I hoped there wouldn't be as much reading involved. I thought I could tape lectures instead of taking notes. I'd learned a few things about getting by. Meanwhile, I could offer myself online for garden design and maintenance. Rick hadn't exactly made us sign noncompete agreements.

I wondered if other people, people my age, were having as much trouble figuring out their next steps, their places in the world. The ones I'd gone to school with, the friends I still kept up with, seemed settled enough. Why couldn't I just join the army or do telemarketing or hawk cell phone plans or have babies or any of the other things they did, and stop feeling like I was missing out on some important life I couldn't even properly imagine?

Rick never called, which fit into the grand tradition of men never calling. I hustled up a few jobs to maintain some properties weekly, friends of my mom's, mostly. Never let it be said she didn't go all out for family. As expected, she got very excited and hopeful at the idea of me taking more college courses. Never mind that it was too late to sign up for summer session, and never mind that the world was full of underemployed college graduates. I was trying to the best of my limited abilities, and that was something to celebrate.

If it hadn't been for the money worries, I might have enjoyed being my own not-very-successful boss. I still got up early and I still hustled to get the work done, and I had enough time, on hot afternoons, to swim at whatever pool was handy, most often one of the two College of Marin pools. I was thinking I'd try Marin this time around in my brilliant academic career, and I liked getting a feel for the place. Which was how, and where, I saw the poster about Viridian's poetry reading.

It was just a sheet of green photocopy stuck on a bulletin board along with notices about kayaking lessons and dog boarding and math tutoring, but they'd put her name in big script so that my eye fastened on it before my brain sorted it out. It was exciting, like seeing the name of somebody you know in the newspaper.

I stopped to read it through. I'd never been to a poetry reading and I didn't have any clear idea of what went on at one. That is, was it a serious occasion, like church, or was it more rip-roaring? (Depends on the poet, I came to learn.) The poster identified Viridian as a winner of various prestigious awards, at least I imagined they were prestigious, and the author of eight books of poetry, and there was a quote (from someone I'd never heard of, but the name was apparently important), calling her "our modern-day Delphic Oracle," which sounded cool, and that she "beguiles us with nets of artful words that contain hard truths."

Well. It all took my breath away, although I had no clue about oracles or beguilement. It was like a code I needed to crack. The reading was this very evening, right on campus. And it didn't sound like the kind of thing you needed an invitation for.

I called Aaron and I could tell from the tin-can sound of the phone that he was in the car driving home. "Hey," I said brightly. "Want to go to a poetry reading tonight?"

"A what?"

"Poetry reading. At College of Marin. It's somebody you know."

"Oh God. Oscar."

"No, the lady. Viridian." I waited, but he didn't say anything. "You there?"

"Yeah, I had to change lanes. Poetry. So you're an intellectual now."

"Yes, it pays better than landscaping. Do you want to come?"

He asked me when it started and how long it was likely to last, the driving would be a pain. I couldn't argue with that. It was the end of a long day for him, so I let him beg off. It was a little disappointing, because I thought he'd be more excited. I knew he'd liked Viridian.

I swam and then I changed into clean clothes and bought a turkey wrap at the market across the street for my dinner. I found the small auditorium where they were having the reading, and since it was still early, I walked past it all casual, like, Poetry, who, me?

There were a couple of other people skulking around the same way, and one of them, a kid my age, caught my eye and said, "The doors are open, we might as well go in."

So we did. I picked a seat on the aisle, in case I decided to duck out early. I'd seen an old Ernie Kovacs comedy routine once, where Ernie was a poet named Percy Dovetonsils, and wore a paisley smoking jacket and spoke with a lisp. I kept thinking about that and while I knew it was meant to be funny, an exaggeration, you figured it had to be based on something.

The guy I'd come in with sat down in the row ahead of me, a few seats over, so he wasn't exactly trying to sit with me, which would have been pushy. The place was still pretty empty. He turned around and said his name was Matt and he was a student at SFSU and he wrote poetry but it kind of sucked. "That's been the biggest part of my education. Learning how much I sucked."

He laughed, so he was at least good humored about it. He was short, or at least shorter than me, with a lot of dark curly hair and glasses. It wasn't hard to imagine him bent over a notebook late at night—for some reason I didn't think poets used computers—all wound up and agonizing over the next word or the next line, getting up, going to the refrigerator or the bathroom, coming back and reading what he'd written, crumpling the page, starting all over again.

I said, "You still write poems?"

"Guilty," he admitted. "Guilty but mentally ill."

"Then you can't think they're all sucky, or you'd stop."

"Yeah, there's these moments when I think I'm a stone-cold genius. But I try not to listen to myself." He laughed again. I guessed he was one of those people who has to make a joke out of everything. "How about you, do you write?"

I could have told him I had enough problems with basic reading, but that wasn't anything I shared in casual conversations, so I just said no. Matt said he'd been to one of Viridian's readings before, had I? Had I read her poems? No and no. "So, what brings you here, if you don't mind my asking?"

"I saw the poster." I didn't care to lay out my brief but eventful history with Viridian. That I had dug in her garden, that she'd watched me while I slept, that I had showed up at her door late at night. People were starting to file in. I looked around the auditorium for Oscar, since it might be awkward to run into him and I wanted to either hide or brace myself. I didn't see him. I said, "Is that her real name, Viridian?"

"Define 'real.'"

"You know what I mean."

"It's the name she writes under. Her professional name."

"Sort of like Sting, or Queen Latifah?"

Right about then, Matt seemed to start wondering just who I was. "I guess like that," he said. "Though she's not really a rock-star poet. More of a cult favorite. She doesn't give a lot of readings nowadays. So this is a big deal."

"I didn't know there were any rock-star poets."

"The ones everybody knows."

"Define 'everybody.'"

"Poets like Gary Snyder. Jorie Graham." He was counting them off on his fingers. "And Merwin, Ashbery, Adrienne Rich, Mark Strand, but they all kind of just died. Um, Nikki Giovanni. Kevin Young. For starters. Everybody has their own list."

"Huh. Are there some rock stars who are poets? Like, Stevie Nicks."

He was getting a little exasperated with me. "They're two entirely different things."

The auditorium was filling up now, getting noisy, and that was an excuse to stop talking. More people were here than I'd expected, over a hundred, I guessed. There was still no sign of Oscar, but I thought I saw a couple of the hens down front, gabbing with each other. The stage was still empty except for a podium and a microphone.

Now, I have to stop here and admit, I wasn't as much of a poetry rube as I made myself sound to Matt. I might not have known his *Billboard* Top Ten Poets, but different teachers had rubbed my nose in enough poems that I'd retained a few things. I'd learned that a poem must not mean but be, that it should be dumb and mute, which would have been a good trick. The teachers had tried, but there was an inevitable, eat-your-broccoli vibe to the whole thing, plus my goofy brain made the words on the page squirm and refuse to mean anything. Every so often the sound of a poem caught and held me, like when the highwayman came riding, riding, the highwayman came riding, up to the old inn door. Although this was said to be an old-fashioned sort of poem, and I was not supposed to like it too much.

I leaned forward to get Matt's attention. "Hey, I was kidding. Stevie Nicks writes songs, not poems."

"Yeah?" He brightened up. "Well, if Viridian wrote songs, she'd probably be like Stevie Nicks."

One of the doors in back opened and there was a stir among the crowd. I turned around in my seat to see Viridian appear, accompanied by a nervous-looking man whom I guessed to be in charge. The two of them made their way down the aisle to the stage.

How much does a poem depend on who wrote it? How can we know the dancer from the dance? Poets die, and even their outline, their ghost, disappears. Who was Shakespeare anyway? Or Homer? It didn't really seem to matter.

And yet here in the present, while a poet was still alive, it did. Matt said that Viridian didn't qualify as a "rock-star poet," and the term seemed so silly. But if there was such a thing as a poetry rock star, it was Viridian on this night, walking into her own reading.

I'd seen her at home, of course, but here she was among people who knew her, who wished to know her better. Here she was a power and a force. She wore a loose white dress over loose trousers, an eccentric outfit that she made seem modish and acceptable, just by wearing it. Her silver-gray hair fanned out behind her and was held back from her face with a scarf of peach-colored fabric. She made gray hair look like something you might want, too. Just as you might want her beautiful, untroubled face, her sun-darkened skin with its freight of history, of things lived and things understood.

And then she caught sight of me on her way to the front of the room and stopped.

"Carla! I've been thinking about you. You must come see me again. Let's talk when I'm done here, shall we?"

I muttered, "Yeah, sure."

I was both dumb and mute. I saw Matt looking at me. Other people, too. I shrugged, unable to explain anything. She probably wanted me to come weed her roses.

Viridian took a seat in the front row and the nervous man stood at the microphone to introduce her. The microphone squeaked and he had to adjust it. "Whoops," he said, and laughed a little. He was so awkward. It was painful to watch him. It was an honor, he said, he was honored—here he unfolded a piece of paper—to welcome us and introduce a great and remarkable poet. "A poet for our, for all, times. All our times. Her voice is her own, distinct and personal, yet effortlessly . . ."

He stopped and started for no particular reason. He might have been running out of breath. I was rooting for him to please get through it. He read off the same things that were on the poster. How Viridian had won this award and that prize, how her books had been received with praise. "It's been said of her poems that they reach us at a level we are not consciously aware of, like radio waves at an unfamiliar frequency. And yet we are consciously changed by them, by their extraordinary—" Here the microphone squeaked again and swallowed his words. "Their extraordinary grace and . . ." He fussed with the microphone and decided to stop talking, thank God. "Please welcome Viridian."

There was applause, and she rose from her seat and climbed the steps to the stage, and laid a hand on the man's sleeve, to thank him, I expect, and perhaps make him feel better about the whole thing. She carried a book and a sheaf of papers, and these she arranged on the podium before she looked up and smiled. "Thank you so much. Thank you and welcome."

At the sound of her voice, low and calm, I think the whole room exhaled. Even the microphone stopped misbehaving for her. It was a relief and a pleasure to hear her, to be soothed by that slow and measured sound. An unfamiliar frequency, the man had said, although I don't think he meant it so literally. What I want to say is, her voice was what broke through all my stubborn misunderstandings and finally let me hear.

"I'm going to start with some older poems, and then move on to newer work." She picked up a book and found the place she wanted, then stopped. "You begin to have these not entirely wholesome relationships with your own work, with different parts of it. There's the poem that's always disappointed you, the one that's always failed to live up to its full promise. And the one you tiptoe around, because you still aren't sure how you pulled it off, and it has its own life by now, like the Frankenstein monster. Then there are the old friends that you turn to with relief. This first poem is one of those."

This is what she read. This is what I heard. For the first time, really *heard* a poem:

BY HEART

I threw a rock into the water of a green pond.
A rock the size of a heart, heavy in the hand,
but dry. Imagine such a heart, unnatural. I said,
"I drowned my heart to put an end to
its thirst." One more extreme solution that
didn't help.

The heart of a tree pumps green blood to the
leaf's veins. If you cut down the tree
and build a boat to cross the water, the heart floats.
You could say that like you've proved something
about hearts. But it's a trick done with words.
The tree is dead.

I hated my heart, how it made the same fool,
greenhorn mistakes, how it would not be turned into
something not myself.
If my heart could answer the phone, it would give out
personal information to strangers. If it could swim
in tears, it would bring a float toy.

Have you heard of green sickness? A kind of
anemia known as the virgin's disease, curable by
intercourse. So say the old books.
Though certain complications, like an unsuitable
heart, might ensue. What can you say? You stick a toe in the
water. You take your medicine.

Such weariness. So heavy. Heart is a paper lace word,
not the thing in the chest that snarls and howls,
the thing you bury in water because it wants to drink and
wants to drown, because you want what it wants, it's
nobody's fault but yours. In the end you are not rock or heart
or pond. You are the ripple on the water, the green echo, love.

She read for nearly an hour. I wanted to know all of those poems, by heart. In between poems she spoke, sometimes humorously, sometimes seriously and with some effort. She said that for her, writing poems was by now a way of processing the world, and she did not know any other way, and she would risk sounding arrogant by saying she thought it was the best of all possible ways. She spoke for a time about the battle for the earth, the warming climate, the oceans filled with plastic, the lands gouged with wells and mines. There had been something about her environmental work on the poster, I remembered. She was charming, and tired, and formidable. It was like watching an actor make a stage their own, except here the only script was herself.

When she was done, and when people had applauded her, I got up and made my way to the front of the room, since she'd said to do so. There were people crowding around, wanting to talk to her, wanting her to sign books, so I hung back.

She saw me and smiled and spoke to me over the others. "I'm so glad you're here! Will you come over to the house some afternoon? I'm always there."

"Sure. Whenever you want me to." I wanted to say something about the poems, but I didn't trust myself not to babble or gush.

"Tomorrow. Or the next day." Someone else claimed her attention then and I watched her listen, nodding gravely, holding their hands in hers.

Matt was standing just outside the auditorium, not even pretending not to wait for me. "I thought you said you didn't know her."

"I said I didn't know her poems."

"Huh." He considered this. "I should have been more specific."

I waited for him to finish being mad about whatever he was mad about. He was the one I didn't know, although he was acting like I did. It was dark by now. A wind rattled the eucalyptus leaves overhead. I was impatient to start home, to be alone in the car and think about everything I'd heard.

He said, "So you weren't just trying to make fun of me? Pretending you didn't know anything about poetry."

"I don't."

"You're kind of a strange girl."

"Thank you."

"I don't suppose you need a—"

I held up my car keys. "Been very nice talking to you."

He muttered something that sounded like "Yeah, whatever," and walked away, hands jammed in his pockets. I was pretty sure he'd go home and write a poem about it all.

PARTY

Viridian didn't have a Wikipedia page or a Facebook account, wasn't on Twitter or Instagram. How could she ignore all that? Was it even legal? When I went online to find her books, all but one, *The Doubter*, were unavailable except in digital form, which was depressing. Maybe she had a thing about social media and privacy, but I didn't think she wanted her writing to be a private thing. Matt had said she was a cult favorite. I had to wonder if she was obscure for reasons of her own choosing, or something else.

I had better luck finding her in anthologies, where a number of her poems had appeared. It took some time nosing around different websites, but I found a couple of the ones she'd read aloud. I held my breath looking at them now in black and white, but the magic held. Now that I'd heard them, they were mine. Here was the one about doors, the choice of doors, golden, silver, or lead, which I understood was the fairy tale riddle, and you were meant to choose the virtuous lead rather than be misled by greed or pride. Yet the poem was also about unlocking a lover's nature, and here the triumphal choice was gold, gold, gold, because that was the lover's worth.

When Aaron asked me about Viridian's reading, I'd said it was interesting. I'd said I was glad I'd gone. But I didn't tell him or anyone how it had changed and rearranged something needful in me.

The internet served up a few more answers, and a lot more questions. I found some stray bits of biography, mostly in essays or chapters about other poets. Her name, one of them, was Linda Rose Cunningham. Or Linda Ricker. Or Linda Ricker Boone. I guessed the different names had come from different marriages, though I also liked to imagine her having aliases, like the fugitives from justice that appeared in the newspaper. When and why she became Viridian, it didn't say.

How old was she? Somewhere north of seventy, to judge by the other poets she was "linked to," which I hope did not just mean "slept with." She was born in Michigan and had lived in New York and Texas and now California. In New York she was "linked to" the famous alcoholic and suicidal poet, Mathias. In Texas she had lived for a time in an artist's compound funded by a tech billionaire. Useful facts, but incomplete. I found a newspaper photo from a few years ago, Viridian reading on an outdoor stage with signs demanding an end to nuclear power. And then a picture of her much younger self that made me stare and keep staring.

The picture was taken in 1970, when she would have been around twenty-five. It was a color photograph on a bright day, and she sat on a rock at the edge of an ocean, it seemed. Her hair was a surprising coppery brown, and the wind blew it in streamers around her face. She wore jeans and a red shirt, and her feet were bare. Her face was both the same and yet different, not so wide open as it was now, but unlined, and with an expression that seemed, in my imagining, to be looking from that past into this present moment, as if she saw straight into the life she would lead and was curious about it.

I found an interview she gave to a literary magazine. I was only now realizing there were such things as literary magazines. But I was glad I found it because the interviewer was just as clueless as I was:

Interviewer: How old were you when you decided to be a poet?

V.: I don't think it's anything you decide. You write poems because you want to take hold of an aspect of experience and examine it, push it a little further, find out why it speaks to you. You want to speak back at it. I don't know when the world starts calling you a poet. It's a frightening moment when you call yourself one, when you have to take yourself seriously. To answer your question, I suppose I was in my early twenties. Which is awfully young, but if I'd been much older, I might have talked myself out of it.

It requires a certain amount of foolhardiness to launch yourself at the world that way.

Foolhardy, interesting word. The fool has the quality of hardiness.

Interviewer: Does it bother you that so few people read poetry nowadays?

V.: It will bother me when I am no longer around to write it.

Interviewer: You chose a life devoted to art, to poetry, not an easy or a conventional life. Do you have any regrets?

V.: I have countless regrets. But none of them have anything to do with poetry.

Oscar Brasco was a lot easier to find online. Strangest thing: he wasn't exactly the national poet laureate, but he had his share of lauds and honors. Being a poet seemed like it was a kind of secret identity, like Peter Parker ducking out of high school to put on his Spiderman costume.

A biographical note said that Oscar was of Portugese-Jewish heritage, and that his poems "brought a certain playfulness to established poetic forms." I didn't know about any of that. But I was able to puzzle through one of them that began this way:

> *Old blue moon*
> *over and over*
> *old boo hoo*
> *another sad night*
> *like the lid of a box coming down.*
> *like blue smoke in a curl*
> *like a glass bead at the bottom of a pocket*
> *or one blue eye*
> *looking at the moon. Where are we going tonight?*
> *To the moon. They're having a party*
> *For refugees and lepers*
> *We'll kick up our heels.*

I couldn't have said exactly what was going on here, except that whoever it was at least seemed aware that he was having a lot of fun feeling sorry for himself.

It was three days before I went to Viridian's house. Maybe she'd only invited me out of politeness, and I didn't want to presume that she, or anybody else, actually wanted to see me. I took my gardening tools, since those might be called for as an alibi.

There was a smell of smoke in the air from a grass fire in the far northeast corner of Sonoma, and a hazy look to the sky. Fire season had started early. It made everybody nervous; we'd all lived through big fires by now. It was only two years ago that the Tubbs fire had burned 5 percent of the houses in Santa Rosa, way too close to home. Driving to Fairfax through the back roads, past fields of blond grass, it was easy to imagine a high wind snaking through the valleys, driving lines of fire before it.

Which is why I was alarmed to reach Viridian's courtyard— the gate stood open—and find that a big portable firepit had been set up there, an oversized bowl on legs. It stood waist high, and a fire of wood logs, the kind sold in bundles at the grocery, was burning and snapping, unattended, it seemed.

I parked and looked around for the mesh dome that fit on top and put it in place so that at least embers wouldn't fly up onto the roof or overhanging trees. I still didn't see anyone. It was probably five different kinds of illegal to leave something burning like this.

I rang the front doorbell. Oscar answered. He sighed. "You. What did I do this time?"

"You left your fire unattended and you could burn up the whole county."

"What, you're the fire patrol now? I'm going to barbecue some oysters. It's not a crime." His hair was slicked back, still wet, and he smelled faintly of shower products. He wore jeans and an orange shirt that glowed like a bad sunburn. He was one of those men of whom it was said, He's not afraid of color.

"Where's Viridian?"

"Making the salad dressing. You're early."

He was already walking away, into the house. Early for what? I followed him, trying to get my bearings. Here was the living room, and a room beyond that which I hadn't seen—an office, I guessed, with a trestle desk and files—and a wide space like a gallery, and beyond that, the kitchen, where something involving a lot of garlic was cooking.

Viridian stood at the one clear space of countertop, whisking something in a bowl. If she was surprised or dismayed to see me, it didn't show in her face. "Carla! How nice that you're here. Do you eat mushrooms? I can't decide if I should put any in the salad."

All around her, different cooking projects were underway: a large pot of red sauce on the stove, loaves of bread on a cutting board, a pasta machine disgorging wide noodles, an open canister of flour sifting over everything. Heaps of vegetables: tomatoes, summer squash, eggplant, peppers, onions. A bowl of cut-up peaches, cheese and cheese grater, the sink full of greens, a tub of butter, jars of this and that, honey, olives, pickles. The kitchen, which was not large, looked like one of those puzzles where you're supposed to find hidden objects.

Viridian looked completely serene and untroubled by any of the kitchen wreckage. Tonight she wore her hair pulled up on the top of her head, in stripes of gray and silver, and a white apron over a floating light blue dress or caftan. I wanted clothes like hers.

"No mushrooms," Oscar said. "I need them for the ratatouille."

"No mushrooms," Viridian agreed. "Just plain greens with vinaigrette."

"Bacon," Oscar suggested, but she shook her head. "Vegetarians," he said to me. "So rigid."

I shrugged, as if I might agree. I wanted to renounce every cheeseburger I'd ever eaten.

"I'm sorry," I said. "I didn't mean to barge in and interrupt you."

"You're not interrupting anything, you're paying a visit. Now that you're here, you should stay for dinner. Shouldn't she, Oscar? We certainly have enough food."

"Sure. Get the boyfriend to come, too. I haven't been humiliated in at least a couple of weeks." I spied the remnants of a scar bisecting his right eyebrow.

"I'll only stay if I can help." I wanted to stay. I wanted to sit at the table, taste all the food.

I followed Oscar outside to see about the dinner table, which was set up in the garden. But first I made him stop and check on the fire. "Seriously," I said. "You always need to make sure it's not a red flag day. Unless you're cooking enough food for the fire department."

"Sure, fine," he murmured, poking at the logs. "I guess I should let this die down for a while. People aren't coming for another couple of hours. I wanted to see how hot I could get the fire. I don't think Virdie realizes that you kill the oysters right here on the grill. Don't tell her, okay? I had to fight to get her to serve anything like fish."

"Who's coming?"

"Who isn't. Oh, I don't mean you. Some local writing types. A couple of the hens, you can't keep them away. And Lorenzo the Magnificent."

I waited for him to explain his joke, which went right past me. "Lorenzo de Medici. A fifteenth-century Italian patron of the arts—"

"Yeah, great, who is this other guy?"

"A high mucky-muck at the Artists United Institute." My face must have stayed blank. "In San Diego," he prompted me. "God, you really don't know anything, do you?"

"Why is he magnificent?"

"Money. They're swimming in it down there. He's like an art gangster."

"Is his name really Lorenzo?"

"Larry."

"Larry the Magnificent."

"Whatever. He's thinking of naming Virdie to an endowed chair the Institute has."

I considered this. "Would that be a good thing?"

"Yeah, since she's broke. Did she show you where the plates are?"

I went back to my truck and called Aaron and convinced him the dinner would be a great good time. I did not mention the vegetarian menu. I told him to bring my striped sundress, my red sandals, and some earrings. Then I went to see about the plates.

A long table had been set up between the flower beds and the breezeway, covered with a number of white linen cloths. Ten chairs were in place and there were two more in the screened porch that would do for me and Aaron. Strings of small electric lights were hung overhead, and there were candles set out in earthenware saucers. The garden plantings could have used some attention, but at least they'd been watered and nothing had died.

It makes me sound criminally naive when I admit I hadn't realized that a poet might worry about money, but I really hadn't. For one thing, any poet who came to my mind was already safely dead and beyond money troubles. And wasn't being broke a kind of badge of honor for artists, a testament to how detached they were, how devoted to their art?

It was all right for me not to have money; I was young and unserious and nobody expected me to amount to much anyway. But I didn't like to think of Viridian as broke, or whatever Oscar meant by broke.

I set out the plates and silverware. I have an unexpected and generally useless talent for folding napkins. It was something I'd taught myself from youtube videos when I was supposed to be doing homework. I considered fans, tulips, hearts, and pinwheels, but all that seemed too fussy and housewifey. I finally settled on a simple diamond fold with the silverware tucked inside. I got my clippers and snipped sprigs of rosemary and flowering ninebark to set across each napkin. I thought it looked nice. I wanted it to be nice.

I walked through the kitchen and found Viridian in the gallery beyond it, putting wineglasses on a serving table. "What else can I do?"

"In that cupboard? Bring out all the red wine and put the white in the refrigerator. As many bottles as there's room for. We need the serving dishes out, but I'm the only one who knows where they are, and I'm not sure what Oscar has in mind. He's put together the whole meal."

That explained the mess. "Just point me in the right direction." I wanted some difficult task, something I could accomplish that would astound and please her. I arranged the wine bottles, then opened more cupboards to bring out the bowls and trays. I made an effort at tidying the kitchen, starting at the edges so there might be some clear space.

"See?" Viridian said. "You're exactly what I needed. An extra pair of hands."

"I'm happy to help." Her praise made me shy. But it was the first chance I'd had to be alone with her, and I blundered into what I wanted to say: "I loved listening to your poems. I've never heard anything like them."

She stayed silent. I couldn't look at her; I was keeping busy with the pot I was scrubbing. I said, "I don't read poems, I can't. I mean, I have a learning disability, I have trouble with reading even basic stuff. But when I heard you read them, it all made sense. It all ended up inside me. So, I just wanted to tell you."

Still, she didn't speak. I felt my face burning. I thought I must have said something wrong, monstrous, without at all meaning to. I wanted to apologize, although how, and for what, I didn't know. I began to stammer, something about how I hadn't meant, hadn't meant to presume. But she rescued me from myself, finally.

"Thank you. That's lovely to hear."

"It's not like I know anything at all about poems." I shrugged. "It's not like anybody needs my opinion."

"I'm very glad to have yours. And there's no one way to enjoy a thing."

"I guess that's good." I still felt a little raw, as if I'd said too much. "I didn't know you were going to be there. I just saw the poster."

"That's a lucky thing then. Every so often, the universe sends you a gift."

"A dishwasher," I said, encouraged enough now to make a joke, and Viridian laughed and said that yes, the universe was generous that way, and so we got through the moment, and if I still felt like sort of an idiot, I was glad I'd spoken up.

What the universe sent next was a couple of the hens, Barb and Chloe, their names were, who arrived carrying bouquets of flowers, two trays of hors d'oeuvres, more wine bottles, and a cake decorated with fondant roses. Barb was the one with the spiky black hair and joke-shop glasses. Chloe was blond and brittle and made me think that my mom was probably right about sunscreen.

Viridian said, "You remember Carla, don't you?"

They did but I could tell that they would rather not have. They ignored me and crowded into the kitchen, deciding where the things they'd brought should go, and what should be refrigerated, and what needed to be done first, and clearly it was their show now. Although it would have been entertaining, in a sick way, to watch when Oscar came in and found them adding salt to his tomato sauce, instead I went out and sat in the truck to wait for Aaron.

He pulled up twenty minutes later. I hadn't told him to dress up, but he had, in a black shirt and tan pants, and I loved him for coming and for looking so good, so tall and badass.

He got into my truck. "You," I said, "are the sexiest bald guy in two counties."

"Thanks, I guess. What's going on here?"

"I mean it, you look awesome. You look like one of those preachers who holds services for biker gangs. It's a dinner party with a lot of poets coming. It's a cultural occasion. Did you bring my dress?"

"Yeah. And a six-pack. They drink beer, right? What are we doing here anyway?"

I said I'd been working on the garden and she'd invited us to the dinner. It was close enough to the truth and it made me sound a little less like a stalker. Aaron considered this.

"When did you turn into a poetry groupie?"

"What's that supposed to mean?"

"Oh wow," he said, seeing Oscar, who had come out of the house and was poking at the firepit. "Orange."

Oscar and Aaron seemed happy to see each other, which surprised me a little. Maybe it was a guy thing to bond over your stupid drunk escapades. Aaron offered Oscar a beer and the two of them stood around the firepit, which was another guy thing, although by rights they should have a haunch of beef or elk to grill.

I went inside to look for a bathroom to change clothes. It was the weirdest house, with half flights of stairs leading to rooms that opened directly into other rooms, and hallways that zigged and zagged. I found a small bathroom not too far from the front door. Viridian and Barb and Chloe were back in the kitchen; I heard them laughing.

The sundress was candy striped, with straps that crisscrossed in back and a long, flippy skirt. It was my best summer dress, and I liked the way I looked in it, at least, if I decided not to think about my patchy farmer's tan. My red sandals gave me another inch of height. I ran a comb through my hair and pinned part of it back from my face. Aaron had remembered earrings, god bless him, had even brought two pairs for me to choose from. I decided on the long silver drops and nodded at myself in the mirror.

When I went back to the kitchen, the others stopped talking.

"Don't you look nice," Viridian said, admiringly.

"Thank you. Aaron's here, he brought me different clothes. Can I help with something?"

How did Barb and Chloe look? They looked all right, I guess. They'd both gone in for large scale, abstract prints, like they might have bought their outfits in an art gallery.

I was put to work setting out the rest of the bar, the glasses and ice bucket and cocktail napkins, the tongs and corkscrew and saucers of olives and almonds. I wasn't part of the kitchen conversation, but I could overhear it.

"What does Larry drink?"

"Whatever he wants. He'll bring his own bottle."

"That's rude."

"No, that's just Larry."

Somebody, Barb or Chloe, murmured something, and Viridian said "No, not a bit, and please don't say anything."

"I'm glad Sacha's coming. She'll keep things cheerful."

"I assume Anders is coming with her. Talk about bringing your own bottle."

Someone, Viridian I think, shushed them, and there was some giggling. I wished I knew everybody they knew. I wished I knew all the jokes.

Viridian came out then and I asked if there was anything else I could do.

"I don't think so, dear. I'm going to lie down before anyone else gets here. Calm before the storm."

"Of course," I said. She was smiling, but there seemed to be some effort in it, as if she was already tired. "Everything's under control." Then, quickly, "If you'd like, I can come back and do some work in the yard. Anytime you want."

"Could you? That would be lovely." She patted my arm. "What would I do without my young friends."

I heard her light footsteps receding. She'd called me a friend. Even if "young friend" might be something other than a real friend, some lesser subcategory, or just a way of speaking.

The front door slammed, and Oscar rushed past me into the kitchen. "Hags! Get away from my food!"

I hurried outside to find Aaron. Perhaps things were not entirely under control.

Aaron was poking around in a galvanized pail full of ice. The oysters, presumably. "You do clean up nice," he said when he saw me. "How long are these guys supposed to cook?"

"Until the shells open. Five minutes. Then the sauce goes on. I wouldn't start them until everybody else is here." A couple of

Adirondack chairs were pulled up to the firepit. I pulled one out of the stream of smoke.

"Who's everybody else?"

"Poets. Their friends and allies."

I waited for him to offer some opinion about weirdo poets, but he sat back in his chair and looked up at the canopy of trees shifting in the late-day breeze. "The fire jumped the lines. They have a warning out for Geyserville."

"That's still forty miles." I meant, from Petaluma. It was closer than that to Santa Rosa and my mom.

He was peeling the label off the beer bottle. A nervous habit. "God, it stresses me out. And it goes on for months."

"You have to try not to think about it every minute." I didn't want to think about it right now, with this particular evening ahead of us, but I could tell Aaron was working his way through something, the way he did in that big bald head, building up arguments until he convinced himself.

"You ever wonder about moving?" he asked, not entirely a change of subject, if you were paying attention.

"Moving where?"

"I don't know. British Columbia, maybe. Vancouver. It's a whole different climate."

"It's a whole different country."

"Would that be so bad? Look at the shitstorm going on. California's about the only sane state left. And it's burning up. And nobody can afford to live here. I can get another IT job. They're everywhere."

"I thought I was going back to school."

"They have schools in Vancouver, too. Okay, it doesn't have to be Vancouver. Haven't you thought about living someplace different? Someplace we haven't been all our lives. A fresh start."

The truth was, I hadn't. But Aaron was four years older than me. He thought in terms of the future, of planning things out, while I was still, Whatever. He was right, he could get other jobs. And he wanted me to come with him, which told me something I needed to know. But it was his idea, not mine. And this was home. Why would you want to leave home?

"I don't know," I said. "It's a lot to think about. It's not so bad here. All right, the fires are kind of bad."

"There's times I just want something new."

I didn't answer. I'd thought that being in love with someone, as I was with Aaron, as I believed he was with me, made everything new every day. But I guess that wasn't what Aaron meant. Then some of the guests arrived, and we didn't have to take things any further.

Though I kept thinking about it. We did love each other, didn't we? I don't just mean sex, although we had it good there. And it wasn't like love in dopey movies or in songs, something giddy and perfect. No, this had more to do with contentment, and calm, and not wanting to be with anyone else, or anywhere else. But Vancouver?

Ed and Doug, the newly arrived couple from the city, started in talking about how rustic and charming everything was here, like they'd crossed the Golden Gate Bridge and found themselves in Croatia. Then came Sacha and Anders. Sacha was fine-boned and pretty, with a lot of curly fair hair and a silvery laugh. Anders kept his eyes on her. Did she want a drink? A sweater? A chair? Anything at all? he asked. Viridian and the others came out to greet them. The party was underway.

But where was the famous Larry? How long were we expected to wait for him? Oscar told Aaron to grill most of the oysters but to save out a dozen more for any latecomers. "We can build up the fire again later if we have to."

"Is he coming straight here from San Diego?"

"No, he's been in the city, there's some conference at Fort Mason Center. I hope he can tear himself away." Oscar looked grim. He didn't say it, but I knew what he was thinking: it would not be a good omen for Viridian's potential job at his institute, the endowed chair, if Larry and his magnificence never showed. The whole party must have been for him.

Everyone else had found their way out to the backyard and seemed to be having a good time. The electric string lights were on and the candles were lit, and the last bits of sun shone through the trees in bars of rose and gold. Viridian sat at one end of the table, talking with Sacha, while the others held wineglasses and hovered around the hors d'oeuvres Barb and Chloe had brought: pastry envelopes of mushrooms, of crab, of cheese. So far it was a pretty normal party, like something my mom might go to at a doctor's house.

I found myself next to Ed or Doug—I hadn't sorted out which was which—who asked me what I did.

"I'm a landscaper."

He nodded. "Oil or water?"

"What? No. Not painting. Landscaping. Dirt."

"I thought you meant—"

"No, that's okay. I guess everybody else but me is some kind of artist."

"Some kind, yeah." He lifted his wineglass and surveyed the yard over its edge. He and his partner—Ed or Doug—looked rather alike, slender, with glasses. They both wore beautiful summer clothes: linen jackets; soft shirts in gray and cream, one pinstriped, one checked; jeans so perfectly fitted and frayed, I found myself wanting to take notes.

"So what kind of artist are you?" I prompted him.

He shook his head. "I'm an attorney. But I work in artist representation."

"I'm acting like I know what that is, but I don't."

"We represent visual artists, mostly, but writers, too. When they have contract issues or property disputes. Mediations. Copyright questions."

So some artists, big-time painters, say, had wealth that needed lawyers attached to it. He said, "Doug's the artist in the family. The poet. And he's been the editor of *Compass Points* for a few years now. That's how we know Viridian."

I hadn't quite understood everything, like, what was *Compass Points?*, but at least now I knew I was talking to Ed. I said, "I guess I know her sort of by accident. I mean I don't really know her. I'm going to do some garden work for her,"

Ed looked at me, in a measuring way. "That's nice. Viridian has a talent for finding useful friends."

I wasn't sure what that meant. It felt as if I was being implicated in something. Luckily, I saw Aaron walking along the breezeway. He spotted me and waved.

"Excuse me, I think my boyfriend's looking for me."

"I don't suppose he's an artist," Ed murmured, and I said no, sorry. Aaron was like gay catnip. We always joked about guys hitting on him, he was a good sport about it. Then I saw that Ed wasn't looking at Aaron, but at Doug, who was, and before things got too complicated, I said it had been nice talking to him.

"Come help me with the oysters," Aaron said once I reached him. "Oscar went inside and left them to me."

"They're really easy." Which was true, but that didn't mean you couldn't screw them up. We went out to the courtyard and counted out the two dozen oysters that Oscar had told Aaron to get ready, put them on the grill, and waited. "Do you need another beer?" I asked him.

"That guy who looks like a Nordic serial killer took the last one."

"Oh. That's Anders. He's, ah . . ." I wasn't sure what he was.

"Carla? We're not staying real late, are we?"

The oyster shells opened, so we knew they were fresh. Aaron pried them the rest of the way and pasted them with barbecue sauce. We loaded them on trays to take into the house.

"Thank God," Oscar said, when we reached the kitchen. He was pouring a pan of boiling water into a colander in the sink, and the steam turned his face nearly as florid as his shirt. "Get those outside, try and make people sit down and eat them while they're hot."

We did our best, showing everyone the trays and inviting them to take a seat. It was the kind of thing you might expect the hostess to do, but Viridian remained a benevolent, detached presence at the head of the table. People did sit, and Barb and Chloe fussed over refilling the wineglasses. I went back to the kitchen to help Oscar.

He was pulling things out of the oven, sprinkling chopped herbs, tossing pasta, everything all at once, like a grill cook at a diner. "Here, careful, it's hot." He handed me a breadbasket and a pot of whipped butter. "No, I'll take this one, it's heavy."

Aaron came in to help, and we got a staggering amount of food out to the garden in a very short time. There was a bowl of green salad served family style, two kinds of pasta, one with red sauce and one with spinach and cream. A ratatouille layered like a stained-glass window, a caponata served cold, a cheese soufflé, a tray of spring rolls, roasted asparagus.

"Good Lord," Sacha said, contemplating it all. "Oscar, take a bow."

Which he did, after mopping at his face with a napkin. Then he rapped on the edge of a wineglass with a knife for our attention.

> To the Looking-Glass world it was Alice that said
> 'I've a sceptre in hand, I've a crown on my head.
> Let the Looking-Glass creatures, whatever they be
> Come and dine with the Red Queen, the White Queen,
> and me.'

Then he sat down. People applauded. "Do you remember the rest of it?" Doug asked.

"I remember everything I ever read," Oscar said glumly. "I have that kind of brain. It's a burden."

"So you're Alice?"

"No, I'm more like the Mad Hatter."

Viridian said, "Well, the White Queen has untidy hair, so I guess that's me."

"I'll be the Red Queen. She's always cutting people's heads off," Sacha said cheerfully.

I kept quiet. I'd only seen *Alice in Wonderland* on television, another of my cultural failings.

There were some more jokes about Eat Me, Drink Me, and then people settled in to do just that. Aaron was sitting next to me. "Good oysters," I said, and he gave me a stoic look.

Barb was sitting on my other side. We didn't say anything at first, then we agreed the spinach pasta was good, then we had the kind of conversation that can happen when you're both drinking a lot of wine. She nodded at the two empty chairs. "So much for the guest of honor."

She meant Larry and his entourage, I assumed. I said, "Maybe they're just late."

"Everybody else managed to get here on time."

You couldn't argue with that. I put my fork down. I was already getting full. I said, "Is he really that big a deal? Larry. I don't know his last name."

"Larry Nagel. Sure he is. He's big in po biz. Like show biz," she explained, because I was doing my famous impression of being slack-jawed and clueless. "Po biz is everything poets have to do to get their poems published and recognized and read and make some kind of a name for themselves and then they can get more stuff published and win a contest or two and then you can get a small press to do a chapbook and sell three copies of it at a literary festival and go home and write more poems."

She set her wineglass down on the table a little harder than necessary for emphasis, and looked around the table, as if challenging anybody to disagree. Her pink glasses made it hard for her to look entirely serious, even when she was mad.

After a moment I said, "I can't tell if that's supposed to be a good or a bad thing."

"It's just the way it is."

Neither of us said anything for a time. "So, do you write poetry?" I asked, thinking it would be polite to take an interest.

She turned her head so the glasses stared at me. "I do. Night and day. Day and night."

I tried to think of what else to say to that, something respectful and encouraging, but she said, "Never mind me. Viridian's the one they'll be talking about a hundred years from now."

"Yes," I said, fatuously, as if I had any business even offering an opinion.

"She's the queen."

"Yes," I said again, wondering if we were still talking *Alice in Wonderland.* I didn't think so.

Barb slashed her portion of ratatouille into small pieces but didn't eat it. "Goddamn that Larry Nagel. He should have some respect."

"She doesn't seem upset," I said, watching Viridian at the end of the table, smiling and looking lovely and untroubled.

"That's because she's above all the petty, grubby things that drive the rest of us crazy.

Her soul is larger than ours."

"Oscar's a good poet, too, isn't he?"

She sniffed. "All he ever writes about is his wee-wee."

"And the others?" I prodded her. "Are they, um . . .?" I didn't want to say *famous*, because I hadn't heard of them.

She must have taken pity on my ignorance or decided that I was harmless. She explained that Sacha was a big enough name in poetry circles, even a celebrity of sorts in the wider world, due to her television appearances (which I had never seen), where she discussed her feminist critique of Mary Shelly's *Frankenstein*. Anders was the principal translator of a Nobel Prize–winning Swedish poet, in addition to writing his own poems, which were "very dark. Very." Doug was a good and worthy poet, but he was mostly known as the editor of *Compass Points*. "God," Barb said moodily. "What I wouldn't give to get something into *Compass Points*. Excuse me."

She got up from the table and went into the house. Aaron was having a conversation with Doug, on his other side, so I ate a little more and took the opportunity to sit quietly and watch everything going on around me. Anders, who did in fact have a hollowed-out and sinister look, was tending to Sacha, filling her plate with food as if he had a mind to devour her later. Ed and Chloe were sitting next to each other but not finding anything to talk about. I didn't assume that Doug was flirting with Aaron, I mean come on, people can just talk to each other, but maybe Ed was crazy jealous. Anyway, he didn't look like he was having a great time. As for Chloe, I didn't know her at all and couldn't speculate, but she had a pinched, anxious expression, like she was waiting for a stack of dishes to fall off the table.

Sacha, Viridian, and Oscar were at the far end of the table, talking and laughing, eating and drinking, as if they were the ones delegated with having the best time. It was completely dark now except for the candles and the lights overhead and the lights from the house. I could only hear bits and pieces of what they were saying. Sacha reached across the table and put a hand on Oscar's wrist. "You were on fire."

"No, drunk."

"Don't be modest."

"I'm not. I was magnificently drunk."

Viridian said, "We thought you weren't going to get through it. You kept interrupting your own stories and rambling and changing the subject. We were all frozen with horror—"

"Come on. Not horror."

"Horror because we thought one of us was going to have to get up on the stage and help you down."

"And then you finally shut up—"

"And started to read—"

"And I swear, the hair on my head blew straight back, listening to you."

"Shucks," Oscar said. "I had a good night."

He was beaming. Modest noises were coming out of his mouth, but it was clear he was loving it all, as the two women loved him, in ways that were generous and large-spirited. And I thought that poetry must be love, or maybe love was poetry. My head was muzzy with wine. The table was an island lit by glowing lights.

Those of us who loved Viridian—because I was coming to love her—those who she loved, we were all, at this moment, poets. As were Ed and Doug playing their jealousy games, even scary-looking Anders, waiting silently at Sacha's elbow. I hitched my chair closer to Aaron's and waited for him to turn in my direction.

The kitchen door slammed, and Barb ran up to us, wheezing, out of breath. "Somebody call 911! The fence caught on fire!"

FIRE

Aaron and I looked at each other, dumbstruck, *oh shit*, vaulting out of our chairs. We raced around the back corner of the house, the others behind us. Fire was eating at the tall board fence between the courtyard and the neighboring property. The wood was scorched and smoldering along its bottom edge. Lines of bright flame climbed upward.

We hadn't put the top back on the firepit. It was nobody's fault but ours. Mine.

Aaron got to it first, kicking at the base of the fence. He shouted at me to get a shovel, hurry, and I ran to my truck. The truck was parked in one corner by the gate, out of the fire for now, though *shit* Aaron's car and a couple of others were way too close. There was nothing to keep the flames from spreading.

I grabbed the planting spade and a heavy rake and ran to join Aaron. Oscar threw what was left of the ice bucket on the flames. The oyster shells scattered on the bricks.

Aaron took the spade and dug into the narrow border of earth between the bricks and the fence. "Smother the fire, pack the dirt

onto it," he yelled. Wherever I piled on dirt the smoke billowed
up, dark and choking. My sandals were useless, I kept sliding out
of them. Somebody got the garden hose going but the water pressure was pitiful, and the stream barely reached the flames.

There was a lot of shouting and people yelling one thing and
another, to wait, to be careful, to step back. The smoke made it
hard to see. Anders was next to us, swinging a broom to knock
embers out of the air.

Sirens, and the fire truck came in at the gate, its lights whirl-
ing. Aaron pulled me back by one arm. "Watch out!" I stamped
my feet on the bricks. The bottom of my shoes started to smoke.
"Are you all right?" I nodded, though I wasn't all right, not really.
His face was sooty, streaked where he'd wiped at it. I must have
looked the same.

The firemen moved slowly in their gear and boots and heavy
coats. I expected them to drop off the truck and start running
around, but maybe it was just another day at the office for them.
They spread out along the fence, and some of them sprayed a layer
of foam along the base, while others opened the tank on the back
of the truck and let the fire have it with the hose.

They had the fire licked in minutes, though there was a lot
more to do. They went back and forth to the truck, bringing
out different tools, talking into their radio. The fence, or a lot
of it, was going to have to come down, and the ground on both
sides dug up to keep the fire from traveling along any roots.
The neighbors on the other side of the fence would need to be
consulted. Nothing was over yet, though the active catastrophe
part was.

I watched all this from behind my truck, near an untouched portion of fence. Nobody saw me slipping away to hide there. Nobody had missed me yet. I was too far away to hear everything, but I could see the group of them in the courtyard, talking with the firemen and with each other, everyone excited, holding towels and water pitchers, taking cell phone shots. I couldn't be part of it. I'd screwed up too badly and there was no way to be sorry enough or to undo what I'd done.

Viridian stood next to the island of plantings, talking to the fire chief, at least I guessed it was the chief. She'd wrapped a white shawl around her shoulders and stood very upright and calm, and I imagined her saying something like, No harm done, it was just an old fence, and how prompt and helpful the firemen had been. Oscar was walking around the firepit as if trying to determine how it had failed him. The others had retrieved their drinks and were talking to each other in ways they might not have if they'd stayed at the table, as if burning something down was the best thing you could do for a party.

Aaron came out of the house and I guess he was looking around for me, which made me feel bad, but I couldn't face him either.

I got my work clothes, my shirt and jeans and shoes, out of the front seat and squirmed into them. The striped dress and red sandals were probably ruined. I mopped at my face with the droopy fabric of the skirt. The fire truck was still blocking the gate and I couldn't drive out, so I walked around the back of it and down the lane in the dark. Maybe it was childish of me (as Aaron accused me later), but I felt cast out, as if I'd been pretending that I fit into any portion of Viridian's world, and now I had been revealed as my true, stupid self. Not to mention the authorities, who might want to talk to a fire-starter.

I reached the end of the lane and the canyon road, and I hesitated, since it wasn't the safest place to walk. People went tearing around the curves without expecting anyone to be there, and most of the time that was the case. Anyway I didn't want to go far; as soon as the firemen left, I was hoping to sneak back in and start the truck and make my getaway. Just leave. That was as much as I'd thought through. I felt my shame as a weight, like a stone in my mouth.

Headlights came toward me on the road, and I stepped back. But the car stopped, and the window came down. "Excuse me," a man said. "Is this still Fairfax?"

The passenger side window was down and he was talking to me across the passenger, a woman. I stepped closer. "Yes, this is Fairfax."

"That's good to know. The GPS on this thing is useless." It was a big, dark Mercedes. The idling engine made almost no noise. If the car was cruising in water, it would have been a shark.

"The GPS is fine. You didn't want to believe it," the woman said. There was just enough light from the instrument panel for me to see that she was Asian, and extremely beautiful, with her hair pulled back into an elaborate topknot. She was wearing a dress with a halter-style top that left her shoulders bare. Her eyes and mouth were made up as precisely as an engraving.

"It's a rental," the man said. "Give me a break." I couldn't see him as clearly, but he was white, and older than the woman.

"I don't suppose you know where we could find Sixty-eight Meadow Way?"

"Right here." I pointed up the lane behind me. Larry? It had to be. "But you can't drive up there just yet, they had a fire."

"A fire? Jesus."

"Can we go now?" the woman asked. "I mean, if the place is all burned down."

"What happened? Anybody hurt?"

"No, it was like, a grass fire." That wasn't quite accurate, but close enough. "Everybody's fine. But there's a fire truck blocking the entrance right now."

There was some conversation between the two of them. "Can you walk up to the house?" the man asked. "I mean, you don't have to go through flames or anything."

"It's a dirt lane and it's kind of steep."

They spoke some more, and then the man said, "It was just an idea."

I walked around to his side of the car, and he rolled down his window. He had a big square head, like an actor's, and what I thought of as an ordinary handsome male face, one that would look good in newspapers, handing out checks at banquets. Square chin, wide forehead, and I expect his teeth photographed well, too. I said, "My boyfriend's helping out up there. I'm waiting for the firemen to move out of the way so I can get our truck." I didn't know why I was talking to him. I was curious about him, I guess. Or because he didn't know me, or anything about me, and I could practice being someone else.

Just then a car came toward us from farther up the hill, and I had to jump back out of the way. "You want to wait with us?" the man said. "Might be safer."

I know all the usual cautions about getting into a stranger's car, but he was only technically a stranger, and besides, it would be a really nice car to get abducted in. "Thanks." I opened the back door and slid into the cool, expensive leather of the seats.

The woman muttered something. I said, "I bet you're here to see the poet. The lady."

Larry (it was surely him), put his arm on the seat back and turned to look at me. "You know her?"

"Sure. Everybody knows Viridian. She's famous."

"Huh."

"I went to a reading she gave. It was packed." I didn't know if anything I said would make any difference. "People get very excited about her poetry. Passionate, even."

"Northern California," the woman said. She waved a hand dismissively. A gust of swooning fragrance reached me.

"Thank you, Maura. So helpful." Maura turned her elegant neck to stare at him.

We waited in silence. I could make some excuse and hop out of the car if I needed to. Larry fiddled with the air-conditioning, gave up, looked around him at the dark road and hillsides.

Maura sighed. "I don't think we should barge in on them. They're probably going through all their burned stuff."

"It wasn't that kind of a fire. And they're expecting us, we're just late." Again Larry turned around to speak to me. "It's been a long day for us. We started out in San Diego."

I said that would make for a long day. I said I thought the

people in the house were having a party. Larry said, glumly, "Oh, it's all business, no party for me." Then, switching into what I thought of as his toastmaster mode, encouraging and enthusiastic, warming himself up, perhaps, "So you're a big poetry fan."

"Huge."

"That's encouraging in a young person. You want to see our cultural heritage passed on."

"Absolutely."

"You can't go wrong, investing in the arts."

"Sure you can," Maura said. I wondered how she got her hair to stay in such an intricate mass of loops and braids.

"I was speaking about ideals. Truth and beauty. Maybe you've heard tell of them."

"We're staying forty-five minutes, tops," Maura said. "And the countdown starts now."

"It's been a long day," Larry said again. Just then the fire engine came down the lane backward, a complicated process involving two of the firemen walking ahead with flashlights to head off traffic. Larry had to move the car up the road and turn around, a thrilling procedure, given how narrow the road was and how enormous the Mercedes.

We started up the lane. "You can let me out at the gate," I told them. I was feeling nervous and sick about running into the rest of them. "Have a good evening."

"Forty minutes," Maura announced, as I got out of the car.

I watched from behind the gate as they drove a little ways into the courtyard. The fence, the burned part of it, was a pile of ruined, soaked boards. There was a bad smell in the air, wet and unwholesome. Ed and Doug were eating plates of cake on the front steps, together again. I guess they all knew each other, because they put the cake plates down and shook hands with Larry. Maura waited for Larry to open her door, then she got out and looked around her, clearly unimpressed. "Northern California," I imagined her saying again.

I waited until they had gone inside, then started the truck and got myself out of there as quick and as quiet as I could. I took my phone out of the center console. It had about forty texts and voice mails from Aaron. I waited until I was out of Fairfax to call him back.

"Where are you? What the hell happened to you?"

"Nothing happened. I'm fine." I was almost to the expressway in San Rafael. I pulled over. "I had to get out of there, I didn't want to talk to any of them."

"Did you not want to talk to me, huh?"

I didn't answer. I could tell he was angry, and I didn't have anything to say that wasn't totally stupid, as stupid as I felt.

He went on. "I told people you felt sick from the smoke and had to leave. So now everybody's worrying about you."

"Well, nobody asked them to."

"Carla? Are you going to tell me what's wrong?"

"The fire was my fault." I watched the cars going by on the overpass. Across the street was an Italian restaurant with people eating dinner. I wanted to be one of them, somebody who had never heard of poetry.

"That's completely dumb. It was an accident. Or it was at least my fault, too. We were both doing the grilling."

"I told Oscar he shouldn't be lighting fires. I made a point of it. And here I'm the one who practically burned the house down."

"Would you stop talking like that?" I guessed he was outside. His end of the line had a windy sound. "Nobody thinks it was your fault. Are you at home? I'll get there as soon as I can."

"I'm going to stay at my mom's tonight. I'm not mad at you. It's okay if you're mad at me. I'll see you tomorrow."

I hung up. I waited to see if he'd try to call me back, but he didn't.

It was late, past ten, when I got to my mom's house. At least she hadn't gone to bed yet, so I didn't feel quite as bad, showing up with no warning. She opened the door and said, "For God's sake, Carla," which told me how gnarly I must have looked.

"What happened?" was her first question, and the one after that was, "Why do you smell like smoke?"

I started crying. Total meltdown. She hugged me, smoke and soot and all, and told me it was all right, all right. What can I say. She was my mom.

She led me to the couch and let me cry a while longer. She brought me Kleenex, a damp washcloth, a 7 Up in a glass. When I'd calmed down a little, she said, "Did something happen with Aaron? Did you have a fight? Did he—"

"He didn't do anything." I'd reached the nose-blowing part of crying and it took me a lot of Kleenex to clean myself up. My mom waited for me to finish. She was wearing her blue quilted bathrobe and her hair was pulled back in a headband so she could do her nightly facial routine. When I stopped crying enough to get words out, I said, "I did something really stupid and I had to get away."

"Are you going to tell me what it was?"

"It doesn't matter. Why am I such a loser?" I was sniffling again.

"Who called you that?"

"I did. It's true."

"Not true."

"I'm never going to do anything right! Anything important. I'm going to spend my life working at some dumb job and hanging out with dumb people and die watching television."

"Carla Marie Sawyer. I haven't heard you whine like this since you were five years old."

I muttered that I wasn't whining. But you can't argue against that particular mom-voice, because then you are whining.

She went on. "You are a beautiful, capable, talented, smart—"

"Hah."

"You have a learning difference. That's the only reason school's been difficult for you."

"Yeah, what am I talented at, exactly?"

I thought that would stump her, but she came back with, "You are a fast learner, and you have an adventurous soul."

I didn't imagine that was anything you could cheer yourself up with on a bad day, but it shut me up for a minute. Then I said, "Aaron's talking about us moving somewhere. He wants to live somewhere different."

"Oh, really?" That surprised her. "Where does he want to go?"

"British Columbia. Vancouver. Maybe. Or somewhere else."

It had only been a few hours since he'd brought it up. It was possible that my latest escapade might change his mind about bringing me along. But it was still out there. It was part of what was making me feel so wretched, although I hadn't realized it until just now.

"Well," my mom said after a moment, "I'd be sad if you went so far away. But I expect you'd have new opportunities in a new place. You might find some kind of work that hadn't occurred to you, something worthwhile that would be just the right match for your skills."

"What kind of work?" And what sort of skills were we talking about, I wondered, but I didn't want to ask.

"My goodness, Carla, how would I know? You haven't even started looking yet."

I couldn't help thinking she made it sound like what I needed was a sheltered workshop of some sort. But now I was only feeling sorry for myself. "Can I stay here tonight?"

She made up my old bed for me and put out towels in the bathroom and found an oversized T-shirt I used to sleep in. She kissed me and told me things would look better after a good night's sleep.

If only. I had too much confused unhappiness cresting inside me to fall asleep easily. I didn't know why I was so scared of moving somewhere with Aaron, why I wasn't like the girls in old music videos who jump on the back of the guy's motorcycle and head out to wherever. Not that Aaron was a stranger, or even had a motorcycle. Not taking into account that he might be seriously p.o.'d at me by now, and might rescind his offer, even kick me out of his house in disgust.

This was how my thoughts were spiraling down.

I kept checking my phone, nothing.

I'd tell Aaron that I'd freaked out about the fire. And I had. I didn't want to try and explain how miserable it made me, thinking I'd cast myself out of Viridian's presence forever. Not that I had any real reason to be there in the first place. Just the ache and the hunger that her poems both awoke and soothed in me. I hardly knew what poetry was, only that it had shaken something loose, the same way music sometimes did, the way it tapped into the messy longings I had that had always embarrassed me, everything that was restless, urgent, and unknown, that I'd pushed away.

And if I was honest, the misery of the last few hours was another kind of extreme sensation and was a thing I valued.

My mom had to work the next day, so she was up early. I heard the hair dryer running in the bathroom while I was still in bed. "Good morning, sunshine," she greeted me, once I reached the kitchen. "I don't know if you eat a big breakfast nowadays."

I said that coffee and toast would be fine. I sat at the table and watched my mom cross and recross the room, gathering all the things she needed for her day. She was wearing a black sundress with red trim and a necklace and earrings set made of red beads. On somebody else it would have looked too matchy-matchy, but on my mom, it was smart and put together. She saw me watching her. "What?"

"Nothing. You always look so nice. I wish I did."

"We could go shopping. I could help you pick some outfits."

"Outfits for what? I don't ever need to look fancy." I thought of my clothes from yesterday, still in a smoky heap in the truck.

"They say to dress for the job you want. So if you don't want to be a lumberjack or a field hand—"

"I get your point."

When she was ready to leave, she bent down and kissed me. She smelled powdery, fragrant. "It doesn't matter so much what you end up doing, honestly. Not to me. You just do it the best you possibly can."

She was my mother, nobody was ever going to love me more than she did. But she didn't entirely believe in me.

There wasn't any reason to stay once my mom left, so I got myself together and headed back home. The house was empty, except for Batman, who rolled over on his back for me to rub his tummy. Aaron was at work. He hadn't left a note or anything for me, which was both good and bad. I mean, no love letter, but no good-bye letter either.

I showered and left again. I didn't want to screw up with the clients I still had. I weeded and watered and planted. It wasn't like I hated what I did. A landscape you've shaped and tended is a gratifying thing. Plants and flowers have such infinite variety, so many ways of growing or failing, combining or striving against each other, coming into season then falling away. I guess they had everything going for them except words.

I didn't have that many clients, but I put off going home as long as I could so that Aaron would be there first. I didn't want to be the one sitting there waiting for the stroke of doom to fall. So I went for a swim at the Indian Valley pool, bought a six-pack of some IPA as a peace offering, and pulled into my usual parking space next to Aaron's car.

"We have to talk," he said, as soon as I opened the door. He was on the couch, watching the television news.

"Okay," I said. I sat on the couch, too, but not right next to him. I put the beer in between us. We didn't talk right away. We watched the television, where the president was giving a speech in front of a crowd. He was moving his mouth in an ugly way, pulling his upper lip back to show his teeth. He was saying that somebody or something was no good, worse than no good, the worst, the absolute, lying, disgusting, putrid worst. I couldn't tell what he was talking about since the news anchor was cutting in. The crowd fell all over themselves, cheering and stomping.

"Who are all these people?" I asked. "Why is it so thrilling for them to hate everybody?"

Aaron lifted the remote and clicked the television off. "That was some stunt you pulled yesterday."

I didn't say anything. I stared at the blank television screen, like some invisible broadcast was playing.

"It was childish. Among other things. It wasn't your house and it wasn't your party and it wasn't your responsibility to watch the grill. You want to know what people were talking about? How you jumped right in to fight the fire. You're their little hero."

"You were there ahead of me," I said.

"Yeah, I'm wonderful, too. I'm trying to tell you, nobody thought you did anything wrong. They're big fans. You can stop acting like you killed somebody's puppy."

I kept quiet, trying to sort it all out. I had been acting like I was in charge, or that the party had something to do with me, when it didn't. I'd only wanted it to. It was part of my stupid yearning, like a little kid desperate to tag along.

I said, "I really did think I'd done this horrible thing. I thought I practically burned the place down. I'm sorry I made you worry about me."

"Even if you did burn something down, I'd still think you were cute. Come here."

We moved in closer on the couch and hugged sideways. I loved touching him. Always always. I felt better, but still tired and beat up.

"Carla? Why do you want to hang out with these people anyway? I mean she's sort of cool, Viridian, but they're a different kind of crowd. I'm not sure we've got a lot in common."

"I don't know. I never knew anything about poetry, I couldn't even read it. I still can't, not like normal people. But I want to learn more about it." I shrugged. "I guess it's not really a career path, is it." As soon as I said it, I saw how it might be. How you might study poetry, become a student of it, and that might lead to the next unknown thing. It would be a little like jumping on the back of that stranger's motorcycle.

Aaron got up from the couch. "Viridian gave me something for you. A couple of things."

He went into the kitchen and came back with a paper shopping bag. "Here." He handed me a thick paperback, an anthology, it looked like: *Modern and Contemporary Poetry*. "There's an audiobook, she made sure of it. You can follow along."

I was still turning it over in my hands when he gave me a second book, a slim one this time. "This is hers. She says she'll read the poems to you if you want."

The book was called *Lost and Found*. It had a picture of a black dog, or its back legs and tail, walking off the right edge of the cover, while the front end of the same dog appeared on the left edge. There was a picture of Viridian on the back, a formal black-and-white portrait that made her look like someone from another century, like she used to hang out with Emily Dickinson.

"Thanks," I said. "That's great." I didn't want to let on how excited I was.

"Her phone number's in there. You're supposed to call her. Come help me figure out dinner."

"Did Larry ever get there? The guy they were all expecting?"

"Somebody came after the fire was out. I wasn't paying a lot of attention at that point."

I followed him into the kitchen and we made pasta with bacon and mushrooms and a tomato salad, and we drank the beer I'd brought, and got in bed and made everything right between us.

It was only a couple of days later that I realized he hadn't brought up moving again, not since that first time.

STUDY

I must have listened to that audiobook, the poetry anthology, three times all the way through, then more for the parts I liked or didn't get. There were a lot of both. I listened to it driving to work and then again driving home, until even the parts I didn't understand, I knew by heart, a chorus of sounds that made words and words that made thought and feeling.

It was an eccentric book, though I didn't realize it at the time. What did I know? It was arranged in purely alphabetical order, with centuries and nations all jumbled together. So that it began with Anna Akhmatova, followed by Maya Angelou, followed by W. H. Auden. Billy Collins came right before Emily Dickinson, and Dylan Thomas after Gertrude Stein. The book made it seem they might all be acquainted.

Each poet was read aloud by a different reader or voice actor, I guess they were called, so that there was a chopped salad effect, this that and the other poem coming at you fast and furious. It wasn't a bad way to immerse myself, all those scraps of word and thought competing for attention. I didn't have to consider them or render judgment, not at first. I only had to let them in.

At the very end of the book was William Butler Yeats, and I recognized the poem about the girl with the yellow hair that Oscar had recited the first time he'd seen me. I still wasn't sure if Oscar had been making fun of me, just as I couldn't tell whether Yeats hadn't been somehow making fun of Anne Gregory, like he knew something about her that she didn't know about herself. I tried to imagine what kind of a poem Anne might have written back, something about what a drag it was when old men tried to get your attention with words.

I wanted to read Viridian's book, and I tried, but it was like trying to break a rock into gravel. Here was a piece of poem I could chip off and understand, and here was the mass of it I could not. She had a lot of poems with one-word titles, like "Fever" and "Bartender." These started out in places I understood, then took a twist or turn that lost me. I thought about asking Aaron to read them to me, but he'd tell me to call Viridian. Which I was going to do, as soon as I got my nerve up.

I was still embarrassed about the fire, not so much my accidental, incidental part in causing it, but my chickenshit stunt of running away. I didn't trust myself to explain it without sounding like the fool that I was. When I finally did call, it was because I realized Viridian already knew I was foolish and ignorant and anxious to please. I guess she might know things about me that I didn't know myself.

"I hope I'm not disturbing you," I began.

"Carla!" Her deep glad voice came over the phone line and enveloped me. "Of course you aren't. I've been thinking of you. I've been out in the garden, trying to curb its excesses."

That was such a funny way to say it; it made me smile. I told her I'd come over and get everything in shape.

IT HAD BEEN more than a week since the party and the fire. The pile of burned fence boards was gone and the fence line was scraped down to bare dirt. Some of the fence panels were still standing, and there was a fan-shaped scorch mark on one. It could have been a lot worse. All of Fairfax could have burned, and all the wooded acreage around us, up the slopes of Mount Tam, across the ridge line and down to the ocean. It was too enormous to think about. The thought actually made me relax a little and let go of some of my remaining guilt. How could one insignificant person like me have that much destructive power? I wasn't some tragic figure. I was more like Mrs. O'Leary's cow that started the Great Chicago Fire.

I parked the truck and took my tools out to the back garden. I was still shy about ringing the front doorbell, though I'd done it before. I wanted to be occupied with something when I first saw Viridian, not standing there looking useless.

The plantings had been left to get too dry, so I set a drip hose all around the main bed. The rhododendrons weren't happy. Foxtails and wild carrot had crept into the borders. It felt good to yank them out and set things to right. I didn't have a hand in the vegetable garden, but I tied the drooping tomato plants to their stakes and pulled up some seeding lettuce. There was a patch of lavender that was doing just fine.

I'd been working about twenty minutes when Viridian came out through the breezeway. "There you are. Leave that for now and come talk to me."

I followed her into the kitchen, which was back to its usual clean-but-cluttered state. "I had a taste for lemonade," Viridian said, opening cupboard doors and bringing out two glasses. "And there's apricot cake from the bakery. How does that sound?"

I murmured that it sounded just fine. I carried the plates and napkins into the living room, while Viridian brought the rest on a tray. She settled into what was clearly her seat, the brown velvet sofa, while I sat on one of the upholstered chairs. Viridian took a drink of lemonade and set the glass down. Today she was wearing another of her white linen kimono-style outfits and a pair of slippers, blue satin with a dragon print, like something you'd get in Chinatown. She said, "Oscar will be sorry to miss you. He's at a writers' conference in Maine."

I nodded, like I knew what that meant, then I thought better of it.

"What's a writer's conference?"

"It's like summer camp for writers," Viridian said. "People who want to practice writing pay to take classes with different authors, and listen to readings, and there are parties and more than a little drinking and carrying on." She made a wry face when she said 'carrying on,' and I guessed I knew what that meant.

"Do people get their money's worth? I mean, do they learn anything?"

"I expect that some do. It can be very intense, very heady, all the talk talk talk about writing, all the exposure to ideas and personalities. It's a little like a religious retreat, I imagine, though I've never been to one of those. Anyway, Oscar will get a big kick out of it. He'll get paid for reading and showing off and being made much of." She cut a slice of apricot cake and put it on a plate for me. "Now you have to tell me what you thought of the book."

Which book? Hers, that I couldn't read? I fumbled with my plate of cake. I wanted to ask more about the writers' conference and what sort of people went there, but first I had to come up with opinions. "I was saving your book. I was hoping there was an audio version, or something—"

"I'll read it to you. Some of it. We'll probably both get bored. Tell me how you liked the anthology."

"I liked a lot of the things. The poems. I guess they're all supposed to be good, if they're in a book, right?"

"Carla, you need to get over the idea of supposed to be. You need to develop your own standards, your likes and dislikes. That's part of critical thinking."

"Okay." I would do that, sure. As soon as I figured out how. "I have trouble with the ones that are, you know, messy. When there's only some loose words here and there, floating around."

She set about explaining the difference between narrative and lyric, between prose and poetry, and how in a poem the thing not said might be just as important as the thing said. About the associations of words, how they triggered other words in our minds. About sound and rhythm, how they reinforced meaning and feeling. How the first lyric poems were songs, sung to the lyre. How the first narrative poems were ballads or epics, meant to commemorate heroes and battles. She would look for a book she had about Navajo storytellers, who passed down creation myths in oral form, over years and years and years. Not everything was about reading.

We kept on talking, or rather, she talked, and I took it all in, and when we reached a pause, a space of silence, I said, "I think I've just been to a writers' conference. My very own. Thank you."

Viridian leaned back into the velvet couch, stretching her neck and shoulders. "You'll want to listen to more than just me."

But I wanted to listen to her for at least a while longer, so I asked if she'd read some of her poems to me. I could tell she was only too pleased to be asked, in spite of what she'd said about boring me. She sat on the velvet couch and I closed my eyes to listen.

We made it through most of the book she'd given me, and we only stopped when I felt I'd been too greedy, used up too much of her time. One stayed with me, *Honeybee*:

Flower food. Honey hive.
Dance to work. No. We are not fanciful.
Nor sentimental. We have no need to see ourselves
as you see us. We forage, build, swarm, sting, die.
We are filled with purpose. Our queen is all.
Are we happy? Leave us alone. We know
everything we need to know.
Huddled in the warm center of the winter hive
we dream the same dream. Always there is life, life.
Leave us alone. The honey's not for you.

I asked her if the poem was about bees or maybe something else. "It's always about something else," she said, and I said I thought I had known that.

I said, "I wish I was better at poetry. Knew how to understand it. It must be—" I turned shy again.

"What?"

"It must be the best life. Writing. Being so very good at it, like you are."

She shook her head. "Don't make too much of it."

"No, really. It must be like times I wish I could sing, or dance, except I'd actually know how. Never mind."

She could tell how much yearning there was in me, how unsure I was. Her voice was patient. "I've had a long life, and it's had its grand moments, as well as awful ones. I've been lucky, I was able to leave the bad behind me. Lucky that I had readers and could keep doing what I wanted."

"Lucky, you're more than that. You're—" I was going to say, a genius.

"Carla, don't take me for something I'm not. Don't make people into idols. It doesn't do anybody any good."

"I won't," I said, too quickly, because how was anyone to prevent me? There was so much more I wanted to ask her. But I already sensed what I would come to learn later: how resistant she was to being known, how she guarded herself from any easy intimacy. And of course I was the opposite, in spite of the shyness, which was not natural to me and was soon overcome. But I didn't want to be overeager, like a Labrador retriever, shoving my nose underneath people's hands, begging for attention.

Now that Viridian was no longer speaking, she looked tired, even old, a suddenly old woman, and my heart sank. It was as if everything had just now declared itself mortal. I said I would finish up in the garden, and she said yes, thank you, that would be lovely.

As I was clearing the plates and glasses, she said, "You remember Ed and Doug, from the party? They're stopping by. Maybe you'll get to see them and say hello."

I heard a car pull up while I was still tending to the plants. Ed and Doug's, I imagined. I took my time, hoping I'd have a chance to see them. I still didn't want to make too free with the house and go sauntering in looking for them. I was finishing up with watering when Doug came through the breezeway and opened the door of the screened porch. "Hi there. Viridian wants to know if you're staying for supper."

Was it getting that late? It was. "Ah, no, I need to be heading home." I had a new attack of embarrassment, wondering if I looked like I was loitering around waiting for invitations.

"You're sure? Ed brought one of his stuffed manicotti dishes. It's killer."

"I can't, really. But tell her thank you, would you?"

"I will." He didn't leave right away but came out and took a seat on a bench. "It's so much hotter here than the city. I always forget."

"I don't get down there much," I said, just to be making conversation. I was trying to take care of all the dry areas without overdoing it. You were supposed to be mindful of water restrictions and I didn't want Viridian getting nasty letters from the water district.

"We're in Pacific Heights," Doug offered.

"That's nice." It was more than nice. It was home to some

of the juiciest real estate in the city, and therefore the planet.
I couldn't tell if he was bragging or just finding something to
talk about. "What brings you up into the hills?" I spoke before it
occurred to me that it really wasn't any of my business.

"Ed needed to talk lawyer-talk with Viridian."

Lawyer-talk, boring.

"Sure you can't stay? We brought plenty of food," he said
encouragingly. "Stuffed squash blossoms. You can't say no to
that."

I said I already had plans, thanks. I wondered how old he
was. Forty or more. He wore a faded red T-shirt, vintage, or at
least they were sold as vintage, and jeans in the palest of blue
denims. Nobody ever dressed their age in San Francisco. He was
the better looking of the couple. He wasn't wearing glasses today
and it suited him. He had a fringe of soft, fair hair and light
eyes that matched his jeans. When he was younger, he must have
been more than pretty. I hadn't spent any time talking to him at
the party and didn't have an opinion of him yet, except that he
seemed good at striking up conversations, like he did it a lot.

Now he said, "Viridian tells me you've taken an interest in
poetry."

I turned off the hose. "Yes." Taking an interest. It sounded
stupid, like I was learning to play the harpsichord.

"I wonder if you'd like to be on hand when we put together
the next issue of the magazine."

I wasn't sure what he meant. "Be on hand?"

"Help out. Make phone calls, keep track of author queries.
Pick up the lunch order."

I was trying to get it straight, what he was saying, and how it all worked. A magazine.

"Nothing too exalted. But you can learn a lot. And we're always looking for unpaid labor."

I was still rummaging around my head, looking for words. Could I afford to work for free? Not for very long.

"We're an excessively casual workplace," he added. "No dress code. Perish the thought."

"But I can't do proofreading. Just so you know. I have a disability, a reading disability. I mean, I can read, but I'm not reliable like that." I was aware that what he was offering might be a thing of value, and I wanted it fiercely, but I didn't want to disappoint anybody.

"No proofreading. Lucky you." He smiled, as if my total lack of qualifications was a plus.

"When were you thinking? And how long? I have to still see to my paying clients, and they get crabby when things die."

Doug said they'd start work on the winter issue next week, and since I wasn't on the payroll I could come and go as it suited me. A few mornings or a few afternoons or a mix of both. I said that I would come sometime next week, he could decide if I'd be any use to them.

He said he was sure I would be. He took out a business card with the magazine's name, *Compass Points*, and his name, and street address—he worked from home, he explained—and then he wrote his cell number on the back and said I should call him if I had any questions, and that parking was a bitch, I should expect that.

"No problem," I said. I was trying to keep my face and voice steady and neutral, though I felt like one of those starlets discovered by a talent agent at a lunch counter.

"Outstanding. How's Aaron?"

"Fine. He's good."

"You're sure he's not a firefighter? The way you two pitched in was amazing. Please give him my best."

I told him I would, and I loaded up my tools to head home. Everything was banging and clanging inside me all at once: Viridian and the poems I'd heard, and the magazine, and what I might be expected to do there, and Doug and Ed, and how anybody could afford to live in Pacific Heights, and maybe if Doug had a thing for Aaron or just liked guys who would dress up in uniforms.

It wouldn't be the last time I'd wonder about people's motives.

AARON WAS AMUSED, mostly, by my poetry pals, as he called them. He did point out that I wasn't getting paid for any of it, Viridian's garden work or whatever Doug would find for me to do at the magazine. I said it was like an internship, trading labor for a chance to learn things.

"Learn what, exactly? It doesn't sound like vocational training."

I guess it always came down to that. Some version of, Show me the money or you're wasting your time. "They're not doing so bad. These guys live in Pacific Heights," I pointed out.

"Yeah, well one of the guys is a lawyer."

"So?" I knew what he was saying. Poetry didn't pay the bills. "Different people make different contributions."

"You don't even know them," Aaron said. "You don't have to defend them."

"I just think, there's such a thing as learning for its own sake."

"There's such a thing as gas money and bridge tolls, too."

I didn't like it that he kept holding money over me. Why was he trying to piss me off? "I'll keep track of everything I spend. I'll pay for it all myself."

"I just don't want you to get too carried away with all this."

"All this what, exactly?"

He muttered something about people I just met, and I said there wasn't anything wrong with meeting new people, was there? I didn't know what he meant then, and maybe he didn't either, not really. It had not yet taken shape. All this enthusiasm for things that did not include him, that might take me far afield. Money was just the easiest complaint.

"Fine," he said, giving up. "I kind of wish you'd gotten fascinated by, I don't know, stocks and investing."

"You have no poetry in your soul," I said, fake punching him in the stomach, and that was how we left it.

I'D ARRANGED WITH Doug to come in on Tuesday morning. I got up extra early and stopped at my clients' yards in Petaluma and San Rafael on the way, doing what needed to be done so I could play hooky the rest of the day. It was almost nine when I was able to get on the freeway south. It was clogged with rush-hour traffic, of course, and there wasn't anything you could do except relax and enjoy the world's most beautiful commute. Past the glimpses of the bay, of Sausalito Harbor, through the tunnel with the rainbow arch in my rearview mirror. Then the Golden Gate Bridge itself, my tires humming, the bay and the ocean spread out below me like a blue plate dotted with sailboats, the city skyline as sharp as cut paper on this beautiful clear day.

Aaron and I didn't get into the city that often. Every once in a while for a concert, or to see someone we knew. I thought we could make more of an effort to do so, not pretend that San Francisco was a world away. Yes, it all cost money, but it might be worth it.

Something else that cost money: Pacific Heights. I got off on Fillmore and cruised the neighborhood, already jazzed from the traffic and the crowds of people coming and going, the prosperous, the oddballs, the prosperous oddballs, and all the storefronts where I could imagine myself buying pottery or expensive coffee and living some different, utterly cool life.

I found Doug and Ed's address and was glad to see they didn't live in some historic mansion, although it was still a pretty nice pile of real estate. One of those houses that was either a real Victorian, modernized, or else a new place fitted out to look old. It was tall and gray with white trim, squeezed in between two other swell-looking houses. It had a grand flight of stairs leading up to the front door; tall, narrow windows ornamented with plaster half-pillars; and on top, diamond-shaped windows set off with some gewgaw fretwork. It wasn't remarkable in San Francisco for houses to be this elegant, this visibly expensive. But it wasn't like I ever got to see the insides of them.

I rang the doorbell and a scratchy intercom said something, presumably in English. I spoke my name and said that I was here to see Doug about the magazine.

After a time, the door was opened by a slim guy in a black T-shirt and black jeans.

"Carla, right? I'm Jonathan. Welcome welcome! We're going to the top floor. Thank God there's an elevator. I only use it to go up. Exercise." He was a little breathless, though maybe that had something to do with taking the stairs.

I followed him through the foyer, past a large, open living room, trying to see as much as I could. I'd imagined that people who owned Victorians would go whole hog with fringed lamps and period furniture. Ed and Doug went the other direction, everything sleek and contemporary, aside from a fireplace with old-fashioned plaster moldings. There was a lot of white upholstery and a white furry rug and I was pretty sure that the paintings on the wall were Art.

I would have liked to slow down and look some more, but Jonathan kept us moving, down a hallway with a quick glimpse of a kitchen featuring a lot of stainless steel and blond wood. Past a couple of closed doors to a single small elevator.

"This is some house," I said while we waited for the door to slide open. You just about had to say it and get it over with.

"Isn't it amazing? There's a sauna in the basement. That's where I live. I mean the basement apartment, not the sauna."

"Aren't you lucky." The elevator door slid open and we stepped inside. It chimed and whooshed. I guess it made sense to rent out your extra space if you wanted to keep an expensive roof over your head.

"Yeah, it's part of my compensation. Which is good, because otherwise I'd be living in like, Stockton or somewhere."

Like, Petaluma or somewhere. I kept that thought to myself. Doug already knew I was a backwoods rube type, it wouldn't be any surprise. I wondered about Jonathan's job, and how exactly he was compensated. Then the elevator settled, and its doors opened.

Reggaeton music, turned up loud. And a big, bare room, the furniture all pushed to the sides. In the center of the room, beneath a large skylight, was a hammock, and in the hammock was Doug.

"Carla! Important question. Do you speak Spanish?"

"A little." I'd picked up enough to swear back at the landscape crew when I had to. I hoped I wasn't going to have to translate any poems.

"What is she saying?" He waved his hand and I understood he meant the music, the singer.

"Ah, she's . . . she lives fast, she can't change . . . *con altuda*, with height? Or maybe it means something else, like, going as high as you can, anyway, she's going to die young," I finished, lamely. The rest of the lyrics were one long Spanishy blur.

"Well bust my buttons." Doug seemed happy with even that much translation. He hopped out of the hammock. Today he wore a hoodie and jeans, a ball cap and sneakers. He was too old to be dressing like a skateboarder. "You are the most useful girl. Come here. Show you something."

He told me to take his place in the hammock, which I did, though it made me feel like an idiot. From here, he said, there was a view of the bay. Yes there was, past the marching rooftops. A piece of blue water against the blue sky. "Wow," I said, dutifully, then got myself out again.

"You ready to work? Excellent. Show her where the coffee is," he said to Jonathan, who led me over to a side of the room that had been outfitted as a small kitchen. I poured a mug for myself, and Jonathan told me that Doug took his coffee with extra cream. My first job in po biz. Coffee girl.

Under another skylight was a big table with stacks of the actual magazine, *Compass Points*. "The finished product," Doug said, handing me one, rocking a little on his heels.

It was about the size of a phone book for a medium-sized town, with a glossy cover. The cover was black, with some jagged shapes in different colors scattered here and there, like broken Easter eggshells.

"This is where we do the Lord's work," Doug said, which I understood was meant as a joke. "We get submissions from all over the country. All over the world, really. You can imagine how important it is for writers to find readers. Imagine somebody sitting alone at a desk, practically writing in blood—that's how it feels sometimes—they send us a poem and they get a response. They get validation."

I imagined that most of them got a rejection, but Doug's phone rang just then, and we didn't have to get into such fine points. The phone call took Doug across the room. I sat down with my copy to take a look.

There was a title page, and a table of contents, and a list of the magazine staff. Doug was Doug McGregor, editor-in-chief, and there were other names that didn't mean anything to me, nor did the names of contributors, though I hadn't expected to know any of them. I opened the magazine in the middle and started to read.

The kiss of the sun. Grow old with me.
The fleur de lis on your shoulder
The tortoise and his friend
All on the very edge of falling
into dysfunction

I did not find this encouraging. Maybe it was just me, my brain, turning words into slop. But no, I was meant to develop my critical thinking skills. I was pretty sure it was slop to begin with.

Doug came back from his phone call. "What do you think?"

"It's very handsome."

"It better be. We pay enough for glossy cover stock. All right, let's get you started on something." I followed him to another table, where Jonathan was already staring into a computer screen. "That was the Spring/Summer issue. Winter's next."

It was only July. I said, "I guess it takes a long time to get an issue to the finish line."

"Time. Also blood, toil, tears, and sweat." He pulled out a chair for me. "Jonathan's going to show you what to do, I have to go out." To Jonathan he said, "She can help you pull pages."

As soon as Doug had disappeared into the elevator, Jonathan got up and turned the music off. "There's only so much Spanish screaming I can stand, if that's okay with you."

He showed me what he was doing, opening different files on the computer screen, then making a note of certain pages, which I was to print out using a separate computer. These pages had problems or questions, he explained, and Doug would need to go over them. Doug handled all the edits himself. He insisted on actual pages, he made his notes in actual ink. He was a real old-school editor. Which wasn't a bad thing, Jonathan added loyally.

"What does an editor do, exactly?"

"They're the guiding intelligence. The one that shapes the vision of the magazine. Doug picks the poems for the issues, and then he works on the poems to make them better."

"And the writers are okay with that?" It was hard to imagine they would be.

"If they want to be in the magazine. And everybody wants to be in *Compass Points*."

Did they. I stored this information away to revisit later. "Are you a big poetry fan?" I asked. Testing the waters.

"Not really. More of a film guy. Doug knows a lot of people in film. He's going to help me get a foot in the door. Learn the business."

"What kind of film, exactly?"

"I'm working on some script ideas. That's all I better say right now."

"You want to be a film editor, I guess."

"No, I want to be the director. Film is different."

It took me a few tries to get the hang of the printer, but then I did, and it was easy enough to do my tasks, and talk with Jonathan at the same time. He was from Wyoming, he said. Not the best place to be a gay boy. Had I heard of Matthew Shepard? I had. Well, he was from Wyoming, too. That was the kind of thing that happened there. If you stayed.

Doug and Ed had been, like, his fairy godfathers. Jonathan had a job waiting tables at a place in Noe Valley. He was trying to put a little money aside. He loved San Francisco. He loved Doug and Ed, they were angels who walked among us. He owed them everything. "I don't want to get into the details, but seriously, they saved my pitiful, scabby little life."

"They sound great," I said. It made me a little uncomfortable, hearing him go on about Doug and Ed, singing their praises, which for all I knew they entirely deserved. It reminded me that even the most sincere admiration, the most devoted hero worship, can make you sound foolish.

Doug came back with our lunch, pizza slices and some fizzy fruit sodas. So far I had no complaints about the working conditions. We finished with the page printout and Jonathan said it was time for him to get ready for his waiter job. He waved as the elevator door closed on him.

"I should think about getting back, too," I said. The afternoon rush hour started early, and I didn't want to get slammed twice in one day.

"Absolutely," Doug said. "First let me show you something."

I followed him to an alcove under one of the diamond-shaped windows. An old-fashioned bookcase with glass doors was there, and Doug opened a door to show me a line of small bound journals. He drew one out. "Here. *Compass Points*, spring 1943."

It didn't look like much. Limp, a little grimy and worn, and with a plain cover of rough blue paper. "Yeah, it's been around for a while," Doug said. "Not continuously. There was a break in the sixties, and another one in the eighties. It kind of dragged along in the nineties, then went under again. I've had it for the last eight years."

"So it's not really the same magazine," I said, then wished I hadn't, since Doug gave me some side eye.

"It's a heritage. A heritage of excellence. *Compass Points* published e.e. cummings. Pablo Neruda. Bertolt Brecht. Marianne Moore. I expect you may have heard of some of them."

I said something that might have been yes and might have been no. It never took me too long to lose whatever self-confidence I had, whatever altitude I'd gained, and crash into the glass roof below. I wanted to get to that elevator and get myself out of there. But Doug reached into the bookcase and handed me three or four issues. "Here. Promise me you won't sell them on eBay. They're worth some real money."

I took them without examining them. "Sure. Thanks."

"Read them. Keep them as long as you need. What I'm trying to do, Carla? Build on the glory days. Bring *Compass Points* into the present. Keep the tradition but make it contemporary. Give it that edgy vibe. You follow?"

"Sure," I said again. I was pretty certain I wasn't the least bit edgy.

"Take this one, too." He reached for another issue. "It's from sixty-nine. One of Mathias's first published poems."

That name again. By now I knew a little of Mathias, that meteor of a poet. A streak across the sky. Famous at twenty-five, dead by thirty-five. Everything he touched, he scorched. "Wow. Thanks."

"One of two surviving copies. The other's in a safe deposit box. A poet like him doesn't come along very often. There weren't that many of his poems to begin with, so they're especially valuable." He fixed me with a serious look. "He killed himself, you know."

I tried to give the magazine back to him.

"No," he said, "you hang on to it. Please. Show it to Viridian. I expect she's mentioned him to you?"

Had Mathias been a friend? Lover? I remembered a picture of him in one of the anthologies. His wild black hair, his smudged, desperate eyes. Doug made it sound like suicide had been a good career move.

"She hasn't said anything to me," I told him, and Doug nodded and repeated that I should show it to her, he knew she'd get a kick out of it. He thanked me for being here and helping, he could tell I was a quick study, and I should come again because it only got more interesting as the deadlines approached, as well as a little crazier, and it wasn't all work around here. There were parties from time to time, maybe Aaron and I would come?

Seeing his face this close was a little unsettling. You wouldn't have guessed he used to be pretty.

I said we would certainly try to be there. Doug was being nothing but charming, as if to make up for any earlier unpleasantness, but still I felt relief at leaving, at finding my way to the front door and out to the street. I drove home trying to sort out how I felt about it all. I didn't have any great powers of intuition or foresight, but I was pretty sure that Doug was not an angel walking among us.

GOSSIP

Oscar returned from Maine and the writer's conference spent, exalted, and in love.

Heartsick, he went for long, solitary hikes up Mount Tam and returned to Viridian's scratched and sore. Or he holed up in his room, writing furiously, emerging only for supplies of alcohol and sandwiches. The lady was a fiction writer, another one of the conference staff. She lived in Montreal. They were going to see each other again as soon as possible. He couldn't find his passport; it was expired anyway. How long did it take to get a passport renewed? Or wait, somebody told him you only needed a passport to enter Canada if you flew. He could drive. Then he would only need a driver's license.

They'd met the first night and talked for hours. So incredible! It was as if they'd been saving up words their entire lives, just to share with each other. Things had progressed from there. She was brilliant, or as Oscar said, "blazing brilliant." He'd bought all her books, he was reading them straight through. She was reading his books, too. She completely got them, what he was doing, what he was trying to do. He was writing new poems. For her, about her. He hadn't stopped writing since they'd met. They'd both cried when they had to leave. They were inconsolable! They'd talked every day since, emailed, wrote.

"He always falls in love at conferences," Sacha said. She and Viridian and I sat on the screened porch. Oscar had been pacing back and forth on the breezeway, oblivious to us, then he stalked into the house. We were drinking iced coffee and watching the sprinklers I'd set up send fine bands of spray through the air. If you looked into the water just right, you saw a rainbow.

"He's not the only one," Viridian said. "These shipboard romances." She sighed, as if she'd witnessed too many such cruises.

"At least it's not a student this time. I know Irene, she's quite nice," Sacha said. "I'm fairly sure she has a long-term partner in Montreal. I hope she's decent to Oscar, lets him walk away with his poems and some beautiful memories."

"We're shocking Carla," Viridian warned.

"No you're not. But they sound like teenagers."

This made them both laugh. "Exactly," Viridian said. "It's always passionately sincere and it's going to last forever. "

"I'm so glad I'm not young anymore," Sacha said. "That helps. My God, the abject humiliation of falling in love." She might not have been young, but she was pretty enough to be able to say things like that and not seem pathetic.

I didn't know if she was talking about Anders, who seemed to be in love with her, in a slightly berserk way. He was in Sweden this month, doing research, or, as Viridian teased her, on a mission of errantry designed to win favor in his beloved's eyes. Sacha just smiled. You had to wonder about those two.

I'd gotten into the habit of going to Viridian's in the late afternoon, doing what needed to be done in the garden, then sitting with her and whoever might be visiting. Sometimes it was Barb or Chloe or another of the hens. Sometimes other poets, friends of hers, who either lived nearby or might be in San Francisco for one or another reason. I didn't talk much, just listened, soaking everything up. I wanted to keep living this way, among people who talked about writing, sometimes frivolously, sometimes seriously, often both in the same conversation. I wanted to spend my afternoons eating macarons or panna cotta or whatever treat somebody showed up with. I wanted the clothes they wore, the lives they'd lived. I guess you could say I had a poetry crush.

I was learning a lot, in a disorganized way. Viridian kept loaning me more books, as had Sacha and Oscar. James Wright, H.D., John Berryman, Elizabeth Bishop. Sexton and Plath, Roethke and Snyder. Newer poets just starting to make a name for themselves. I found that if I read the poems out loud to myself, I could make some headway with them. This was a relief, although I didn't want to make too much of it. I didn't want to be a curiosity, like those people born mentally handicapped and blind, who are geniuses at playing the piano. I'm just saying, I was a little self-conscious.

I read all the books they lent me. There were those moments, rare but wonderful, when a particular poem would make me feel as if a huge bird inhabited my chest and now it was struggling to take flight.

I'd gone back to Doug's a few times as well. I wasn't a member of the Doug fan club; I thought he was a little too full of himself, or maybe a lot. But he wasn't in the office that much. I liked Jonathan, and I had to admit, I liked the beautiful house as well. I liked being around the enterprise of the magazine, which was literally taking shape under our hands. I made phone calls, took messages, helped Jonathan make changes in a master file. Sometimes poets showed up here too, most often to meet Doug for lunch or dinner.

There were a variety of these, or as Oscar liked to say of them, "great rats and small rats, lean rats and brawny rats." In person they might be odd, eccentric, unimpressive, vain and quarrelsome, but on the page, they blazed. There was Philip Kirby, ancient now, who had once known Ferlinghetti. And Lucca Benin, a sorrowful little bald man who wrote so beautifully about death and immortality. Lolly Robinette, who had lived in a Buddhist monastery for five years under a vow of silence. Pyotr Bogrov, who played his mandolin for us.

On such occasions I was part tour guide, part hostess, showing the visitors around, fetching them drinks. I didn't mind, even when men went out of their way to make sprightly conversation with me. It wasn't any worse than putting up with the landscapers. And all the while I got to listen to them, their enthusiasms, their feuds and rivalries. Nobody ever seemed to think I was listening. I was slowly working my way through the poems in the magazine's winter issue. I decided I liked some of them better than others, which was the way it was supposed to be. I decided I wasn't particularly edgy.

I'd given the issue of *Compass Points* with Mathias's poem to Viridian. She read the poem, studied the page, then handed the magazine back to me. Isn't that interesting, she had said, and I should thank Doug for letting her see it. Which I did. If Doug had expected her to say more, I couldn't tell. He'd nodded, put the magazine back in the bookshelf, and climbed into the hammock to make a phone call. No one was going to tell me anything.

I got up to change the sprinklers' path and when I came back inside, Sacha said to me, "We have an idea. Please hear us out and don't take it the wrong way." She turned her curly head to Viridian, waiting.

I looked from one of them to the other. Viridian said, "There's a writer's conference the end of August, up near Placerville. A number of us will be there and we were wondering if you'd like to go as well."

"I'm not a writer." My first reaction.

"You would be on the staff. Help with setting things up, running the conference. There's a little bit of money in it and you could go to the readings and some of the class sessions if you wanted."

"It's sponsored by an environmental foundation," Sacha said. "Harnessing the power of the arts to heal the planet."

"All very worthwhile."

"Into the Woods. That's what we always call it."

"Of course, it has a more serious name."

"Absolutely. Serious stuff." Although they were both trying not to laugh, as if at some past joke.

"I don't know," I said. "I mean, it sounds great, and it's nice of you to think of me, but I'm not sure I could get away."

"It's only what, five days? Maybe six," Viridian waved a hand. "Our friend Tony Presto's in charge this year. He said he's still looking for assistants."

"I don't know," I said again.

Sacha said, "Now, we are not trying to set you up for some scandalous love affair. That's your own business." She smiled her pretty smile.

"She has a perfectly lovely boyfriend already," Viridian said.

"See? Not an issue."

"Anyway, it's a very high-minded conference. Everyone's expected to be on their best behavior." More of the not-laughing.

"No one will harass you. We'll see to it."

"They'll all just write poems about her."

"I expect some of them already do."

I didn't want anybody writing poems about me. I didn't want to be Anne Gregory. I reached for my keys. "I have to be heading out. You'll need to turn those sprinklers off in another hour."

I was starting the truck when Viridian called to me, walking across the courtyard. "Carla! Wait up."

I waited. She leaned in at the truck's window. "I'm sorry. We were teasing you and we shouldn't have been."

I stared straight ahead, not wanting to answer. It seemed like I was always getting my feelings hurt, then running away like a baby.

"We really did think the conference would be something you'd enjoy. Something you'd be good at. But you don't have to have anything to do with it."

I turned the engine off. "I guess I didn't know what to think."

"Well. Open invitation."

If I was supposed to say either yes or no, I couldn't manage either yet. "Can I just ask, why would anybody go out of their way for me? Why do you? I don't know anything."

She shaded her eyes with her hand. There were times when a trick of light or an angle of vision made her look either younger or older. At this moment she looked older, tired, the skin settling loosely into the grooves of her face. I began to feel bad for distressing her.

She said, "It's exactly because you don't know anything. Not yet. But you want to. Because you're excited about learning, because it's all new to you the way it has not been new to me for a long time. Don't feel embarrassed about being young, Carla. My God. Glory in it."

By now I wasn't sure which of us should be apologizing to the other. It was thrilling to hear her speak about me, just this once, in such personal terms, for her to lessen the distance between us. Maybe she still felt bad about upsetting me.

I said, "I could never be a writer. I mean a good one. I don't have the talent. I could probably be a bad one, lots of people seem to be. But I could never do what you do."

"You wouldn't want to live this way."

I shook my head. I would. I'd want it more than anything.

"You think writing poems has something to do with talent? Not much at all. It has to do with pure, stubborn determination to keep doing it, to not be discouraged by the thousand thousand things that are meant to discourage you. Nobody cares if you do it or not. No guarantees that anybody is going to read any of it."

"But that hasn't stopped you."

"Because I have been absolutely selfish about my art. Do you know how hard it is for a woman to be selfish? Not to give in to her own nature?"

She stopped then, and neither of us spoke. I didn't understand her, at least not until much later. Below us on the road, a car accelerated up the curves, trailing music. Then it was quiet again. She said, "Please don't worry. About anything. Least of all this silly conference."

"Can I think about it some more?"

"Of course." She straightened herself and stepped back from the truck, smiling, already distancing herself, stepping back into herself. "I expect there's another week or so before anything gets decided."

"I wanted to ask you about something different."

"Yes?"

"If you're going to San Diego. If you're going to be part of the Institute."

"Ah," she said, and now she was entirely remote again, although still smiling. "That's been taken under advisement. One more thing you don't have to worry about."

Taken under advisement, meaning, she wouldn't say. Don't worry, meaning, none of my business. I started the truck again and headed down the lane. In the rearview mirror, Viridian turned toward the house and out of my sight.

I was about halfway to downtown Fairfax when I saw Oscar shambling along the side of the road, and I slowed to see if he wanted a ride. "Thanks," he said, hauling himself into the passenger seat. A gust of heat and, I couldn't help noticing, sweaty odor accompanied him.

"You look terrible," I told him, and he said "Yeah, so what." But he did. His long hair was unwashed and stringy, and his big, loose face was mottled with uneven sunburn. I wouldn't dream of saying anything so disrespectful to Viridian. But Oscar was different. He all but invited you to participate in his problems.

"Seriously, are you all right?"

"Seriously, I need a drink. Come with me."

"I can't," I said. But he looked so miserable that I told him I'd have one drink, one, then I had to meet Aaron for dinner in San Rafael. Oscar said oh sure, he got it. Celebrate, fornicate, don't worry about him for a minute.

"'That is no country for old men. The young in one another's arms, birds in the trees—'"

"Stop." He was always quoting Yeats for some twisted reason of his own.

We went to one of the live music bars, too early still for any event crowd. The bartender knew Oscar, as did the waitress. We settled into a corner booth and the waitress brought him a red-eye beer, which I guess was his usual. I ordered an IPA. "How's Irene?" I asked, figuring that love had everything to do with it.

"That's all over." He got some of the red-eye into him and looked around the empty room at something that wasn't there.

"What happened?"

"Nothing happened. And kept happening. After a while, you get the message."

"Was there somebody else?" I asked. "Did she have, a, uh . . ."

"Of course there was somebody else." He swatted away a piece of hair that was interfering with his glass. "I knew that. I knew it from the start. We could have worked it out."

I didn't dare ask how. I said I was sorry. I didn't know what else to tell him. I was unaccustomed to consoling grown men about their sketchy love affairs.

"She was an honest person. I valued that in her."

"You shouldn't talk about her like she's dead."

"To me she is."

I took out my phone and texted Aaron: NEED HELP ON MISSION OF MERCY RE: OSCAR.

It was a couple of minutes before he got back to me. Oscar complained he thought there was something wrong with his heart, no joke, not a metaphor. He had these episodes of light-headedness. I said he hadn't been eating or sleeping right or taking care of himself, but he should see a doctor just in case. He said what was the point. I said then what was the point of complaining about it. He said I was one of those heartless, practical people, wasn't I? My phone blipped. YOU'RE KIDDING, Aaron had texted back.

LOST LOVE. DEATH TALK. PLEASE.

LET ME GUESS. YOU'RE AT A BAR.

I texted the emoji for crying, and one for a glass of beer, and he texted back asking which bar.

I put my phone up. "Aaron's going to join us," I said brightly.

Oscar signaled the waitress for another beer. "Lucky him." But I think he was glad there would be some addition to my inadequate company.

It would take Aaron some time to get here. "I've been helping out on the next issue of *Compass Points*," I offered.

Oscar gave me a look that seemed at least briefly interested. "How did that come about?"

"Doug was at Viridian's with Ed one day and asked if I wanted to see how it was done."

"And how's that working out?"

"Fine, I guess. I'm doing the no-brain stuff. Sharpening the pencils." Oscar seemed skeptical at this account of my contributions. "He's not paying me."

"No, he wouldn't."

"Is *Compass Points* a good magazine?"

"Often enough. When Doug holds off on the logrolling."

"You want to tell me what that means?"

"The exchange of favors," Oscar said wearily. "He publishes poems by other editors and they publish his in their magazines. Everybody's happy."

I was quiet, considering this. Then I said, "But it's a famous magazine, isn't it? It goes way back."

"It's been famous. And Doug wants to be famous. Don't we all."

"How did he end up with the magazine?"

"Same way he ended up with that swell house. He had a wealthy lover who died and left the place to him. And enough cash to start the magazine up again. Not that Ed doesn't pull his weight. And puts up with a thing or two, I imagine. He's a good guy, Ed. Why can't I ever find any wealthy lovers?"

"Then I guess you'd have to kill them off."

"So funny. Doug's such a tease. He's always on the verge of taking my poems for the magazine and dangling some real money in front of me. Then it never happens. Well screw him. He should do something for Virdie, she really needs the money." He glanced at me. "I shouldn't be telling you any of this."

"Somebody needs to tell me things once in a while so I'm not always the only clueless person in the room."

"Not clueless. Innocent."

"Now you're pissing me off."

The bar was beginning to fill up, people drifting in for happy hour or bar food. Somebody got the jukebox going. Emmylou Harris singing "Boulder to Birmingham." That song for a perfectly broken heart. I said, "Tell me about Mathias."

"What about him."

"Why he's supposed to be such a big deal. Why Viridian doesn't talk about him."

"That's old gossip."

"But it's still going around."

Oscar pushed his hair back with both hands and sighed and said that first he needed to finish his beer.

You have to understand, he told me, it was all a long time ago. The good old days in good old grungy New York City. Days that would kill you if you tried to revisit them now. That had, in fact, killed Mathias. He, Oscar, had only begun to poke his head above ground, writing poems, hanging out with other poets, trying to figure out what the hell it meant to be a poet, how to live and work and walk and talk like one. And they were older, Mathias and Viridian, they were actual poets. Already riding the train. No, Mathias wasn't a lot older than Viridian. How did that one get started? They were pretty much the same age. It was just that Mathias had been so celebrated at such a young age, like the child Jesus in the temple.

It wasn't like Oscar had been their good friend back then. It was a whole scene, a whole way of life. Imagine a constellation of people, poets and punk musicians and artists and underground cartoonists and wannabes and hangers on and hustlers. You saw each other at parties, clubs, events. He couldn't say he'd known Mathias well. There hadn't been enough time to know him well, since he was nearing the end of his stay on the planet. He was brilliant. He was crazy. The drinking didn't help. His poetry readings were theater, the kind where you were never sure if the actors were going to jump from the stage and throttle someone in the audience.

Of course, they all drank a lot back then. But Mathias was an extremist in that as in everything. He'd shown up one night with a big bloody gash above one ear, he wouldn't say how, and he wouldn't let himself be taken to emergency, and the thing had festered and become infected and landed him first in detox, then a hospital bed for a week. Good times.

He would have been intolerable, a true pain in the ass, if he hadn't been so smart and so unhappy. In spite of all his talky fun and hijinks. He was probably diagnosable, there was probably medication nowadays for whatever they'd call him. Depressive, bipolar, both. Whatever name you'd hang on that core of churning disquiet in him.

And Viridian. She wasn't called that yet, she was Linda, Linda one thing or the other. Mathias gave her that name. I thought you knew that. Can you imagine how beautiful she was? That clean, wide-open face standing out in all those grubby rooms. Like the light in a gloomy Rembrandt canvas. A number of the artists back then had painted her or had tried to. Of course, she had to kick and fight her way free of so many assumptions. That she was a lovely lightweight, that she slept her way to success, and most humiliating of all, that she was meant to be the muse for someone else's life work.

She'd married young and had shucked off that husband. She'd married again later, either because of or in spite of Mathias. They were on-again, off-again. True love, of the blood-curdling kind. Like Romeo and Juliet, if Shakespeare had made Romeo a binge drinker and Juliet was always calling the police. One of them probably had to die.

All that detachment and calm I saw now? She didn't come by it naturally.

He wasn't doing them justice, either of them. But here was what I needed to know now: Before he died—that is, before he ingested a double fistful of pills and a couple bottles of high-powered codeine cough syrup—he destroyed his newest poems, an entire cycle of them.

Here's where I broke in. "Destroyed? Why? What happened?"

"Oh, he burned them. Burned them alive, I guess you'd say. In public. He was giving a reading somewhere in the city. No, I wasn't there. You know who was? Lolly. You should talk to her."

Lolly Robinette, the little Buddhist lady that I'd met at *Compass Points*. I didn't know her that well. "Okay, but why did he—"

"Spite. Despair. Dragging everything down with you, like the dead Vikings and their burning ships. Short answer? Crazy poet syndrome. But you can get tired of hearing that one."

Oscar was cracking peanuts and tossing them into his mouth. He wasn't crazy. Just untidy and unhappy and maybe a little foolish. A poet could be all kinds of normal, at least on the outside. I knew that by now.

Oscar looked up from the peanuts then and raised his hand in a wave. "Here's your boyfriend. The other thing you need to know? The cycle of poems he burned? It turned out that Viridian had a copy of the whole cycle."

I thought again about Doug bringing up Mathias, offering me a spot at the magazine in the first place. He must have thought I could help him get the poems. So much for people wanting to help me on my journey of discovery. I'd been such an idiot. I wondered why I had been offered a job at the writing conference. I wondered if some dark motive lurked behind every kindness. And if it was easy to be mistaken about what you thought was true love.

AARON AND I were going to a party at Doug's and neither of us was happy about it.

Aaron complained about hauling ass all the way down to the city, just to stand around in a room full of *pew-ets*. People he didn't know and had nothing to say to. He didn't know why he was doing it. "Because the last party was so terrific, you know, with the fire truck and all."

We were on 101, crawling toward the bridge with all the other Marinites out to have their city fun. "It's not just a magazine party," I said, although I wasn't entirely sure of that. "All kinds of people will be there. Besides, you like Oscar," I pointed out. Aaron had liked drinking beer with him and agreeing that women were no damned good, present company (me) excepted, possibly.

"Oscar doesn't act like a poet."

"Meaning what, exactly."

"Just for once, maybe you could not challenge everything I say."

Meaning, I guess, shut up. Which I did. We rolled forward, onto the bridge itself. Traffic sped up. They must have switched the lanes around so that we had the extra one.

"Okay, here's the deal," Aaron said after a time. "I'll put on my party face. It just isn't my kind of scene."

"The house alone is worth the trip." I was at least looking forward to seeing more of it than the glimpses I got between the elevator and the front door. I wanted to see the place all decked out for company. I wanted to eat food I couldn't even pronounce.

"Maybe we can set it on fire."

"Nice." I wasn't exactly at ease about the party myself. I expected that at some point Doug would ask me to start emptying ashtrays or some other service job, just to make my status clear to people. The issue we'd been working on was almost done. I wouldn't be spending a lot more time there.

Viridian had been invited but she wasn't coming, which somehow had turned into my fault.

"Can't you talk her into it?" Doug had asked me, annoyed. "Tell her I'll send a car for her."

But Viridian said her party days were over. I guess Doug was at least glad he hadn't invested in me as a paid employee.

I wished I could ask Viridian about the Mathias poems, or Mathias himself, but I didn't dare, didn't want to risk upsetting her. I found more of his work online, and maybe it was the awfulness of his life, the waste of it, that made me shiver, reading it:

A room, a roaring room. Through the door, an enemy will come.
Are you ready? This dream
is your death foretold. The air in the room is the exact weight
of the brick thrown through the window
you neglected to account for.

And what about the lost poems, the ones Viridian was said to have? My guess, which turned out to be pretty good, had been that Doug wanted to get his hands on them for the magazine. He wanted the attention and the glory. I didn't much like Doug or how he operated, but maybe the magazine would be a worthy home for Mathias's work. And Doug had money, maybe he would pay Viridian a lot to publish them, what she needed, however much that was. I thought about how Viridian would hate my knowing even this much about her circumstances.

How much was a legacy of poems worth anyway? Was it the exact weight of a short life subtracted from a long one, the difference in years?

We crossed the bridge in silence and began our climb to the Heights. "You look nice," I said to Aaron, mostly to be saying something. And he did. He wore a white open-collar shirt, gray jeans, and sandals. Casual casual casual, Doug had told me, and we'd done our best.

"So do you," Aaron told me. I'd decided on a dark blue shirt with a pattern of sequins on one shoulder, and my best jeans. I'd put my hair up on top of my head and used two fancy picks, like chopsticks, to keep it there. I hoped I looked effortlessly and eccentrically chic, not just weird.

"How about, if the party's awful, we can go somewhere else. One of the bars you like."

"Yeah, sure."

He still sounded grudging. I gave up. It wasn't like I was making him go to court with me. I couldn't help thinking that he'd liked me better, I'd been easier for him, before I had any new interests or enthusiasms. When I was aimless and adorably incompetent, and he had to keep giving me advice.

"THOSE STUPID CATERERS," Jonathan said. "They dumped everything off and left, and I don't know what's supposed to be heated, what's cold, and what's room temperature."

"Does it matter?" I asked. We were in the enormous space-age kitchen, assembling trays of tiny, perfect food from the caterer's boxes. There were, in different combinations, figs and pomegranates, mint, pink peppercorns, glazed tofu, duck breast sliders, curried lamb skewers, pear tart slices, and other things I couldn't identify. I hadn't intended on helping but I'd seen Jonathan's anguished face poking out of a door, and I'd gone to investigate.

"It's going to be fine," I told him. We'd already hustled the cheese and charcuterie trays out to the grand dining room table. "Heat up the sliders. And the lamb. The tofu. Everything else, people will think it's supposed to be that way."

"Doug hired a bartender. And valet parkers, even. I don't know why he couldn't get servers."

"It's fine," I repeated. "They'll eat it and like it." I wanted to get back to Aaron before he decided to be bored and blame me or drank any more Aperol cocktails.

I'd left him near the bar, in conversation with a man who either sold commercial real estate or else made commercials about real estate. It was a mixed crowd. There were some "pew-ets," but also people who could have been stockbrokers or porn stars or anybody. Aaron spotted Lolly Robinette and asked if she'd had cancer, and I had to explain that no, she'd been a Buddhist monk, or maybe it was a lifetime thing and she still was one, anyway, she'd decided she liked keeping her head shaved. I waved to Lolly from across the room. I wanted to make sure I got a chance to talk to her.

"So this is your new posse," Aaron said, in the kind of tone that invites you to say, "Screw you," though I ignored him.

When we first came in, Doug had greeted us in the living room, standing barefoot on the white fluffy rug. "So great you could come," he said, shaking Aaron's hand. We hadn't yet seen Ed. Doug was wearing (in addition to no shoes), a pair of camo pants and a black polo shirt. I always felt that his clothes were trying to send some message, and I hadn't yet cracked the code.

"Thanks for inviting me," Aaron said. "Beautiful house. I've been hearing a lot about it."

"Yes, this is where Carla's been slaving away all this time." Doug grinned at me, as if he was hugely pleased. It was a little bit frightening.

"Yup," I said. "The old sweatshop." Ha ha.

Aaron said, "I guess I should read more poetry." Like he read any.

"Our next issue's going to focus on social justice and the poetry of incarceration. As well as some Venezuelan poets in translation. You should check it out," Doug said encouragingly.

Aaron said that he would. We didn't dare look at each other.

"Oh, Carla? Before I forget, Tony Presto's here. He wants to talk to you about the conference next month."

I said, Sure, of course. New guests were coming in behind us, and Aaron and I moved away to let Doug greet them. "What conference?" Aaron wanted to know, and I said it was something Viridian had been talking about. I hadn't yet told him since I hadn't really imagined myself going. I spotted the bar and steered us toward it, and then there was Lolly and a couple of the other regulars to greet.

I hadn't been trying to keep things from Aaron, though he certainly was starting to feel that way. But he'd been either uninterested or begrudging or negative about so much of what was new with me that I'd gotten into the habit of not bringing any of it home with me.

JONATHAN AND I got the food out to the serving table, and people crowded up to it, trying to look casual instead of like hogs at a trough. We got some extra trays ready to set out as needed, then stood against the wall to make sure there were enough forks and napkins and coconut shrimp wraps and everything else. Jonathan fretted that he needed to get out of the kitchen and circulate. There were supposed to be some film people here tonight.

"It's under control for now," I said. I saw Aaron, still near the bar, talking to two girls wearing black T-shirts. One of the T-shirts said Pancho, the other, Lefty. I guess it would work as a conversation starter. The girls weren't twins, but they both had hair dyed a shiny cellophane red. They were all laughing together. Aaron was holding up one hand, then the other. He appeared to be trying to determine which was his right and which his left. Fine. I wasn't going to worry about him for the moment. "You should go," I told Jonathan. "Hey, where's Ed?"

"Trouble in paradise," Jonathan said, lowering his voice. "I think he's hiding out in the magazine office. He and Doug had a big fight about money."

"What happened?"

"The phrase that kept coming up was, 'down the toilet.' Ed said they shouldn't be having a big expensive party when they were already spending so much to keep the house going. The magazine came up, too. And not in a good way. Here's hoping they don't raise my rent. I'll just take a quick lap. Do I need to fix my hair?"

I stayed where I was, trying to process this news. When you knew people with money, not that I knew a lot of them, you wanted to think of the money as solid and inexhaustible. You grew comfortable with your envy and your imaginings of just what you'd do if you were rich. You admired their houses (or in my line of work, their gardens), you were happy to accept whatever little crumbs of leftover wealth might come your way from them.

Then I told myself that in addition to being so not my problem, people with money probably spent a lot of time worrying about money.

I couldn't find Aaron in the crowd, but I was still nursing my bad mood about him, so it didn't matter. Lolly was filling a plate with shrimp toasts. "Can I get you anything?" I asked her.

"I can't think of a thing I need but thank you." She smiled. She wore plastic-framed glasses on a chain, and a cardigan over a print blouse. She would have looked like my grandmother except for the shaved head, which I admit took some getting used to.

Now or never. "I wanted to ask you something. About Mathias."

Her eyes behind the glasses considered me. How old was she? I wasn't sure, but I thought she'd been old for a long time. "Yes, what about him?"

"Nothing in particular, or I mean, not one thing. I'm trying to, ah, understand him. Understand his poems."

"All you need for that are the poems themselves."

"I guess I meant, why he was so . . . extreme. Troubled."

"Oh well." Lolly nodded. Her scalp was faintly blue. And smooth, which you might not expect, given the age her face showed. "You should ask Viridian. I see you don't want to do that. I walk in the Presidio every afternoon around one. Meet me there sometime, we can have our conversation. It doesn't matter when. When you get this old, one day is pretty much like any other."

I thanked her and she made her way down the buffet table. The party was getting louder; some kind of Afrobeat music was pounding through the speakers. People were loosening up, not that they appeared to need much of an excuse. I wondered if the little hunks of food were going to be enough ballast to counter the bartender's heavy pours. I was drinking mineral water. The official beverage of party poopers.

Doug was waving to me from the doorway of the next room. He stood next to a short man, making big swooping gestures over his head, pointing and mouthing something that I translated as "Tony."

I waved back and did my own pantomime, pointing to myself and then to the kitchen, holding up one finger. I ducked into the kitchen, then went through the door to the back hallway. I didn't want to be put on the spot about the conference. I didn't think I was going to say yes, but I didn't want to have to say no.

The noise of the party was distant, like a football crowd heard on television. I pushed the elevator button. I could say hello to Ed, hang out with him until the coast was clear. The elevator traveled up to the third floor and the door opened. The room was dim except for the sconce lights on the far walls.

I took a few steps forward. "Ed?"

"Not here," said a man's voice, a figure rising up from the hammock as I yelped.

The elevator door had already closed. I reached behind me, scrabbling for the buttons.

"Whoa," the man said. "Ed went downstairs for something, he'll be back."

I was trying to unfreeze my breathing. "Somebody said he was up here."

"And he was." I couldn't tell anything about him, except he didn't sound like a kid. "You just missed him."

"Okay, good, never mind," I said idiotically. The man started to get out of the hammock, then seemed to think the better of it. I realized that I'd taken one of the picks out of my hair and was holding it in my fist, dagger style.

"How about I just stay here," the man said. "In case you're some kind of ninja." I couldn't see his face; he was just an outline in the dark. There was a light over the elevator panel so I guessed that he could see me. When I didn't say anything, he said, "There's supposed to be a view from here. Hard to tell at night."

"There's a sort of view. You have to work at it."

"How's the party going?"

"Going good." I was trying to find a way of casually putting the hair pick back, but part of my hair had fallen down, and it wasn't going to work. "I'm just taking a break from it. To see Ed."

"I guess Ed's been taking a break, too. I'm sure he'll be back up in a minute."

"That's all right, I guess I can see him later." I pressed the elevator's down button. It was one of those nervous situations that you didn't want to turn into a crime scene.

"Sorry if I startled you."

"Sorry if I was getting ready to attack you."

"Don't apologize. Excellent reflexes."

We had to wait another minute for the elevator to get there. When it did, I got in. "Well, goodbye. Enjoy the view, if you can."

The elevator door was already closing when he said, "Hold on a second."

I blocked the door with my free hand. "You're really pretty," he said, and I let the door slide closed. I don't know if he saw me smiling.

In the elevator I tried to put my hair back up, but it wasn't happening, and I took out the other pick and shook my hair loose. I wondered what time it was. I'd had about enough party fun. I could check on the food, collect Aaron, and we could make a break for it.

The elevator let me out on the ground floor. The party was still buzzing, I could tell from the noise. On my way to the kitchen, I almost collided with one of the red-dyed Pancho Lefty girls. She was coming down another hallway, from a bathroom, I guessed. I couldn't say which one she was because her shirt was inside out.

She gave me a what-are-you-staring-at look, and walked, less than steadily, out to the front of the house.

I thought for a moment, then headed down the corridor she'd come from. I heard Aaron's voice, and another. I reached the door. It was closed but they hadn't thought to lock it. When I opened it, I didn't look for long, but long enough to tell that this one was Pancho.

AARON

I spent the night in Jonathan's basement apartment. He'd gone home with somebody he met at the party, a film guy who worked in postproduction. I woke up early, borrowed one of Jonathan's sweatshirts, made myself toast and coffee in his tiny, meticulous kitchen. I found a paper bag to write on and a purple crayon. "Hey," I started out, and then I stared at what I'd written for a while. "Thanks for letting me stay here. I hope it works out with . . ."

More staring. I guess the film guy had a name. I didn't know it but I hope Jonathan did. ". . . with everything," I finished, which was lame, but I was too tired to care.

It only took me a few blocks of walking to find a Muni stop for a bus that would take me to the toll plaza at the bridge. From there you could get Golden Gate Transit to Santa Rosa. I changed buses in San Rafael and slept the rest of the way. When we reached Santa Rosa, I called my mom and asked if she'd come get me.

I told her I didn't want to talk to Aaron. I didn't want to talk about any of it. I settled in as best I could in my old bedroom.

But a couple of days later, my mom and my sister took me out to dinner so they could gang up on me. Anita was six years older than me. My mom would swear up and down that she didn't play favorites, but Anita was just easier for her. She didn't have a learning disability or attention deficit disorder or whatever it was that kept me in low-grade trouble all through my school years. Anita applied herself, my mom said, like that was something I knew how to do and was willfully refusing to. Anita had put together enough scholarships and loans to get through Sonoma State. She'd gotten her degree in art education, and she taught kids in disadvantaged schools how to make compositions out of toothpicks and glue and tissue paper and other low-cost supplies.

She got married, of course, and her husband was kind of a jerk, but she seemed okay with him. She'd picked out the names for her two kids years before: Sailor Johanna and Raymie Cole. Since my mom was who she was, she still worried and fretted about Anita, but not in the global ways she worried about me. Anita's life was on track. Mine was missing a wheel and running on fumes.

The dinner was billed as a treat for me, something to cheer me up and distract me from my personal setbacks and betrayals. I was pretty sure it was going to involve some effort at reeducation. We went to a restaurant that featured oversized salads and sandwiches, also drinks served in fishbowl glasses. I ordered a strawberry margarita. It didn't taste like much of anything, but it gave me something I could occupy myself with.

My mom knew what had happened at the party, in a general way, and that meant Anita knew, too. They were both being super nice to me. Was I comfortable? Would I like a fried onion blossom? Anything?

"How are the kids?" I asked Anita. You could always get her talking about them.

"They're great. Well, Raymie had pink eye last week, but the rest of us didn't get it. Sailor starts Teeny Ballereenies this weekend."

"Take lots of pictures," my mom said. She looked pretty tonight, her hair pulled back in a ponytail, like a girl's. She wore little pearl earrings and a white linen blouse. I was still wearing Jonathan's sweatshirt.

"So cute," I said, chiming in. They really were cute kids. I hoped I'd still like them when they got older.

Anita and my mom traded looks. Here it came. "So, Carla," my mom began, but just then our food came, and we had to figure out who got what. Everything, burgers, salad, sandwich, seemed to have bacon and avocado on it.

We settled in to eat. Anita and my mom were so much alike. Despite two small kids and a job, Anita never had ragged-looking nails or run-down heels. She'd gained maybe two pounds for each baby and she thought she was fat. She made special pop-up cards for each of her students who had birthdays. For Halloween and Christmas, she practically bought out the craft stores. She and my mom had a hot thing going on Instagram. And she made the whole enterprise work. I was happy for my sister, and in awe of how she could power through obstacles. But I didn't want to be her.

"Have you talked to Aaron yet?" Anita asked. Finally, down to the real business of the evening.

I found some watery alcohol at the bottom of my drink and slurped it. "Nope."

"You have to, sooner or later."

"No, I don't."

"Come on," my mom said. "You have to give him a chance to explain. It was only—"

"A blow job in a bathroom? I don't think that needs a lot of explanation."

For a moment I was sorry I'd said it, then I thought, why not. They both looked pained. My mom addressed someone in the vicinity of the ceiling, asking where she went wrong with me. Then she said, "So all right, he's a man. He's not perfect."

Anita said, "You need to keep some perspective. Honestly, worse things happen at bachelor parties."

"I guess that makes it okay, then."

"Sweetheart," my mom said. It seemed they were going to tag team me. "You have to grow up enough to see the big picture."

"I saw plenty in the bathroom, thanks."

"Aaron's such a good, steady guy, and he works so hard."

"And he's totally hot," Anita said. She was cutting her bacon-avocado burger into quarters. I wish for once she or my mom would just chow down on their food. "If you kick him to the curb, he's not going to be alone long."

"Especially if he keeps dropping his pants."

"Really, Carla, you're going to have to get over that. If there had been an extra female in the Garden of Eden, the original sin would have been Adam screwing her."

I couldn't remember hearing my mom say "screw" before. She seemed to realize what she'd done and reached up to smooth her ponytail. "I just mean, he's a normal man. And aside from that, he's smart and good-looking and employed. You heard that last part, right? Employed?"

"You're saying, what, he's a good catch?"

"You've been happy with him up to now. Don't let this one stupid night ruin everything."

But it wasn't just one night. He'd been bored and resentful for a while now. I wasn't saying that Pancho and Lefty happened because he'd wanted to punish me for being distracted or inattentive or unavailable. Or not exactly because of that. But you could draw a line from one thing to the other.

Anita said, "I don't suppose he's called you."

I said he hadn't. "That's not a good sign," my mom said. "You don't want to let this drag out too long."

"How about we talk about somebody else's personal business for a change?"

My mom shook her head. "Not mine. I don't have any."

"How come, Mom? Why aren't you out there finding yourself some no-good man you can make excuses for?"

"I already did," she said crisply. "And I don't need another. I don't have to settle for some grown-up baby. I can take care of myself."

"And I guess I can't," I said. I meant it to come out sarcastic, but I saw the truth of it in their faces. It wasn't really that Aaron was such a great catch; they just thought I couldn't do any better.

PRETTY MUCH BY accident, I found a video of Mathias giving a poetry reading. Not the famous one, the last one, but new to me at least.

I was killing time online. I had plenty of time to kill these days, since I was an underemployed single girl. I'm still not sure how I got from puppy videos to poetry. A few stops in between at a cowboy love song I thought I remembered better than I did, and somebody's Twitter feed and who was the guy playing saxophone on what looked like a subway platform? It had a melancholy urban vibe, and the next run of videos were jazz performers in dark and smoky clubs, and I wasn't paying much attention until the camera cut to an empty stage. Then Mathias stepped into the small circle of light.

He was young here, or at least, younger than other pictures I'd seen. Every time I saw a photo of him, I had to decide all over again what I thought of his looks, if he was handsome or freakish or both. In this film clip he was a skinny kid wearing a white T-shirt and jeans. His black hair was cut short and he kept his eyes down. Nervous, you'd think, from the way his body jerked, stiff-shouldered, as he stood and rummaged through his pages, but when he started reading, suddenly and without introduction, his voice boomed:

Who is the Lord's anointed, the crazy holy man
shouting on the street corner. His eyes
are wiggling loose. His tongue is black in the furnace of
his mouth. Airplanes bother him. They get in through his
ears and buzz like flies trapped in a window, because everything
turns into something else. Himself is not himself. The Lord has
gobbled him down and excreted him out.

Here Mathias paused and addressed the audience. "In other words," he said, "Holy shit."

After a moment people laughed, some of them, because what else were they supposed to do? Mathias returned to the poem. He read the whole of it, hammering the words into place. When he was finished, people applauded, Mathias left the stage, and another poet took his place. I could see how he might not be someone easy to like, but you would have to pay attention to him.

It occurred to me to search for footage of the poet who had read after Mathias and here another video popped up, a different camera or different angle, and it swept the audience to show Mathias and, yes, Viridian sitting together. It was only a few seconds of film, but the camera seemed caught by their remarkable faces. I started and stopped and started the video again and again, and I hated the way she looked toward him and how he looked away, but maybe I was imagining things, and anyway it was all over a long time ago.

EVEN THOUGH FIRE season had stayed quiet so far, there were still fires up north, and sometimes that smoke drifted south and turned the sky to a thin no-color. If I wrote poems, I would write one about how the world brooded and smoldered, even as I did the same over Aaron. Then I decided it would come off as grandiose and cheesy, so never mind. I guess I was becoming a better critical thinker, to realize that I'd be writing slop.

A couple of days later, in the afternoon, I went to the Presidio in search of Lolly Robinette. The sky lightened as I drove south, and by the time I reached the city, it was blue overhead. I'd only driven past or through the Presidio before. A big place, with woods and promenades and old military barracks, a golf course, a Disney store, crowds of people strolling or on bicycles and scooters, tourists clutching maps. The odds of finding one small old lady didn't seem good. But here Lolly was, exactly as she'd said she'd be, on a bench just off one of the plank walkways. She waved as I approached. "Lovely day," she said, not at all surprised to see me. I was sort of relieved that she was wearing a hat, a kind of knit turban, so I didn't have to either look at her bald head or pretend not to look at it.

"Shall we walk?" She took my arm. We went slowly. Sunlight sifted through the trees overhead, eucalyptus and Monterey pine.

Lolly said, "I like the cemetery overlook. It's got the best view of the bay."

Cemeteries were right up my alley these days, all gloom and death and misery. I didn't want to come right out and bring up Mathias, so we talked about one thing or another, the trail, the trees, and then everything opened up and there was a little space to sit, and the view below us of the rows of white tombstones, the scallops of blue water, the cloud tops, the towers of the bridge. And you could forget, until of course you remembered, that those white stones were not just scenery, but that each one marked a fallen soldier.

We settled ourselves on a bench and Lolly sighed.

"So, Mathias. He was what I call a loud poet. Everything at top volume and maximum intensity. There are other registers, you know. And everything was self, self, self! You have to at least try to get beyond that."

I thought that was probably Buddhist-talk, though I didn't know enough to say anything more about it. "I guess you didn't like him."

"Liking or not liking, one more thing you try and get beyond. I felt sorry for him. He wasn't a happy person. Or anytime he was happy, it was too much like his poems, big and loud. And of course, unsustainable. I don't know what, exactly, was wrong with him."

"That was going to be my next question."

"Depression? Mania? Both? But he certainly made the most of it. Oh, he had charisma. But he took up all the oxygen in the room. Fighting the universe, instead of letting it take its course. Self again. Self-dramatizing, self-indulgence, and finally, self-destruction."

Lolly stopped speaking and we looked out on the trees and clouds and water for a time. I thought I was pretty self, self, self also. I didn't know any other way to be. The rows of white stones made me a little dizzy, a little sick. Who wouldn't want to be more than that, one of many, anonymous, forgotten?

I hadn't read many of Lolly's poems. The ones in *Compass Points* were excellent, small and graceful. But she'd probably never be famous, notorious. People seemed drawn to messy lives and bad behavior.

I asked Lolly to tell me about the reading, the last one Mathias ever gave. She sighed.

"It was awful. He was in such bad shape by then. Some writers get themselves so worked up, so full of doubt and anxiety, they can't write. It hadn't been going well for him, he hadn't produced anything new for a while. He was supposed to be coming out with a new collection and it kept getting pushed back. And everybody knew. By 'everybody,' I mean our little circle of poets, serious poets. There were never that many of us. But we regarded ourselves as so important!

"The reading was Mathias's idea. He was going to read his new poems, and we were all mad curious about them. It was at one of those awful bars we went to back then, with cheap beer and an open stage. Mathias showed up looking terrible. He'd pretty much given up eating or sleeping. Viridian wasn't there. They'd probably had one of their famous fights. Did he ever abuse her? I can't say I know for certain. But I would not have been surprised.

"He started off by saying something about writing in blood, and about running out of ink, and the poems were his last will and testament. Typical melodrama from him. We all rolled our eyes. He read the first poem. It was good, it was more than good. When he was finished, he held it up by two fingers and set it on fire with a lighter. Another of his stunts. Once it was nothing but ash, he picked up the next poem and read that, and again it was good, rich and strange and potent, it's stayed with me all this time, and again he set it on fire.

"By this time, it was clear that there was something wrong, very wrong, and a couple of people tried to stop him. But he held them off, reading, burning, reading, burning. I'd started scribbling notes, off in a corner where he couldn't see, everything I heard, everything I could remember. I got the titles and a few first lines and maybe a bit more.

"He finished. The air stank of smoke. People sat him down, bought him a drink, tried to get him to eat something so as to change the awful, skull look of his face. People talked to him, wanted him to get help. My point is, people tried. But you can't keep somebody alive if they're determined to die. Two days later, he was gone."

I waited a moment before I asked about the poems. "The ones he burned. I thought—"

"Somebody found out that Viridian had copies. I guess they saw them in her apartment, she hadn't been quick enough to put them away. It turned into gossip and the gossip got around and next thing, Mathias's publisher took her to court to get them. Viridian testified that she'd found copies in the garbage, she had to go through the alley cans to find them. I don't know what to think about that. He'd meant to destroy them entirely. And now she had them, and she wouldn't give them up, not to his publisher or anyone else.

"I had to give a deposition, because I had those notes, you see. Viridian won. She had herself named his literary executor. And there the matter's stayed, for all these years.

"Everyone wanted those poems. They still do. It's like Sylvia Plath and Ted Hughes all over again, or sort of. Passion, drama, death. There have been a lot of offers. But she won't budge. Why not let someone publish the poems, or publish them herself?" Lolly stopped speaking, raised her hands and let them fall back again. "Because she doesn't want to."

*   *   *

I MISSED AARON, even though I was the wronged party, even though I was meant to be fatally offended. I kept going back and forth between different fantasies. In most of them, he begged and pleaded for me to forgive him. Sometimes I did, sometimes I stalked away, forever lost to him. The only fantasy I couldn't sustain was one where the whole thing had never happened at all. I was pretty thoroughly miserable.

Our friends knew there had been some kind of a fight. I hadn't provided the mortifying details. It wasn't anybody's business, and I didn't want another chorus of people telling me that drunk party sex wasn't any big deal.

I went back to the house during the day a few times when I was sure Aaron was at work, to retrieve clothes and things I needed. I'd take Batman for a walk, because I'd missed him, too. I hadn't thought I was much of a housekeeper, but left on his own, Aaron had given up on cleaning the bathroom and the kitchen counters and taking out the trash. Maybe he wasn't spending much time at home. Maybe the filth was some really unattractive way of expressing brokenheartedness.

One morning I cleaned the whole place. I hadn't meant to. The neglect of it just tore me up and then I felt sorry for him. Anyway, it was too disgusting, one step away from insect infestations. I guess he hadn't hooked up with a new girlfriend yet, or if he had, she was a slob, too, goddamn him to hell.

This is how it went with me, both sad and mad, one and then the other, and then starting up all over again.

Batman was confused when I showed up and confused when I left again. The only times I cried were when I had to say good-bye and he'd put one paw on my arm to tell me not to go. He was getting to be an old dog now. One of these days he was going to die, and that would be awful, awful. A couple of times I sat next to him, bawling, imagining it all, and he'd burrow his nose into me for comfort.

I watered my apricot and plum and olive trees because, clearly, nobody else was going to, and they shouldn't have to die because of human unhappiness.

My mom wasn't going to kick me out anytime soon, if ever, but living there wasn't exactly a refuge. She tried not to say too many helpful, anxious things, but still there was a constant slow drip of them. Wasn't it almost time to register for fall semester classes? Had I met with an advisor, somebody who could help me get started off on the right foot?

I hadn't. I wasn't sure I had a foot that ought to be put in charge. Going back to school had been my all-purpose answer to any questions about my future, but in truth I hadn't thought much about it lately. Breaking up with Aaron (if that's what we were doing) seemed to knock the props out from under whatever version of myself I'd started out with. But I told my mom I'd looked through the course offerings, I'd be ready to roll, I was all positive attitude.

It had been almost two weeks since the party. That Monday, when I made another of my sneaking visits to the house—I was starting not to think of it as ours, or mine—I found an envelope with my name on the kitchen counter, and a note inside. He'd typed the whole thing, which I guess you'd expect from an IT guy, but I had to admit, I wished he'd written it out by hand.

Dear Carla,

You know I'm sorry. It was stupid. I was drunk. I guess I thought I
could get away with it. As much as I was thinking.

Can we talk? I've been too chickenshit to call. But I will,
and if you want to hang up on me or cuss me out, well,
who could blame you. Not me.

Love,
Aaron

PS Thank you for cleaning the house.

It was funny, the one part of his note that touched me was his
saying he thought he could get away with it. That at least seemed
honest. I decided to wait for him to come home. Get it over with
one way or the other. I went to sit on the front steps. I wanted to
keep it all outside, with plenty of space.

His car turned down our street and then in at the drive. He
got out and I watched him trying to figure out what it might
mean that I was there.

"Hi," he said, finally.

"Hi yourself." He looked big and tired and slow-moving, and
I was simultaneously remembering and forgetting every time I'd
ever seen him before, everything jamming up in me.

"You want to come in?"

"Not especially."

"Did you let the dog out already?"

I said I had. He went in past me and a couple of minutes
later he came out with two IPAs and gave me one. He sat down

next to me on the steps, but at the opposite end. Fighters, go to your corners.

"I've been staying at my mom's," I said.

"I figured."

We sat for a moment, watching the evening traffic roll by on the roadway beyond us. The sky was a dry and powdery blue. A breeze had picked up and cut the heat of the day. I could sit there all night and the sky and weather and traffic would change around me and my heart would still be a block of wood and I'd still have no place in any of it.

"I'm sorry."

"Yeah, I know."

"Those girls were crazy. They said—"

I held up my hand. "I don't want to hear about them."

"Right. Sorry. I mean, about that, too."

I knew what he meant. I guess this was my fantasy, or at least the real-life version of it without any big speeches. But he was trying.

He said, "I wake up in the morning feeling crummy and I go to bed the same way. I miss you."

And I missed him, too: his hands and his voice and the rise and fall of his breath at night, and a hundred small things I'd taken comfort in. I said, "I miss you. But there's things I don't feel good about."

He didn't say anything, just let out his breath in a big, windy sigh. Like Batman when he was depressed.

"My mom's on your side."

"Is she."

"Yeah, because men are hopeless horndogs, and it's just something you have to get past."

"I'm not sure I want her on my side."

At least we were talking, which was better than not talking, even if we couldn't get anything settled. I said, "I guess I'm supposed to decide how long to be mad, or how mad, or whatever. You know, make the punishment fit the crime."

Aaron was trying not to look too hopeful, like maybe he'd get off on probation. I'd wanted him to be sorry and to want me back, and he did. But that wasn't everything.

I said, "I don't think I want to be everybody's favorite under-achieving fuck-up anymore."

"Where did that come from?"

"God forbid I try anything new. God forbid I might be good at it."

"Give me a break. That's not how people think of you."

"You don't like Viridian."

"What? She's fine. How much am I supposed to like her?"

"You don't like anything I've been doing lately, with her or with the magazine."

"If you mean, I don't understand why you want to hang around with some of these characters who crack jokes nobody else gets and look like they belong in the hippie museum, then no, I don't like it, and I don't understand what you get out of it. It's like you've joined a cult."

"I like poems."

"Well can't you read them in the library?"

We weren't talking sorry anymore. We were back to unhappy

and impatient. I said, "I think I might have a calling for it. Not writing poems but getting inside them. Understanding how they're put together and how somebody's mind works and how once in a while they make you feel like you grabbed onto a live electric wire." What more could I say? I hadn't yet read Shelley, but if I had, if I'd said that poets are the unacknowledged legislators of the world, I doubt if that would have moved the argument in my direction.

Aaron was waiting for some better explanation, and when none came, he said, "So is there a job in all this?"

"An education."

"Fine." He was giving up on me, at least for now. "How about you tell me what to do. What you need from me."

"Time."

I guess he wanted me to say how much time, but I wasn't ready to measure it out.

After a moment he said, "Could I ask you to text if you're coming over? Let me know, so I don't get nervous about walking in the door and looking around to see if you've been here and then get . . . disappointed."

He almost had me there. I saw how much grief I was putting him through, just as he'd put me through a lot, and I almost said let's stop this, let's either go back or start over, I give up, uncle. But I guess there are reasons you don't do things, even as there are reasons you do. I stood up and said I had to be getting back to my mom's.

He walked me to the truck, and we hugged, one of those awkward hugs where nobody knows what to do with their chins or elbows. When I was getting ready to drive off, he said, "Remember me talking about Vancouver?"

"Yes?"

"I'm still thinking about it. I found a couple of interesting gigs. I might take a trip up there to check them out."

I wasn't allowed to ask about when, either. "Well, let me know if you need me to take care of Batman."

"Yeah, that would be great."

"Sure." We were down to nothing more to say. And that's how we left it.

I'D ALREADY TOLD Viridian that I wanted the job at the writers' conference. It was a no-brainer by now. I could get out of my mom's for a week, give the two of us a break from each other. It was the slow season for landscaping work. I could point to a paid, productive use of my time. I might learn a thing or two. And Aaron could go right on missing me for a while longer. I would harden my heart and chart my own course.

"I'm so glad," Viridian said. "You'll want to talk to Tony. The job's mostly running around and troubleshooting. Everything from changing light bulbs to babysitting lovelorn workshop students." I must have looked alarmed because she laughed. "It's mostly light bulbs. But there's always some kind of psychodrama."

Oscar was going to be there, too, as well as Sacha and Viridian. They were all teaching workshops and classes and giving readings. It was a big conference, with fifteen different poets, fiction and environmental writers on staff. Also visits by agents and editors who would be prospecting for promising new authors. And the conference attendees themselves, several dozen of them, manuscripts in hand, hoping to be instructed, validated, encouraged.

All this had been explained to me. The conference students came mostly from the Bay area, but a fair number from farther away. They were both young and old, hobbyists and earnest students. They came in all different levels of accomplishment, from well-schooled workshop veterans to the truly talentless. Each of them had purchased access to the staff, who were tasked with reading and commenting on their writing. There would be group critiques and discussion sessions. Someone, or more than one, was bound to cry.

Viridian arranged a phone call with Tony Presto. He sounded cheerful and distracted and said he'd heard such good things about me. I said I was sorry I hadn't had the chance to meet him at Doug's party, but either he didn't hear me say this or he'd forgotten all about it, and he started in telling me what I needed to know. The conference site was an old resort compound near Pollock Pines. Rustic but comfortable. Sort of like, camping but not camping, if I knew what he meant. (I didn't.) Right on a river. Beautiful place. The other assistant, Gil, had been there the last two years. Gil would show me the ropes. Perhaps Gil and I could meet in Sacramento and caravan up together? It would be best if Gil and I arrived there the night before, got everything nailed down and swept out. (Swept out?)

Finally, he mentioned the pay, which was decent, and I gave him my formal acceptance.

Barb filled me in on some of the particulars. She'd been to last year's conference and was going again this year. "It really is pretty up there. You're at a higher elevation so it cools down at night. The river has a little inlet for swimming. But everything depends on where you sleep."

The main lodge and the conference center and the newer cabins were upgraded, central heat and air, good ventilation and so on. But most conference attendees were housed in the old dorm buildings. Last year she'd stayed in one nicknamed House of Spiders. This year she'd booked a hotel room in Placerville, twenty minutes away. She might miss some of the late-night hijinks, but at least she could go to bed without first wrapping herself in plastic.

"Late-night hijinks?" I asked, passing over, for the moment, my questions about spiders and sleeping quarters.

"Somebody always goes skinny-dipping and then loses their clothes. Or people wander off into the woods and get lost. There's always a bear scare or a rattlesnake scare. Or somebody gets comatose drunk and needs to be hauled off to the medical center. Oh, don't worry. There's probably only one real crisis per year. The rest of the time it's all these amazing writers talking to you and each other. It's fantastic." She paused and gave me a measuring look. "You'll be fine. You won't let yourself get too carried away."

"Thanks," I said, though I wasn't sure it had been meant as a compliment. Someone really should have mentioned bears and rattlesnakes in the job description.

I was used to Barb by now, as I guess she was used to me, and though I wouldn't have called us friends, I at least respected that she was serious about her writing. She was a few years older than my mom, and divorced, "of course," she said, and her kids were grown and out in the world, making their own mistakes. One day she woke up tired of feeling sorry for herself and decided to stop caring what anybody else thought. I guess that accounted for the hair and a few other things.

She wrote on her own at first. All of it the purest crap. She began going to workshops and conferences. She'd been at it for a while now, she'd gotten a few poems into small magazines. Nothing she was going to brag about. Viridian's workshops were the best thing that ever happened to her. She'd learned so much. And Viridian was always so patient and helpful.

"I worry about her. I wish she could afford to slow down," Barb said.

"Afford?"

She stared at me. The pink glasses made it seem as if she never blinked. "Nothing."

I stared back until she shrugged. "You'd think after a lifetime of writing great poems, you'd have enough money to get by on in old age."

"Don't you get Social Security, things like that?" My notions of how people, old or not, got by was meager.

"It's not enough. She never earned enough to get much payout. I hope she can keep the house, it's practically month to month lately."

I was trying to think things through. "Could she sell the house?"

"And go where? She loves the house, she's been here almost twenty years. Even refinancing wouldn't help much. It's getting harder for her to do conferences or teaching jobs, the things that bring in money. I know. You look at that face and think she's immortal, like a Greek statue or something. But age is finally catching up with her."

I wondered if Barb was aware of Mathias's poems, what they were worth to anyone. Six months of a mortgage payment? A year?

Barb went on, "Now don't say anything to her. I shouldn't have blabbed. She's super proud, she doesn't want anyone to know."

But Barb knew, as did Oscar, as did I. I thought of all the people who arrived with food, or who offered rides or herbal supplements or the use of their vacation houses, or even me, taking on the gardening chores. It seemed like a lot of people knew something.

I'd never heard Viridian say anything about money. Either it didn't interest her or it was nobody's business or both. Life went on as it always did around her. People came and went, sitting with her to talk and drink wine or iced tea or fruit juice with sparkling water. Oscar cooked up suppers of fish and pasta and vegetables. Viridian presided over it all with effortless serenity.

IN THE TWO weeks before the conference, I saw her nearly every day. I dug up the foxtails and cut back the rosemary. I nursed along the new plantings out back and pruned the trees. The fence was still down and I guess I was getting used to the look of the scorched panels, although it wasn't anything I liked thinking about.

It was Viridian's habit to work at her writing during the morning, then do her yoga practice. She took a nap after lunch, in the upstairs room with the blue curtains drawn across the windows and the ceiling fan whispering overhead. Then she'd make her way downstairs to check the mail and see who or what might have turned up while she slept. It was all so very pleasant: the big, shabby house, the company, the food and drink, the slow afternoons shading into evening. None of us who were part of it that summer wanted it to end or change, certainly not me, living in self-exile at my mom's, no longer at home anywhere.

Surely all of it cost money. All of it, the food we ate, the wine we drank, the fruiting trees, the water in the pipes, the whispering electric current in the walls, the books and paper and ink that made up the enterprise of poetry. Did poems pay for the house, or any part of it? I couldn't have said.

One afternoon I was working on the center island in the courtyard when Viridian came out and sat on the top step. "Don't mind lazy me," she said. Her feet, long and narrow, were bare. She wore a denim shirt and black pants, and her white hair was pulled back in a braid. I had already promised myself that when I was old, I would dress like she did. "You've been working so hard, Carla. Everything looks just lovely."

"Thanks." I had been working hard and I was pleased and shy that she'd noticed. "I love being up here. It's like a whole separate world."

"It can seem that way, can't it." She raised her gaze to the treetops surrounding us, motionless in the afternoon heat. "I love it, too. I've been lucky to have the place."

I was careful to keep my eyes on the weeding in front of me. I hoped she would keep talking if I didn't look at her.

"I bought it back when you could still almost afford California real estate. Now we're all house poor. Ah well. Nothing lasts forever."

"Is everything all right?"

"Everything is fine."

Neither of us spoke for a time. Then she said, "You and Tony have all the conference details worked out?"

"I think so. Enough to give me a running start."

"I'm glad you're coming. You'll be a big help to Tony. You won't let all the titanic egos get to you."

I wondered if Barb had meant something similar. "Well. I hope not."

"You'll be fine. You won't fall all over yourself trying to be nice. What I call 'good girl syndrome.'"

I did look up at her then. "Just remember," she said. "Nobody is ever going to love you passionately for being nice." She stood, brushing herself off. "Don't work too much longer, come in and have some lemonade."

After she'd gone inside, I tried to sort out what she'd said. I thought I only fell all over myself trying to be nice when I was around Viridian.

It was the time of day I found myself thinking about Aaron. How I'd always head back to him when I was done working, how I missed that whole part of my day and my life. I could text him right now, ask him if he wanted to meet for dinner, see what came of it. But I was still hurt and stubborn and I wanted to show him I had a life of my own, a life without him.

I was sweeping up and gathering my tools when Ed and Doug's car, a Mazda MX-5 Miata, came through the gate. I hadn't known they were coming. Ed was driving. He parked next to the gap in the fence and waved to me. "Hello stranger."

"Hello yourself."

He got out, as did his passenger. It wasn't Doug. The man was a little taller, a little heavier, with a wide forehead. An oversized pair of sunglasses hid the rest of his face. He was smiling as he walked toward me. "It's the ninja," he said.

And while my brain was processing this and trying to fit everything together, I heard the door open behind me and Viridian stepped out. "Hello hello! Carla, I want you to meet my son."

BOONE

I turned from the man to Viridian and then back again. "We met already. Well not really. Hi." I was doing my usual feeble job of handling social ceremonies.

"Pleasure," he said, shaking hands with me. "Boone."

"Carla."

Viridian looked from me to her son. "When was this?"

"At Ed's party," I explained. "But just for a minute."

"How fortunate," Viridian said, "that you had the chance."

Neither man spoke. Something had changed that fast and no one looked as if they wanted to be there. Ed lifted a shopping bag. "We brought you some wine. And bread. And antipasti."

"I would have fixed something fancy, if I'd had more warning," Viridian said. "Any time in the last, what, two weeks?"

I excused myself to go check the sprinklers out back. I must have done something wrong, but I wasn't sure what. I watched them file into the screen porch. Viridian opened the door and waited for me to join them. I tried to read her face, but she was capable of being formidably inexpressive when she chose, as she did now. "Come in and talk to Boone. He lives in New York," she said, indicating her son. "At least, the last I heard."

New York, that was the bite I heard in his accent. Boone had been the second husband, I knew. The son must have some other, given, name, but I guessed no one was likely to explain anything else to me. I took my seat and Ed poured me a glass of white wine. I was trying to measure the resemblance between mother and son without staring. They both did and didn't look alike. Both had wide, handsome faces, but his features were notably leaner, less balanced, and his eyes were brown, not her amazing blue. He had dark hair cut short and he wore a button-down shirt, suit pants, and brogues. An unremarkable outfit, except in Marin, where everything seemed to be some version of playclothes.

Viridian said, "How nice that you're here during a spell of such good weather."

"I thought the weather was always good here," Boone said. He regarded the antipasti without much enthusiasm, then speared an artichoke heart with a fork. I figured he might be in his late thirties, but that was just a guess.

Ed said, "When we get a lot of rain in the winter, that's not so great."

Boone shrugged. "Rain, sure."

"Are you visiting for long?" I asked.

"Hard to say. Work, you know." I thought he'd been almost flirting with me when he arrived, but now he seemed unfriendly. Something sullen had settled over the whole group.

"You mean, for much longer," Viridian said.

"It's a little open-ended right now."

I might have asked what kind of work he did. Or how he knew
Ed, or why he wasn't staying at Viridian's house. But all conversation seemed to have been strangled.

Ed tried again to rally us. "Have you talked to Doug?" he
asked me. "You should give him a call. He might need to ask you
some things about the issue." Then, turning to Boone: "Carla's
been working on *Compass Points.*"

"Ah," said Boone. He nodded, as if this confirmed some dark
suspicion he had about me.

· "I'm kind of a subintern."

Viridian said, "I can't imagine you're not doing a fine job."

"Thank you," I said. It worked out to a compliment, I was
pretty sure.

Ed said, "An awful lot of effort goes into the issues. I've seen
it up close and personal. It's not just artistic temperament that
makes the wheels spin."

"I never know what people mean by that," Viridian said.
"'Artistic temperament.'"

"Really," Boone said.

No one had a response to that. We sat in careful silence. Then it
occurred to me that the rest of them were waiting for me to leave.

I stood up and said how nice it was to meet you, and thanks
for the wine. Nobody tried to stop me, though Ed said, "I'll tell
Doug you'll call."

I said that I would. I gathered my tools and got in my truck
and drove back to my mom's. I was aware that things had gone
badly, but I wasn't sure why. Because Boone hadn't told his mother
he was in town? I'd never heard her mention a son, or any other

child. Or anything of family history, her history. And it never would have occurred to me to ask, even as I wondered about it, never more so than now.

I CALLED THE magazine office the next day. Jonathan answered.

"I still have your sweatshirt," I told him.

"Yeah, how about we set up a rent-to-own contract. I'm kidding. Don't worry, it's no big deal. Anyway, I'm in love."

It was the man from the party. The two of them had spent almost every night together since. It was the most incredible rush. Paul, that was his name, was going to try and get him a job. A job in film! They hadn't talked about moving in together yet, it was too early for that, but fingers crossed. Everything was coming together!

I said I was happy for him. And I was, even though, at the same time, everything seemed to be falling apart for me. "Do you know a guy, Boone? Friend of Ed?"

"Short hair? Looks sort of like a lawyer, if Ed looked more like a lawyer?"

"Sounds about right."

"Yeah, he's been up here once or twice. I think he's working on some project, him and Ed and Doug. I haven't been paying a lot of attention because of—"

"Love. I know. What's going on with the issue, do you need any help?"

Jonathan said that would be great, they were getting page proofs back tomorrow. I reminded him that I didn't do proofreading and he said fine, just come in and help keep track of things. I said that I would. I wasn't sure if Boone would be around and I wasn't sure if he was anybody I wanted to see again or wanted to avoid seeing. I guess I'd let the universe decide. I told Jonathan I'd be there in the morning.

The house was quiet when I arrived, and Jonathan let me in. "They both went to some deal downtown. Did you have breakfast? I'll make you an omelet."

I sat at the kitchen island while Jonathan swirled eggs in a long-handled pan. I drank orange juice and ate my omelet while he told me about Paul, who was a grown-up, thank God, in a universe of neurotic, preening children. Not that he didn't have his adorably silly moments. He was handsome but not in an affected way. Confident but not arrogant. And so on.

"At least the party worked out for somebody."

"Yeah, sorry. What's up with the boyfriend?"

"We're taking a break from each other."

"If I move in with Paul, I bet they'd give you my apartment. Well not *give*. But it would be available."

I finished eating and took my dishes to the sink. "Let's wait and see what happens." It was too much to think about, too many unknowns branching into other unknowns, too much of my old life falling away behind me with every step I took forward. But hadn't I wanted a new life? A different sense of myself? I had and I did. But I would have to go forth and meet the future bravely, and there were times, like now, when I didn't feel anything close to brave.

We went up to the magazine office and we looked at the typeset issue pages and once we were back in our old work routine, I felt a little better. And pleased, too, at my part in it. I'd worked on the layout, translating Doug's notes and directives into an orderly assemblage of black type and white space. "You're pretty good at this, you know?" Jonathan told me. "The design part."

"It was a computer program. It's not like I did anything hard."

"But you got it, not everybody does. And you're fast. You could find a real job doing it. If you're still looking around for some other kind of work."

One more step in a different direction. I could tell that Jonathan felt sorry for me, it made him feel bad to see me moping around about Aaron while he was getting three love texts an hour from Paul. Then he would stop and giggle and text him back. I didn't mind. But the more I saw of love, at least of other people's love affairs, the more curdled and gloomy I felt about the whole subject. When I first met Aaron, hadn't I been just the same? Hadn't we spent whole days and nights in bed together, our two hearts pressed together, thanking the universe for our good luck? Well. So much for that.

Love made people act like idiots, at least for as long as it lasted. I didn't share this opinion with Jonathan, who was still in the fizzy fuzzy stage of things, though I did ask him to stop singing "Only Us."

We worked until early afternoon without Doug or anyone else disturbing us, and then I figured I'd logged enough free hours and told Jonathan to call me if he wanted more help. We agreed to keep everything on a loose, as-needed basis. Story of my life right then.

I told him I was headed up to the writers' conference at the end of next week.

"Into the Woods? Lucky you. You're going to have a fantastic time. Just try not to start any fires."

I let myself out and was walking toward my truck when I heard someone behind me, a man, calling "Excuse me. Excuse me." I ignored it and picked up my pace, since you just never know. Panhandlers, crazy people, garden-variety harassment. But I wasn't fast enough, and he caught up to me as I was trying to find my keys.

"Hi," Boone said, because of course it was him. He was out of breath from chasing me. "Sorry, I forgot your name."

"Carla."

"Right." He bent over to rest his hands on his knees. "It's these hills," he said. "Not used to them."

I was still waiting to decide how I felt about him. As before, he was wearing slightly out-of-place clothes, this time khakis and a plaid cotton shirt under a navy blue sweater. The look of a preppy tourist, since I guess that's what he was. He caught his breath, straightened up, and tried on a smile. "Could I buy you some lunch?"

I assumed he meant that we should have lunch together. "Why?"

"You got caught in the crossfire between my mother and me. I feel bad about that."

"Weren't you on your way to Ed and Doug's?"

"It's nothing urgent. Please. Let me explain some things."

It was the promise of explanation rather than Boone himself that got me to say yes. I pointed us toward a sandwich shop. I didn't want him spending real money on me.

When we sat down with our food, I said, "I don't have a lot of time, okay?" Although I did.

"Fine, no problem." He was juggling his sandwich, a fistful of paper napkins, and a bottle of limonata. I was still getting used to the look of him, to Viridian's face translated into his.

I guess I was comparing him to Aaron, as I did with all men. I was going to have to stop doing that, if only because sex was one of those things I was trying not to dwell on. Aaron was in better shape, but that would have been true of nearly anyone. Anyway, Boone was old, and he wore boring clothes. He'd told me I was pretty, but only because I hadn't been able to answer back. One more man who thought he could get away with something.

He looked up and caught me staring. Quickly, I said, "Are you a writer, too?"

"God no." The New York in his voice made him sound especially scornful.

He didn't say what he did or was instead. We ate in silence for a time. Then he said, "How do you know my mother? If you don't mind my asking."

"I take care of the landscaping at the house."

"And how did you wind up working on *Compass Points*?"

"One thing led to another." The shop was loud. I was glad. It helped to have some distracting background noise between us.

"Kind of an odd combination of odd jobs, don't you think?"

"I think I don't want to answer any more questions."

"Fair enough. You can ask me something if you want."

"Do you have a first name?"

"Henry. But I never liked it." He explained this patiently, having explained it all before.

"Even your mother calls you Boone."

"Yeah. I never really know what to call her."

I must have given him a peculiar look. He said, "I didn't grow up with her. She left me with my dad when I was eighteen months old. He died last year."

"Sorry. I didn't know any of that."

"Why would you? It's all right, it's just the way it was."

He spoke with the same practiced matter-of-factness. I couldn't understand how it would be all right.

"I didn't see much of her until I was an adult. Even then, it's been hit or miss. Last time I saw her? Four years ago, and that was because I was out here on vacation."

"But you get along. I mean, don't you?"

"Oh, she's always pleasant with me. Just not very involved. You know how she can be."

I did know. He went on. "So there haven't been a lot of Mother's Day cards over the years. I don't know why she was so injured that I didn't call her as soon as I got into town. She's not entitled to feel that way. Maybe because other people were involved, and it made her look bad."

I was trying to fathom it all and I couldn't. "Was there something, maybe something going on between your parents?"

"There were other things she wanted to do. And I guess being a bad mother was the most transgressive thing she could think of."

Do you know how hard it is for a woman to be selfish? she'd said. Maybe this was what she meant. Still, I didn't like hearing it. How could you leave your own child? I didn't think anyone would set out to be a bad mother just to prove a point.

I said, "How do you know Ed and Doug?"

"Ed's my mother's attorney. I guess I'm her accidental next of kin. I mean there's nobody else. Ed and I are in touch from time to time. We're trying to get her to take care of herself."

"She can already take care of herself."

"She's not getting any younger."

"What do you want her to do, exactly?"

"Ed's an ethical guy. He's looking out for her best interests. I'm sorry, I can't go into any details because—"

"Ethics," I said, and he nodded. "You came into town just to do whatever it is you're doing with her?"

"No, I like it out here. I'm thinking I might even relocate. I do consulting for start-ups."

"A business guy."

"Entrepreneur." A term for somebody who didn't want to work very hard, although I didn't say so. "All I need is a computer and a phone line to do business. I have a friend I can stay with," he added, and I wondered if he meant a woman.

We paid attention to our food for a time. He must have guessed I didn't trust him.

"Look," he said, "she's still my mother, no matter what our history is. And my father would have wanted me to watch out for her, even after everything, so there's that. And much as I think that artists, poets in particular, are a pain in the ass, she's a pretty good one."

He was like Viridian in that he knew how to be persuasive, how to win people over. Still, I wasn't really sold. I said, "She's never been anything but kind to me."

"Then you'll want what's best for her, too. For her legacy."

It was that word, legacy, that made me finish up my sandwich and push back from the table. "Thanks for lunch. I have to get going."

He stood up with me and we went out to the sidewalk. I hoped he wasn't going to follow me to the truck. "Well, thanks again," I said, already turning away, when he did a quick little foot shuffle and crouched down in a fighting stance.

"Ninja," he said, and that made me smile, though I didn't let him see me do it. I didn't want to like him even a little.

Viridian didn't have any money, that was clear, and the house would come with a chunk of mortgage. Was Boone after the Mathias poems, too? Everybody seemed to have designs on them. I suppose it was possible that Boone might have both selfish and unselfish motives when it came to his mother. I couldn't say. But I could usually tell when somebody wanted something from me, whether it was sex or anything else. Boone wanted something, I was pretty sure, I just didn't yet know what it was.

THEN, AS IF Boone was a bird of ill omen, Viridian had a health scare and ended up in the hospital.

This is what happened: Viridian and Oscar were attending a literary event in Sonoma, a luncheon sponsored by a women's philanthropic organization, where they and some other authors would speak and sign books. They had been driven there by one of the event organizers, installed at the head table, and served their first course of citrus and fennel salad.

The room was crowded, and rather warm. Viridian had remarked on this, but no, she hadn't said anything about feeling ill. She'd said she was fine, in fact. Then she had fainted, fallen backward, and hit her head. An ambulance had taken her to Memorial Hospital in Santa Rosa.

My mom called me an hour later. "That poet lady you know? What's her name?"

When I got there, I found them in the hospital cafeteria, my mom, Oscar, and two women who it turned out were from the luncheon event. It took me a few moments to comprehend the sight of Oscar and my mother sitting together, as if one of them had been Photoshopped in. Oscar was punching numbers into a phone, somebody else's, since he didn't have one. "This doesn't work," he announced, and one of the event women said to let her do it.

"How is she, what happened?" I asked, and my mom said that everybody should just calm down.

"I am calm."

"They admitted her because her blood pressure was high, and they want to make sure she's stable. Dr. Gandhi is going to see her, he's very good."

"But she's all right?" I asked.

"Give me that." Oscar took the phone back from the woman, got up and walked to the hallway outside. I saw him through the glass, marching up and down, talking, changing ears.

"She's fine," my mom replied, watching Oscar warily. "They want to do a few tests. Honey, I wish you'd get in the habit of carrying a clean shirt with you. Would that be so hard?"

One of the event ladies said, "I feel just terrible. We should have taken better care of her. But she kept saying she was fine."

"People are like that," my mom said. "Nobody ever wants to think there's anything wrong." She was wearing navy blue today. It made her look a little like a cop.

Oscar came back in. "My pulse is thready," he announced. "I think I am having a cardiac event."

"Then there are those other kinds of people," my mom remarked. To Oscar she said, "Why don't you sit down, and I'll get you some iced tea. If you still feel bad, I'll walk you over to the ER."

He sat. He turned to me, whispering. "Whatever you do, don't mention any of this to Tony Presto."

"Why?"

"He'll freak out and he won't want her at the conference."

"Should she go? Isn't that up to the doctors?"

"Oh, doctors." He waved away the idea. He had dressed up for the luncheon, in his black coat and another eye-catching shirt-and-tie combination. "She'll still want to go. Don't tell Ed or Doug either. Or the sneaky son."

I would have liked to ask him more, but it didn't seem like the time or place. "Can we see her?"

"They said not yet," one of the event ladies said. "Did you want us to stay? We could, if you need somebody here."

I recognized that they were asking permission to leave. I told them I thought we were covered, and thanks, and yes, someone would let them know how Viridian was.

Oscar watched them leave. "There goes lunch."

My mother came over then with a tray. She put it in front of Oscar and off-loaded a plate and two glasses of iced tea, one for him and one for me. "What's this?" Oscar asked, poking a fork at the plate in front of him.

"Mac and cheese with broccoli."

"They were serving salmon rillettes in Sonoma."

"You'll eat it and like it."

"I see where you get your attitude," Oscar said to me. He took a bite. "This is actually not bad."

My mother said, "I have to get back to work. Is he going to be okay? I don't like his color, he looks flushed."

"It might be the shirt."

Oscar looked up from his mac and cheese. "What about my shirt?"

"It's purple," I said.

"Heliotrope," he corrected. My mother sighed.

"Second floor east," she said. "Ask for Dr. Gandhi. Call me if you need me. Let me know if you'll want dinner, I was only going to have leftovers, but I can pick something up. Don't worry, everything's going to be all right."

We watched her walk away, her heels clipping on the tile floor. "What's your mother's name?" Oscar asked.

"Dawn. Why?"

"Dawn," he repeated. "Come on, let's go find Viridian."

It was another weirdness to be at my mom's hospital, where I'd been any number of times before, and to have Viridian here, as if someone had changed the channel on the cosmic television without me knowing. Viridian was sitting up in bed, in a blue flowered hospital gown and one of those plastic wrist bracelets.

Her hair was mussed, as I'd never seen it, disordered and frizzy. I wanted badly to set it straight. Her voice was calm but weak. "All this fuss. I'm mortified."

"How are you, what happened?"

"It was the silliest thing. I drank a glass of wine, which I should not have done, and it went right to my head. And it really was hot in that room, wasn't it, Oscar?"

"Criminally. I called Barb, she's on her way over."

"Now why did you do that?"

"Because I knew she'd want to be here."

Viridian turned her head fretfully on her pillow. "I suppose this is what I get for being old."

"What is the doctor telling you?" I asked. "Is it your blood pressure?"

"They want to keep me overnight. Like that ever made anyone feel better."

"It's a very highly rated hospital," I said, but she had fallen asleep.

"Oh my God," Oscar said. "Get a nurse or somebody."

"She's just sleeping. I expect she's tired, we should let her rest."

He followed me down the hallway to a waiting room. We sat in two poufy vinyl chairs, facing each other. It was starting to sink in that perhaps Viridian was not fine, perhaps this was the beginning (or the end) of something. Oscar said, "How much do ambulances cost anyway?"

"Let's not worry about that now."

"But she will. She'll worry about paying the doctor, the hospital, everything."

"Doesn't she have insurance?"

"Since when did insurance cover anything?"

I made a trip down the hall to the nurse's station to try and find Dr. Gandhi, who was around somewhere, just not here. When I got back to Oscar I said, "If she can't go to the conference, she can't go."

He turned his palms up, signaling exasperation, agreement, something. I sat down again. We contemplated the indifferent furnishings of the waiting room for a time. I had just opened my mouth to ask Oscar what he didn't like about Boone, when Oscar looked behind me, raising one hand. "Oh hi. We're in here."

Boone was peering in at the door. "Excuse me. Where's my mother?"

I stood up and said I'd take him to her. "Who called you?" I asked. "I mean, we didn't have a number for you." Not that I was sure we'd meant to call him.

"The hospital. Accidental next of kin." He shrugged. "How is she?"

I said we thought she was all right, but we were waiting for the doctor to see her. There was the fainting part, and the falling part, and the hitting her head part. We looked into the room. Viridian was still asleep, just as she'd been, sunk into the pillows. I didn't like seeing her like this, an untidy heap of laundry on a bed.

"I'll wait for the doctor," Boone said. He pulled up a chair. The room was small, and it felt crowded with even two of us there. I stood over him and saw the thinning crown of his dark hair, and a shadowy view of skin down the back of his shirt collar. I moved away.

"Thanks for watching out for her."

"Of course," I said. We were keeping our voices low, though Viridian gave no sign of stirring. I told him what had happened at the luncheon, what Oscar had said. And that there had been nothing worrisome before that, at least not that anyone had noticed.

"She's lucky that she has such a devoted group around her."

"We feel lucky to have her."

"I missed out on that. On really knowing her."

I stayed quiet. I didn't think I was allowed to have an opinion.

"All so she could write poems. I hope it was worth it."

I left the two of them alone. I didn't know what to say. She wasn't my mother, my real mother. She was only motherly to me in fits and starts, and always in an amused and distant way. But she had chosen me, singled me out for her attention and instruction. Just as, years ago, she had chosen to leave her own child behind.

It was funny that I didn't feel anywhere near as bad about my dad, about how he'd pretty much checked out of our lives. He called on birthdays and holidays, sent cards with money, and we talked about getting together, and maybe we would one of these days. But I didn't think too much about his absence. Maybe this was the difference between mothers and fathers. Maybe because among people I knew, fathers were often absent. Or maybe mothers weren't meant to leave just to write poetry.

When I got back to the waiting room, Barb had joined Oscar. "He's going to wait for the doctor," I told them. "She's still asleep."

Barb said, "I don't suppose there's anything we can do about that." She meant Boone, his being here.

"What do you have against him?"

Oscar said. "He's got some grievance. A chip on his shoulder."

"I guess he's entitled to have grievances." What was it about Viridian that made us all so jealous of our places next to her?

Barb said. "And she doesn't need to be reminded of things that are over and done with."

"You don't get to be over and done with your own child."

"You wouldn't think," Barb said, in a way that shut me up and made me feel hopelessly young and unschooled and shallow, with a simplistic and sentimental worldview unsuited to the rigors of high art. I was back to disliking Barb.

But maybe it wasn't over and there would still be some time left for the two of them, Boone and Viridian, to connect, or reconnect, or come to whatever peace might be possible between them. That was only one of the things we didn't know. Barb and Oscar were back to talking about Into the Woods and how different possibilities might play out. It was scheduled to begin in four days. In three, I would drive to Sacramento to meet up with my counterpart, Gil, and see just what I'd gotten myself into.

Oscar said, "I'm betting it's no big deal. One of those little medical hiccups."

Barb gave him a look, meaning, we can only hope so. Barb said, "If she does go to the conference, we have to help her. Watch out for her."

"Which she'll hate," Oscar said.

"She'll put up with it if it's the only way she can be there."

I said, "I don't understand why she'd even want to put herself through going. Can't she just stay home?"

Oscar said, "One, it's kind of fun. Two, it pays well. Three, it pays well."

We were back to money again. "Can't she just sell—" I stopped myself as the other two turned to me. "I'm sorry. I don't understand why she won't let somebody publish the poems. The famous ones."

"You mean," Barb said, "the ones that are worth money now that the writer's dead? If only that was some guarantee. We'd all hold hands and jump off the Golden Gate Bridge."

"You exaggerate," Oscar told her.

"If only."

"Your friend Doug," Oscar said to me, "wants to get his sticky hands on them. And it wouldn't be the worst place for them to end up. But he's not the only one. Remember Larry the Magnificent? He'd be only too happy to give the poems a home at his institute. That's why he's been dangling that job in front of her."

"So it's like, a bidding war?" Or logrolling. A word I remembered.

"Or she could make her own deal with a publisher, that's always been an option. But she might be running out of options. You see, Miss Carla," Oscar said, "perhaps this little flutter of the wings of the angel of death will give her a nudge in the direction of selling. Not to mention the medical bills and the rent coming round. But the other problem we have, say if she has some kind of brain event or if she dies, is that she's never told anybody where she put the freaking poems."

DOCTORS

D r. Gandhi had good news. *good* being a relative term. Viridian showed no evidence of heart damage. Fainting could be precipitated by cardiac distress, and that was not the case here. Dehydration, the hot room—those were more likely culprits. However, the fainting and resulting fall were what the medical profession called an unmasking event, one that brought other conditions to light. Conditions often due to normal aging. The blood oxygen levels, for instance. A concern. And her unacceptably high blood pressure. It was very important that they bring the blood pressure down immediately. This was a splendid opportunity. Medication would be prescribed when she left the hospital, and she would need a follow-up visit with a doctor a few weeks from now.

"I don't trust pharmaceuticals," Viridian said. She was still lying back in bed, and her voice was still faint and creaky. She'd asked for a mirror and a comb and had set her hair to rights. She was not happy about being in the hospital. "I avoid them."

"Would you like to avoid a stroke?" Dr. Gandhi asked. "Would you like to avoid not being able to speak because half of your face is paralyzed? Would you like to use both sides of your body? No, you will stay here tonight so that we can keep you stable and do the fasting cholesterol test in the morning, also very important." He liked his job, you could tell.

Dr. Gandhi left the room, and the rest of us—me, Barb, Oscar, Boone—waited to see who would come up with something to say. Viridian had closed her eyes. When she opened them and saw us all staring, she said, "You people look like the wages of sin."

"It's not that bad," Oscar said. "It's actually great. Well not great. But entirely treatable."

Barb said, "You could see a different doctor if you wanted. A holistic doctor. A naturopath."

"Doctors," Viridian said, dismissing them. She had a spasm of coughing and we all stared at our feet until it cleared. Oscar spoke up.

"Yoga and vitamins are great, but they can't handle everything. How's your head?"

Viridian touched the back of her scalp. "Still hurts."

"The ambulance crew seemed nice," Oscar went on encouragingly. "Very professional."

Viridian said nothing. Barb said, "I'm sure they'll take good care of you here."

"Once they start in on you? They don't stop until they've diagnosed you with five more horrible things. That's just what they do."

"Now don't be a butthead, honey," Oscar said.

This roused her so that she sat up, fixing him with her blue stare. "I don't believe I have ever in my life been called a butthead."

"It was a cautionary statement."

"This morning I was a normal person. Now I'm a medical curiosity."

"You're just tired," Barb said. "Everything seems worse when you're tired."

Viridian didn't answer. Neither Boone nor I spoke. I didn't think Viridian needed any more piling on, and maybe Boone didn't consider himself enough of a son to start telling her what to do. I expected that things would turn out all right, and Viridian would get over her distress, and do what the doctor said. I was relieved that there didn't seem to be anything worse wrong with her. High blood pressure, I thought lots of people had that.

Barb said they ought to find Viridian something to eat, it might be a while before dinner, and what were the odds of finding anything healthy? I said there was always a veggie burger on the patient menu. Everybody looked at me, as if they'd just now remembered I was there.

"My mom works here," I said. "In medical records."

"Carla," Viridian said to me. "I'm sorry I had to ruin your day."

"Please don't worry about it."

"You shouldn't be in some stuffy old hospital room. You should be out in the fresh air, with all the green and growing things."

"It's fine. I do that all day. It's fine to take a break from it."

"And who's going to read poetry to you, if I die? Who's going to keep your mind green and growing?"

I looked at the others. They looked back at me, stricken. I said, "How about I go see if I can find you something good to eat."

I turned and left the room. Walking down the hall, I heard the door open and turned and saw Boone looking out of the doorway at me. For the second time, I put an elevator door between us. I didn't feel like talking, to him or to anyone.

I was thinking that maybe I liked poetry more than I liked poets.

I bought an egg salad sandwich and a green salad in the cafeteria. I texted my mom and said not to worry about dinner for me. I thought I'd stay at least a little while longer, but I didn't want to be one more person crowding the space, elbowing the others aside for a chance to fluff Viridian's pillow. I wish she hadn't said what she did. It made me feel weird and a little angry, like I was some underprivileged child she'd taken on as a project. But maybe that was the cost of hanging around with poets. They looked at you through some kind of poet kaleidoscope and turned you into their own ideas.

I had to wonder what the writers' conference was going to be like, and if it was too late to back out of it. But I was somebody else who needed the money. At least there would be plenty of other people there, and no one would have to pay any particular attention to me.

There were times when remembering Aaron, missing Aaron, rose up and clobbered me the way an ocean wave hits you in the back of the knees. Suddenly, this was one of them. Maybe everything I'd done or tried to do these last few months had been a mistake, maybe I should have left well enough alone, as my mom liked to say, and forgiven him. I'd been happy, or happy enough. Everybody had their spells of discontent and fretfulness. They put their heads down and got through them. That was life.

I texted Aaron. Just HI, HOW ARE YOU DOING? I waited a while, but I didn't hear back from him and I put the phone away.

When I got upstairs with my Styrofoam packages of food, the others had left, and Viridian was alone. I thought that she was asleep again. I put the food on the bedside table and turned to go.

"Carla." She was awake.

"Can I get you anything? Did you want me to call somebody?"

"I'm not myself."

"It's okay. You don't feel well." Her voice alarmed me. It was so hoarse, almost rusty. I thought they must have given her something.

"I'm being such a baby."

"No."

"You're supposed to be brave and then you end up a bad joke."

"Says who? You don't have to be anything." She really wasn't herself. She never spoke this way, fretful and aggrieved, as if at some injustice.

"Then you think about everything you've left behind."

"But you aren't going anywhere, okay?" I tried to sound hearty and reassuring. "Think about feeling better and getting back home."

"Time to walk the plank."

"Now that's silly." Here I was scolding her, another new thing.

"Sooner or later."

I wished one of the others would come back. Or some annoying volunteer with a cart full of magazines. I didn't know how to soothe her. Everybody died, and it sucked. "Later," I said. "Not now."

"I was so foolish."

I had no idea what she was talking about. "It's all right," I said. She wouldn't be saying any of this if she felt better. I was embarrassed for her, and now I was glad the others weren't here.

"And weak willed."

"I think you just need to rest more."

"It was such a boy's club. All of them sitting in the sandbox, hitting each other in the head with toys."

"Yes well that sounds—"

"There was really no place for me, except as somebody's fuckee."

I'd never heard her swear before, let alone say something that extraordinary. I waited to see if she'd go on, but she was quiet. I thought that when you got older, everything in your life must echo back at you. The old arguments waged all over again. It made me uneasy to watch it. But I didn't look away.

Her eyes had been half closed but now she opened them, wet and wide and blue. "You're a smart, lovely girl."

"Thank you."

"Make sure you are taken seriously."

I nodded, as if I knew what she meant.

"You need to keep reading. Promise me."

"I promise."

"Even the pretentious, ridiculous writers, because if you don't at least get some exposure to them, you'll be either overimpressed or confused by them."

"All right," I said. "Them, too." I thought she was sounding better, stronger, now that she was talking about poetry. A nurse came into the room then, or at least, a woman wearing scrubs. You never knew who anyone was in a hospital anymore.

"How are we doing?" the nurse-type person asked, not really expecting an answer. "How about we check that old blood pressure?"

Viridian leaned toward me as the nurse reached for her arm on the other side of the bed and wrapped it in the blood pressure cuff. "Read *A Defence of Poetry*," she said. "That's Shelley. Very important."

"All right," I said again.

"It's difficult but I have confidence in you. Now don't disappoint me."

"I won't," I said, although I didn't know how to avoid disappointing her or anyone else.

"Poor Shelley. He drowned at sea, you know. When they found him, fish had eaten his face and hands."

"Now that's not a very cheerful thought," the nurse said.

"'Full fathom five the poet lies.'" Viridian gave me an impish look, as if this was a joke we were both in on.

I left them alone and waited in the corridor for the nurse to come out. The nurse said not to worry, when they brought blood pressure down in a hurry, it could send you on a little ride. Especially if they lowered it too fast, especially in older people. "Is she your grandmother?"

"Just a friend." It was hard to think of her as a grandmother. My grandma had collected Beanie Babies and watched reruns of *Matlock*.

I found the other three in the waiting room down the hall. They stopped talking when I walked in, as if there was something

I wasn't meant to hear. I wasn't going to tell them what I'd witnessed either. It had all been too strange and unsettling, and in
another sense, mortifying.

"I got her a sandwich," I said. "In case she wanted something."

"Great," Oscar said. "Thanks. We were just trying to come
up with a battle plan. Barb's going to drive me back to Fairfax.
We'll both be here in the morning when she's released, and we'll
get her home. Boone's going to stay here this evening in case she
needs anything."

There wasn't any part in this for me. Maybe I would get to see
my mom for dinner after all. "Okay," I said. "I have a couple of
days before the conference, so—"

"The bloody conference," Oscar groaned. "The earth should
only swallow it."

"Try and think positive," Barb said, although she did not
sound especially positive.

I said, "I don't think she'll be able to go."

"Well not if she had to go this minute," Barb said, as if that
was what I'd suggested. When Barb decided to get on your nerves,
she pretty much stayed there. They all stood up. "Should we look
in on her before we go?"

"I think she's resting," I said. I thought everybody else could
pass on hearing about drowned poets.

Boone said he needed coffee and why didn't I come with
him? I still hadn't heard from Aaron, maybe that was why I
said I would. Also, he'd dressed down today, in jeans and a gray
T-shirt underneath his usual button-down. He looked more like
my slightly inappropriate New York boyfriend than my dad.

Me, I could have used a cleaner shirt, as had been pointed out to me.

We wound up at a strip mall coffee shop, sitting across from each other at a table in front of the window. He'd paid for my coffee and I'd let him, because that felt harmless enough. I wasn't trying to flirt with him; in fact, I kept trying not to. I kept looking for Viridian in him, and I both did and did not find her, like a mirror with a flaw. It's not like we were anything except an odd couple. But here we were again, face to face.

He said, "This blood pressure problem? It may explain some things."

"What things," I said, wishing I wasn't going to find out.

"You have to keep this confidential," he said, which annoyed me, because I didn't want to share secrets with him. I shrugged, meaning, Sure.

"Ed's been worried about my mother. Even before this. About her finances."

I didn't want to let on that I knew anything about it, so I nodded and looked noncommittal.

"She has an investment account. Ed helped her set it up. It's meant to provide for her, but she's been spending it down with nothing coming in."

"She has her workshops." Or as Oscar called them, hen parties. "People pay to study with her."

"They don't pay very much. Ed's tried to talk to her. Get her to see a financial planner. But you can't get her to care about money. He tried, then I tried. She blew me off. Why should she listen to me, anyway?"

I watched his fingers tap, tap, tapping against the rim of his coffee cup, a nervous circuit. How much was owed to a child left behind? More than could ever be repaid.

He went on. "I guess it's supposed to be this great yoga-Zen detachment, you know, not letting yourself care about material things. But now I'm wondering if it isn't some kind of dementia. Blood flow to the brain getting squeezed. Something that's been creeping up on her."

I might have told him he was dead wrong, except for what I'd just witnessed in her hospital room. I said, "She writes poetry. You can't do that if you're losing your mind." Or could you? I wanted to deny it and defend her. But my heart was sinking.

"Yeah. Different parts of the brain, maybe. The way musicians with Alzheimer's can still remember songs."

"It's not the same."

"I don't know if it is or isn't."

We didn't speak for a time. The shop was quiet, nearly empty. The two baristas behind the counter were popping towels at each other and yawning.

I didn't know enough to argue one way or another. And whatever had caused the barmy talk I'd heard from her, medication or anything else, it had been an unhappy demonstration. I said, "You and Oscar and Barb were talking about her money problems." He nodded. "And now you're talking about it with me. Why?"

"So you'll know. So you can help her."

"I don't see how anybody can help. I guess we can try to get her to the conference so she gets paid for it."

"That won't be enough to make much difference. Not for long."

I said, "I don't feel comfortable talking about her like this. When she isn't here."

"I understand that, but it's important. She might lose her house."

I couldn't imagine Viridian living anywhere else. I wanted everything to stay the same, and of course nothing ever did. It was selfish and sentimental of me to think that we would all live forever, and that Viridian would always preside over us, gracious and untroubled. But who could blame me for it?

The next thing Boone said was, "How much do you know about Mathias?"

"A little." He seemed to be waiting for me to demonstrate how much, or how little. "He was a poet your mother knew."

"Knew."

"They were together. They were lovers. He was brilliant."

"Do you think he was? Brilliant?" I must have hesitated. Boone said, "She left my father to go back to Mathias. She left me, too. I guess I'm wondering if it was a fair trade, you know, our little paltry human happiness for great art."

"I don't think I can decide that for you."

"He was nuts."

"He had mental health issues. He committed suicide."

"Everybody seems to know that part," Boone said. "It feeds into the cliché that artists are wild and crazy and you have to let them get away with stuff because of their talent." He raised his eyebrows, either kidding or pretending to be.

"I don't believe that." I had my own ideas about it by now.
"Every poet's different. But they're all tuned into another frequency. They hear things we don't."

"Like dogs."

I was not amused.

"Sorry," he said. "I was being flippant."

"Maybe if we had more respect for dogs," I said. "If we took
them seriously. If we spoke their language. Mathias makes the hair
on the back of my neck stand up. The poem about the dead deer?
Those terrible, sparse lines about her unseeing eye, the empty air
full of her death. And then the way the poem turns itself inside
out so it's talking about longing and the death of longing, and
the life cycle of desire, and yes, I think that is extraordinary, yes
I think it is brilliant."

Boone sat back in his chair and gave me a measuring look.
He said, "You're what we call, in sports, a ringer. You know what
that means?"

"I do, and the next two words out of my mouth aren't going
to be Happy Birthday."

"No, whoa, I didn't mean it like—"

"You meant, I'm not as dumb as I look."

"You're angry. I'm sorry. Could we rewind that part of the
conversation?"

"Why don't you say whatever it is you've been going a long
way around the barn to say."

Boone muttered something to the effect of my being a hardheaded woman. I kept staring him down. I wasn't going to make
it easy for him. He said, "My mother has a lot of material from

that time. About Mathias. He's something of a hot property right now. She could write a memoir."

"Could she? You've been talking about her as if she was incapacitated." Material. You had to wonder.

"Someone could help her. Write down what she says, polish it up."

He turned his hands palms up on the table. See? See how reasonable he was being? The word *entrepreneur* started waving in my brain like a banner. I said, "You want us all to gang up on her. Talk her into it."

"For her own benefit. Or fine, she can have a garage sale instead. But if she could get a book proposal to a publisher, she could be looking at some real money."

Now it was a conversation about money, or maybe it always had been about money, and it was naive of me to have thought any differently. And who was Boone, showing up out of nowhere, or so it seemed, to take up space in everybody's business.

I said, "If she wanted to write a book, I bet she would have already."

"Would it be such a terrible thing? Her telling their story? Saving it before it's too late? Not to mention, keeping a roof over her head."

I doubted Viridian wanted her reputation—her legacy, I guess Boone was calling it—to depend on some other poet. Some man. Like she was just the sidekick. "It's really not up to me."

"Hear me out. Do you think poetry's a big seller? Do you think it's what people grab off a newsstand when they're on their way through the airport? But a good story, that sells. And if

it's a good story with poems hitching a ride on its back, what's
the harm?"

I didn't answer. I was thinking how far away what he said
was from the way I'd come to poetry, the way it had gobsmacked
me and sent me out into the world breathing a new, charged air,
how it made me feel that words might burn if you touched them.
I thought Viridian was every bit as good a poet as Mathias. She
just worked in a different key: less angry, less sexualized. More
sorrowful and contemplative. It didn't seem fair that men could
be celebrated for their misbehavior, indulged and made famous,
where a woman would have been dismissed, diminished, labeled
weak or hysterical. In a funny way it put me in mind of my mom,
who always said that men held more cards and could get away with
more. She hadn't been talking about artists, but it still applied.

I didn't say any of this, because then Boone might tell me how
cute I was when I tried to be intelligent. He was waiting. I said,
"I can't and won't talk her into anything she doesn't want to do. I
don't know why you think I have some kind of influence anyway."

"Because you're another green girl. Aren't you? She calls you
that. The same as Mathias called her. Viridian. Green." He looked
at his watch then. A big, expensive-looking watch designed to
impress during business deals. "I should be getting back to check
on her."

VIRIDIAN CAME HOME the next morning and we all held our
breath. She was tired and she slept a lot the first day, and she
complained that the new blood pressure medicine made her head
feel like an overinflated balloon tethered to her neck. But she was

herself, as far as any of us could tell, and we were grateful. She didn't seem to remember any of the unsettling things she'd said to me in the hospital, and that was fine with me. The conference? She wanted to go, she didn't see any reason not to. She was making plans to be there.

I had plans, too. Tony Presto sent me a long memo with different instructions and prohibitions. Many of these had to do with fire prevention. My mom got me some bear-strength pepper spray and paid for a set of new tires on my truck. I studied the promotional materials, the pictures of serene forest and mirroring water, of students and staff sitting in Adirondack chairs or on a rustic front porch, engaged in fellowship and literary communion. I read the profiles of the distinguished staff members, their many publications and awards. Soon I would be among them. I felt like I was going off to camp, a very high-toned and soulful camp.

The day before I left, I stopped by to see Viridian and Oscar, wanting to reassure myself that the crisis was past, and also so they could fill my ears with last-minute advice. Bear repellant, fire extinguishers, sunscreen, snakebite kit, flashlights—all of those might be useful, but how did you manage several dozen amateur and professional authors?

Viridian said, "Honestly, most of the students are lovely. Excited to be there, hard-working, eager to learn. And often very talented."

Oscar said, "There are the occasional problem personalities. Remember Vikram?"

"Oh, Vikram. Poor man."

"Poor? He was a stalker!"

I waited for them to tell me more. We were sitting in the shade of the backyard, enjoying the late-season garden, the tall verbena, the purple asters and yellow sunflowers, feather grass and maiden grass. The air was warm and indolent, and I would have been happy to spend every afternoon of my life there.

Viridian said to me, "Don't worry. If there are any serious issues, Tony deals with them."

"Who was Vikram?"

"He wrote poems about the other students in the workshop," Oscar said, "and he insisted on reading them out loud. As erotica, they weren't that bad. But clearly . . ."

"Inappropriate," Viridian finished for him.

"What happened?"

"Wasn't there some kind of messy . . ."

"Well. The important thing is, he won't be there this year." Viridian smiled encouragingly. She had lost weight, you could see it in her face. Somebody in her writers' group had given her a necklace, a piece of malachite, green with black veins, held by a thin silver chain. She wore it over one of her white shirts. She looked beautiful and queenly, but it was as if a gear had ticked down a notch. Time passing, age accumulating. Or I might have been imagining it. Borrowing trouble, my mom called it.

Oscar said I would mainly have to do a lot of fetching and carrying and worry about things like stocking the break room with enough coffee and bagels. That might sound menial, but it was very, very important. I promised I'd be on top of it.

It's difficult to say exactly what happened next. We were sitting and talking, and Viridian had just remarked how nice it would be to spend a week near the water, how she planned to swim every day, when her speech phased out—that's what I'll call it—and for a space of fifteen seconds she was speaking gibberish: *and I ran away with the king of the bandits hey nonny nonny.* I think that's what I thought I heard. The next moment she was back to normal. She said she hoped the weather would stay fine for us.

I looked at Oscar and he at me, and I could tell we were both unnerved, and neither of us had invented or imagined it.

Viridian had reached the end of her thought and was waiting for one of us to speak. Oscar said, "Virdie? You feeling all right?"

"Of course I am."

"You were talking funny."

"Now don't be rude."

"Yeah, but you were babbling. About the king of the bandits. It's like your mouth took a little detour." Oscar looked over at me.

"I was talking about the weather," Viridian said, sounding impatient.

"How's your blood pressure?" I asked her. "Have you been taking it?" The hospital had sent her home with a cuff so she could monitor herself.

Viridian sighed. "I check it fifteen times a day. It's perfectly normal. Is everyone going to follow me around all day, fussing over me? I swear, I will run away and join the circus."

Oscar and I left her in the garden and went to sit on the front steps. I said that maybe we should call Dr. Gandhi. Oscar said that he would, but what the hell had happened?

"Maybe it's the medication." I hadn't told anyone about the way she'd talked in the hospital, and anyway, this was something different, worse. "Ask him if there are side effects. Ask him if it's safe for her to travel."

"She won't want to go back to the hospital. That's for certain."

"Should we call Boone?"

"She won't listen to him either."

I wasn't sure if I'd wanted to call him or not, so I settled for not. I was out of good ideas, and I guess Oscar was, too. I didn't want to admit defeat, although we'd have to, sooner or later. Oscar had begun tying his hair back in a tight ponytail that made him resemble a gone-to-seed Japanese monk. He was wearing shorts and sandals and one of his black T-shirts, the same clothes as when I'd first set eyes on him and wondered if he was either dangerous or merely what one called a character. By now of course I was well used to him. And he'd proved himself to be Viridian's loyal friend.

I said that he could watch Viridian take her blood pressure and make sure she was doing it right, make sure the readings weren't too high. Or too low. "It might not happen again," I said, and Oscar said, Right, and then we were both quiet, not really believing it.

Finally, I said, "About Boone. Did he tell you—"

"About his book idea. Yeah." We were keeping our voices low, not because there was any real chance of Viridian overhearing us, but I suppose because we felt furtive about the whole topic. "She's never going to write it."

"I think he knows that. I think he wants somebody else to put it together, a ghostwriter."

"And I'm thinking it's just a new way to pry those Mathias poems loose. I wouldn't be surprised if it was really Doug's idea. He could make a big deal out of the poems. A new chapter in American letters, etcetera. Print a book excerpt, essays, critiques. Run a special issue, get a lot of expensive attention from foundations and donors. Do the right thing for the wrong reasons. Because the world really ought to see those poems."

"So you think it's a good idea. You think we should try to help them."

"Only if it would help Virdie," Oscar said.

We were quiet again. We weren't sure anymore just what kind of help Viridian might need. I wondered now if it was love or spite that made her keep Mathias's poems for herself.

Oscar roused himself. "How's that boyfriend of yours? You should bring him around once in a while."

I said that I would. I hadn't told any of them about our quarrel.

In fact, I'd seen Aaron the night before, and we'd wound up in bed, which, if you asked other people about their breakups, a lot of them would admit to having done the same. But it left us more confused than ever. When we tried to talk things through, both before and afterward, we stumbled and didn't say much. I couldn't say what I wanted him to do, except want me back, and I couldn't tell if he did or not. Sex, of course, not counting. I didn't think he was trying very hard. "You should do whatever you want," he'd said, which didn't sound like a man who was going to fight to the death to recover my favor.

"Do you like Boone?" I asked Oscar. "Or maybe a better question, do you trust him?"

"I can't say. I feel sorry for him. He wants to be her son. I mean, he is and he isn't, you know? He wants to be a hero and solve her problems. Present her with a big, oversized check, like on a game show. Maybe a little payday for himself, say, an agent's fifteen percent. What the hell. You can't expect anybody's motives to be pure. He feels like he's owed something. He feels like he has to prove something."

He stood up then. "People are complicated, don't you think? Good thing, too. Otherwise, robots could write poetry. You better get on home and finish packing. I'll let you know what the doctor says."

INTO THE WOODS I

The official name of the conference was Imagination and Environment: Intersections. Although as Gil said, unloading a week's worth of wasp spray, there were some intersections that the nature lovers at the conference really weren't into.

The whole time I'd been texting back and forth with Gil, I'd assumed Gil was a man. No one had told me any different, or anything at all, really. So that when I reached our rendezvous point, a Chevron station just east of Sacramento, I was confused when a woman came toward me, speaking my name as a question. Gil was short and sturdy, freckled and sunburnt. Older than me, I couldn't tell by how much. She pointed out her own truck, a big black GMC with a dirt bike in the bed. A man sat behind the wheel. "That's Rog," Gil said. "He's not really here. I'll explain later."

I followed them on U.S. 50 as far as Placerville, where we stopped at the forest ranger station and then at an In-N-Out. "The food up there's pretty good," Gil said. "They bring in a kitchen crew all the way from some place in Tahoe. But everybody has different weird food ideas, so it's stuff like beet and watermelon salad. Tofu tutti frutti."

Rog was doing his best not to be there. He was tall and skinny and silent, giving all his attention to his cheeseburger. He had sandy hair and pale blue eyes and near-invisible eyebrows and appeared to be fiercely shy. Gil did all the talking for the two of them. Rog wore jeans, high lace-up boots, and a T-shirt with a picture of a buck and the words EATIN' LOCAL BEFORE IT WAS COOL.

Gil said that the two of them lived in Sacramento and worked in warehouses when they needed cash. They spent as much time as they could camping, hunting, and fishing. Sometimes they found caretaker jobs, like the conference. But Rog was a bow-hunter. Which of course would give the nature lovers fits because they were all about walking lightly on the earth, and so on. So Rog was not here. Get it?

I said that I did. Rog would take the dirt bike up to a campground on the reservoir a few miles north of the conference grounds. He might be around the conference from time to time but if I saw him, he wasn't really there, okay? Anyway, I probably wouldn't see him, he was pretty good at keeping under cover.

I said I was cool with it. I didn't know if it was reassuring or not, the idea of Rog patrolling the perimeter with a knife in his teeth, or whatever. But at least the two of them seemed like genuine outdoors people, and I was glad for that.

I asked Gil about the people at the conference, what were they like, and she said, "About what you'd expect. They flap their gums a lot. Take out their own trash? Not so much. Writers. Huh." Gil fixed me with a critical eye. "So what is it you do?"

"Landscaping," I said.

Gil told me to watch out for this one guy, she thought he was going to be here again this year. He kept showing up at women's cabins and claiming he needed to have sex to help his bad back. "I forget his name. Sinner, maybe?"

"Spinner." Ken Spinner, novelist and one of the bigger big deals attending. Okay, pig alert.

From Placerville we got off of U.S. 50 and followed a two-lane road east. It wound through horse farms, tree farms, vineyards, apple orchards. The pines grew closer as we approached the national forest, the trees shading the road surface. The view ahead, when you could get an unobstructed look, was solid green, the land climbing. Five years ago, the King Fire had started just north of Pollock Pines and burned 97,000 acres. They took fire prevention seriously around here. They had to.

Now we came to a junction and we were traveling the old Pony Express Trail, unrecognizable as such except for the signs announcing it. Businesses selling chain saws replaced the orchards as the trees closed in. We passed gas stations, propane services, white roadside crosses marking fatalities. The air was cooler in the tree shadow. The road became the main street of Pollock Pines, with its tourist-ready painted storefronts. Gil's truck signaled a left turn and I followed them away from the highway and into the deeper woods.

People had built big, tree-shaded houses on the hills, but now these dwindled, and we bumped along on a grass and dirt road. We stopped at a gate, chained shut, marked EL DORADO RETREAT—PRIVATE PROPERTY. Gil got out and unlocked the gate and waved us through. Up another hill, then the trees opened up and I saw the timbered lodge building I recognized from the pamphlets, and the long path of lawn leading down to the mild river.

I parked next to their truck and was about to get out and stretch when Gil stopped me. "How about you let me and Rog do a recon first?"

I got back in. I watched the two of them circle around the lodge building and out of sight. Rog was carrying a hatchet.

Other buildings were set around the central clearing. A couple of these, the largest, were probably for meals or gatherings. In an outer ring stood a dozen or more stand-alone cabins of different sizes, and behind them, some barrackslike structures that I guessed were the bunkhouses. Beyond that, the pines were a green wall. The air was perfectly still.

Gil and Rog weren't gone that long, just long enough to make me wonder what I'd do if they didn't come back. Then Gil came out onto the front porch of the lodge from inside and waved at me to join her. "So amazing!" she called to me. "We killed a rattlesnake and she was pregnant, and if you put your finger on the heart, it still beats!" Right about then I was thinking I was too far from home.

It got better. It was fun to explore the different buildings and cabins and have them all to ourselves before the rest of the conference descended. Everything had a woodsy charm, with a lot of pine paneling and log furniture and gingham curtains. Lighted plank pathways were laid out between the buildings so that even the drunks could find their way back to bed safely. Behind the farthest cabins, there was a small stone-edged swimming pool and a hot tub shaped like a giant barrel.

Later that afternoon the laundry service delivered bales of sheets and towels and we made the beds in the staff cabins and wiped down the bathrooms. I still didn't know if Viridian was coming or not. Oscar hadn't called, and anyway the cell phone service up here was spotty. She was scheduled to stay in one of the nicest cabins, along with Sacha and two other of the women faculty. I made sure her room was clean and aired, and I picked a bouquet of chicory and wild carrot and put it by the bed.

I was relieved that Gil (and Rog, too, I guess) and I were assigned to rooms in the main lodge. The lodge had a big stone fireplace and a bar that looked like an old-fashioned saloon, with carved pillars and rosettes and a gilt-swirled mirror. Gil said the liquor supply was kept under lock and key and doled out sparingly each evening by Tony Presto.

Gil and Rog had brought beer and steaks and potatoes and corn for our dinner, plus other things that should have occurred to me but hadn't, like box fans. There was a deck built out over the river landing and we sat and watched the sun go down in glory. The river, tamed enough for a swimming beach, was deep green, then opal in the last light. That was when I thought, Writers, and had a passing wish that no one else would come.

We ate our fill and policed all our food scraps and stored the garbage in the bear-proof back room of the dining hall. I fell asleep to the white noise of the fan and nothing human or animal disturbed me.

In the morning we waved good-bye to Rog as he loaded his hunting bow and other gear onto the dirt bike and took off along the fire road. A little while later Tony Presto pulled up and the conference was officially open for business.

Tony was short, with a halo of fluffy curls, and nervous, either by nature or because he was in charge of everything. He had a habit of asking questions and not waiting for the answers. Had we found everything? Were the outside lights working? The freezer? Good, good.

We helped him unload the boxes of books by the conference authors, available for sale in the main assembly building. Here was Viridian's one book in print, and a number of anthologies in which she had poems. Here were Oscar's and Sacha's books, and those by the younger poets. Like the younger fiction writers, they were all from places like Africa or Cuba or Mongolia. They were Native American, Asian American, Hispanic American, all manner of complicated identities, with genders and sexual preferences likewise all over the map. By now I had been educated as to the importance of diversity and including under-represented voices and avoiding microaggressions, and how all the Dead White Men had held literature hostage for too long. I had been made aware of the pushback from people who sneered at this as political correctness. It was all too much for me to sort through, and I was glad that my job was simply to make everyone welcome and hand out quarters for the laundry machines. Although it reminded me of that time in high school where everybody started wearing T-shirts that said "Different."

It did sort of tip the scales that we had Ken Spinner representing the Not Yet Dead White Men. Several of his large, overstuffed books were for sale. He wrote lengthy, successful novels about men facing elemental challenges in various natural settings. The actual nature writers looked interesting. They took photographs of native plants, they wrote essays about wild and scenic rivers or the Amazon rain forest. One of them had lived for a year on an abandoned oil drilling platform.

The food service crew arrived with great quantities of organic produce and cruelty-free meats. Gil and I helped with that as well. The crew were all Mexican and I went up in Gil's estimation because I could speak to them in Spanish and they gave us ice cream.

Then Gil went down to the gate to let people in and direct traffic. I was set up at a table just inside the lodge entrance, checking off the arrivals and distributing maps and schedules.

Most conference attendees were told to meet up in downtown Pollock Pines, where a kind of super van transported them up to the resort. The idea, I was told, was to minimize the fire risks of catalytic converters passing over dry grass. The first vanload and their luggage arrived and milled around me, excited, chattering, needing a bathroom, allergy medicine, Wi-Fi passwords, and a good deal more. Another van arrived and then another, as I eased one group out to find their lodgings so I could deal with the next one. They were a mix of ages, more middle-aged than young, more women than men. As I was to do all week, I overheard bits and pieces of conversations:

"You could submit it to *Wallop*. They're doing a whole issue on obsession."

". . . mostly into flash fiction."

"Not the kind of editor you bring home to mother."

"Poisonous plants as a homoerotic subtext. Like 'Rappaccini's Daughter.'"

ONE OF THE younger men lingered by my table.

"You don't remember me, do you?" He had dark curly hair and glasses and a serious face. He could have been anybody. "No, sorry," I said, trying to sound cheerful. I was tired of talking and I needed a break before the next batch of happy campers.

"I met you at Viridian's reading. College of Marin."

"Oh my God, that's right. I'm sorry, you're—"

"Matt."

"Matt, sure. I'm—"

"Carla."

I did remember his slightly pissy air of grievance, as if I'd broken some promise I didn't remember making. He said, "What are you doing here?"

"Working."

"Yeah, but how did that happen?" Meaning, how did a person of no particular distinction end up in a position of responsibility? You could get tired of that attitude.

"Sorry," I said, pointing to the next van pulling up outside, "can't talk right now."

He took off. It was so weird, thinking back to that night, not so very long ago, and realizing how much had changed, how I'd landed in the middle of nowhere, which was still a pretty interesting place to be.

Different writers, staff members, arrived as well, although

nobody I knew. The three younger poets, Bettina Cruz, M'beke Ogbo, and Gary Rain Hsu, had all crossed paths before and were happy to see each other again. As were the younger members of the fiction contingent. It was brought home to me how much of a generational divide there was between them and the poets I knew best. These were writers with podcasts, with Instagram accounts, with YouTube videos. They tweeted back and forth, they had graphically compelling web pages. They organized poetry jams and slams, salons, spa weekends where one might also get editorial pointers on manuscripts. They were geniuses at self-promotion.

Which wasn't necessarily a bad thing. A little too market-oriented, perhaps, but not bad. Why not put yourself and your writing out there, scream for attention along with the rest of the noisy world? I'd seen some of their poems; they were interesting, confounding, show-offy, accomplished, sometimes all of these at once. I worried about Viridian and her friends, how they might be left behind. And where were they anyway? Was Viridian even coming?

". . . . so tired of persona poems . . ."

"You had me at autodidact."

"A kind of syntactical vertigo."

"sustainable viticulture . . ."

"Memoir, memoir, memoir."

KEN SPINNER, AT least, was old school, but in ways that were not especially fortunate. The main room of the lodge was crowded when he came in, and he moved through it by draping his arms on and around the different females in his path, then propelling himself forward, like a kid on the monkey bars. He stopped to

talk to everybody, and everybody to him. A guy with long practice at being a celebrity. He was a big man with his silver hair
combed forward, Caesar style. And a strange, mottled complexion, like a piece of unfresh lunchmeat.

"Hello young lady" was his greeting to me. "I'm Ken." He
leaned over the table to shake hands and look down my shirt.
"Who might you be?"

"Princess Leia." The room was loud enough that I thought I
could get away with it. "Carla."

"Carla. Carla Carla Carla. You're new this year, aren't you?"

"Getting older by the minute."

Again, he hadn't quite heard me. "I need to find my cabin.
How about you help me."

I pointed it out on the map. He kept saying he didn't see it. I
moved the map to the edge of the table so I could get his nose out
of my boobs. Really, the guy was not smooth. Or young. But there
was some weird, confounding vanity that must have worked for
him, at least often enough for him to keep making the same moves.

"Tony," I called out, seeing him on the front porch. "Ken
needs you to help him get settled."

Tony was all over it. He picked up Ken's luggage (expensive
predistressed leather) and led him away. Two young women,
workshop students, that Ken had been talking to stayed behind,
giggling to each other.

Finally, in the late afternoon, after almost everyone else had
checked in, Oscar and Barb arrived, weary and dragging.

"Is Viridian coming?" I asked.

"Nice to see you, too," Oscar said. He plopped into one of the leather armchairs in front of the fireplace and tried to fan himself with a birdwatching guide. "Yes, she's coming. Sacha and Anders are bringing her. They stopped for lunch, I expect they'll be along soon."

I said I didn't think that Anders was a part of the conference. "Just try and keep him away from Sacha," Barb said. "He got a motel room somewhere." Barb was wearing a big wide-brimmed straw hat and a tie-dye tunic over skinny leggings. She saw me staring at her and I looked away.

"How is she, is she feeling all right?"

"Never better," Oscar said. "To hear her tell it."

I looked from Barb to Oscar, waiting. Barb said, "There are these little blips."

"Hardly noticeable."

". . . when she might lose her train of thought."

"It's more like another train comes along and she hops on for a while. Nothing she's aware of."

". . . and she usually ends up where she meant to go. But meanwhile—"

I raised a hand. Two of the gentlemen conference members had settled in rocking chairs on the porch, close enough to hear us. I lowered my voice. "What did the doctor say?"

"I think what he said was the medical version of 'just one of those things,'" Oscar said. "He wants her to see a gerontologist when she gets back. Anyway, he didn't say to keep her home."

Barb said, "I'm in her workshop. I'll help steer things if I have to. And Sacha's in the same cabin. She'll be right there. Her reading's on the last night. By then we should know."

"Good. Just don't tell."

"Right," I said. We were all focusing on the short term, on getting through the five days of the conference. Anything much beyond that, we didn't want to contemplate. Oscar said he was hungry, when did we eat? I said there was a wine and cheese reception at five-thirty.

"Vegan cheese and sulfite-free wine. How could I forget."

We left Barb in charge of the welcome station in case Viridian or any other stragglers showed up. I took Oscar to the back door of the dining hall and told the staff that the *señor* needed something to eat. The crew was having their own early dinner, pork stew and rice. They served up a portion for Oscar. Really, these guys were the best. We sat at a table near the kitchen and Oscar polished off the food.

When he was finished, we sat for a time, not wanting to talk much about Viridian. I said it was pretty here, and Oscar agreed, in an absent way. I said I should probably be getting back.

"Can I ask you something? Do I seem old to you?"

"What?"

"Simple question. Do you think of me as an old man?"

Maybe it was my encounter with Ken Spinner that gave Oscar's question that alarming echo of sleaze. But then, Ken wouldn't ever ask such a thing. And anyway, it was only Oscar, and he seemed more melancholy than anything else. I said, "You're older than me. But most of the time you act about fourteen."

"Really?" This seemed to cheer him up. "What about my hair, do you think I should I cut it?"

"What's got into you?"

"Yes or no."

"Yes, cut it. But don't do it yourself, find a decent stylist."

"Yeah, good idea." He was silent again.

"Why are you asking? What's the deal?"

"*Ars longa, vita brevis.* You know what that means?"

"'Art is long, life is short.' Yes, you told me. More than once. Why?"

"It doesn't cheer me up the way it used to. You know, how your art will survive you and transcend your wretched, paltry existence, I mean, who cares? Who wants to be famous after they're dead? What good does that do you?"

I thought he must be depressed about Viridian. I was, too, although it didn't lead me to thoughts of cutting my hair. "Come on," I said, getting up. "Let's see if the others are here."

They had just pulled up when we got back to the lodge. Anders got out first, followed by Sacha. Viridian was in the back seat. She took her time getting out, but I couldn't see anything tired or strained about her. "Did you know," Sacha said, looking around her, "they used to pan for gold on this river. A few of them got rich but most of the prospectors gave up and died broke. Isn't that a perfect parable for writing?"

Viridian said she was glad to see me, and she hoped I wasn't working too hard. Not at all, I said. But I scarcely knew what to say to her, after all the talking we'd done about her. I felt guilty, almost disloyal, even though everything we'd said had been on her behalf and, one hoped, for her benefit. She was dressed in jeans and a black shirt, her hair tied back with a bandana. Standing next to her, I was aware once more that she was in fact a small person; it was only her presence that was large.

"Thank you for getting me the job," I said. "It's a real opportunity."

"Oh, it's a zoo and you're the zookeeper," she said cheerfully. "Who is it that's supposed to be here anyway?"

"You remember Bettina," Sacha said. "And Gary? And April, who takes the beautiful photographs?"

"I'm sure I will, once I set eyes on them."

I saw Tony Presto hurrying toward us to greet everyone, and I excused myself. Gil and I had work to do.

The reception was held in the main lodge and spilled out over onto the front porch and the river deck. Gil and I poured out wine in reusable plastic glasses and kept the trays of cheese and fruit and vegetables coming. I was grateful for Gil. She worked hard and without complaining and she wasn't impressed by anyone's publications.

Viridian sat on one of the front porch rockers and I was glad to see so many people making a point of coming by to greet her and talk with her. She'd changed into a long green dress I hadn't seen before, and the malachite necklace, and she'd pinned and braided her hair into a silver crown. She was still the queen. She smiled and laughed, engaged and happy. So far at least, it seemed like a good idea for her to be here. And how could we have kept her away? We all seemed to be stumbling up and over an ill-defined line, some nervous territory between friends and caretakers.

Sacha sat at the edge of the porch at Viridian's feet, and Anders stood sentry next to her. Sacha's pretty hair made you think of the sun behind a cloud. Anders, on the other hand, with his gaunt, unsmiling face, resembled the sun going down at the start of a Nordic winter.

The other faculty writers had their own groups of admirers. Ken Spinner was holding forth about the research he'd done for his latest novel, how he'd lived with the Bribri people of Costa Rica and learned their creation myth of the sacred tapir, and maybe he had. The fiction writers all seemed to be talking baseball. Oscar was reciting "Jabberwocky" and some of the other *Alice in Wonderland* poems, which he knew in exhausting detail.

Tony Presto announced that dinner was served, and the crowd headed toward the dining hall. Gil and I stayed behind, picking up. Matt approached, holding a manila envelope. "Hey Carla."

"Hi Matt. Did you need something?"

"I was hoping you'd read some of my poems."

"Sure," I said, because I couldn't think of any polite way to say no. "Just set them over there."

"Can you read them now?"

"Right now?" I couldn't tell if he was serious. He seemed to be. Dead serious and staring. "Little busy at the moment." Plus, I didn't want to explain all the contortions I had to go through in order to read and comprehend a poem.

"I can help. You want me to help?"

"No. Thank you." I looked over at Gil, who was making a racket stacking the plastic cups, pretending not to listen. "Can't you leave them?"

"I just wrote them, I don't have another copy."

"Maybe you should let them cool off a little before you have somebody else read them. We really have to hustle here, sorry."

He muttered something like, Figures, and walked off. He always seemed to be stomping away. Fine, let him.

"What was that about?" Gil asked.

"I don't know. Poetry." We hurried to finish and grab some dinner before the night's main event, the first assembly.

The big auditorium in the conference center was the gathering place for each evening's event, the author readings and announcements. Tonight was all about welcoming and introductions. I sat near the back with Gil in case we had to bolt and deal with something. There were nearly a hundred conference students and another two dozen faculty and staff members. A big crowd. I picked out the people I knew, the people I was starting to know. Already I was feeling the peculiar isolation and intensity of the place, perhaps of every such gathering, as if we were all on a spaceship traveling to some distant galaxy. I was starting to grasp how you could fall in love on such journeys or feel bereft when they ended.

Tony was practically levitating with nerves when he stepped to the microphone. "Good evening and welcome to Intersections! We're off to a great start, aren't we?"

Everyone applauded. Tony said there were some basic rules, designed to keep them all safe, and the most important of these was No Smoking. Nowhere, and nothing! No candles! No incense! The only fires were to be in the riverfront firepit and the main lodge. If there was a fire, evacuation procedures would be followed to the letter. Swimming was at your own risk. And there was also the matter of the septic system. Did they want him to go into details, or could he trust them to read the posted instructions in the bathrooms?

Everyone groaned. Tony talked about the workshop schedule, the meal schedule, the upcoming nature hike. I felt my eyes closing. I'd been running all day and it was catching up with me. A Forest Service ranger took the microphone next to talk more about fire danger, and how to avoid bears. One of the environmental writers followed and gave a talk about ecosystems and California native plants and animals.

Gil nudged me and said I was snoring, and I came awake so out of myself, so out of time and place, I could have been anyone, anywhere. Before I was able to get my bearings, my eyes rested on a face that I registered as beautiful, without recognizing it, and only in the next moment did I become aware that it was Viridian.

I don't know if she saw me looking at her, or if my eyes found her because she was looking at me. But she signaled to me and I got up and went to her, leaning over her seat.

"Can you take me home?" she whispered.

She was sitting near an exit and we were able to leave without attracting much attention. When we reached the door, she stopped for a moment to look back. The environmental writer had just dimmed the lights and was showing a series of wildlife slides: coyote, skunk, black bear, owl.

"Look at that," Viridian said quietly. "The animals are watching the animals."

We came out of the building and stepped into the profound quiet of the night. Only gradually did you become aware of the lap and push of river water, the breath of wind in the pines. It was dark except for the small clutch of lights that marked the buildings, and the paths between them.

Viridian looked around her uncertainly. "Is this home?"

"It is for right now."

"Oh of course. Of course you're right." She laughed a little, a breezy sound.

I took her arm and guided her, and we made a slow progress along the paths and toward her cabin. Yes, I was anxious about her, but there was something dreamlike about walking in this way, through the listening darkness. The sky above us was clear and the moon was only a slice of white just above the horizon. "Are you tired?" I asked her. "Did you need to stop and rest?"

She didn't answer, but she did halt and look around her. "Do you know what poetry's for? So that you can make use of a night like this. Make it into something that lasts."

Slowly, slowly along the wooden pathways. The night was cooler and there was a lonesomeness to it, a thrilling lonesomeness with wildness at its center. There were only the two of us, two small human animals at the edge of a vast forest.

We reached Viridian's cabin and I said I'd go in ahead to turn on the lights. But she said No, not yet, and so we sat on the bench of the small front porch in the dark. By and by we heard the voices of the others as the assembly ended and people made their way along the paths, and after a time one of the fiction writers, Jane, who was staying at the cabin, came walking up to us and said, "Oh my goodness, I didn't see you sitting there. Aren't you cold? Can I get you a blanket?"

Viridian sighed and said she would go on in now. "I used to be able to sit up all night. No more."

She seemed entirely herself again, perhaps a little tired. Perhaps it had only been the spell we were under, now ending. I said good night and headed back downhill toward the river, circling around the lodge, where people were already streaming in, ready for a drink or two and whatever uproar might follow.

I wanted to be alone, I wanted to feel again what I'd felt from the night and the silence, carry it in my hands as if in a cup. I suppose I would have wanted to write a poem, if I thought I could do any such thing.

But in a gaggle of writers, I realized, there were always some solitary brooders, and even before I got close to the river's edge I could see at least two other figures stalking here and there, so I turned back. I thought about Aaron and wondered what he was doing right this minute, and how maybe I didn't really want to be alone, and how very far away from him I'd gone.

I crossed the front porch of the lodge, where people had taken their drinks to lean against the railings and talk. Inside, Tony Presto was presiding over the bar. One of the nature writers was busy building a small, careful fire in the fireplace. Somebody had set up a Bluetooth speaker and was running through their playlist, which leaned to ironic British 80s pop. I hoped the fan was going to be enough white noise to drown it out.

Ken Spinner came up behind me and hooked an arm around my neck. "Carla," he said. "Carla, Carla, Carla."

It didn't feel like any particularly personal attention. It never did, with guys like that. There really was something disturbing about his complexion. You wanted to take a Clorox wipe to his face.

"Ken," I said, by way of greeting. I pried his arm loose and gave him a push toward the bar. From the firewood stack, I found a length of flattened board. When I got to my room, I wedged it under the door as a stop. I turned the fan on high and fell asleep.

INTO THE WOODS II

The next morning I was awake as soon as it was light. Gil was up not long after, and we started in cleaning up the party wreckage from the night before: beer and wine bottles, wadded paper napkins, puddles of suspect moisture, furniture that had migrated around the room: everything, Gil said, except a body behind the bar. She said she hoped the party was a good time, and that they'd better be more careful about eating granola bars on the porch unless they wanted a visit from Mr. Bear. She'd tell Tony to say something.

I asked her if she'd had trouble sleeping through it and she said she'd been out pretty late herself, if I knew what she meant, and I did. I guess she and Rog had found a deer stand somewhere.

We ate a quick breakfast and began to set up the side room with coffee and the all-important bagels and helpful information. The full schedule of classes and workshops was underway and there was a first-day-of-school feel to the groups as they came into the conference center. I hoped there wouldn't be any problems with Viridian's workshop. She seemed to do better earlier in the day, before she grew tired. There was nothing I could do about it anyway; we were all at the mercy of brain chemistry. I was starting to settle into a mindset of numbness and dread, waiting for the next bad event, balanced with a nervous hope that it wouldn't come.

We got through that first morning without anything too remarkable happening, except for the thin, waiflike older woman who plopped herself down in front of the bagels and ate six of them, one after another. She was to do this every day of the conference. Breakfast was free; all we could figure was that she really liked bagels.

Gil and I watched her making steady progress through the blueberry cream cheese and the peanut butter and the strawberry yogurt spread. "Orange juice?" Gil asked, handing her a glass, and the woman said thank you in her pipsqueak voice and drank it down. Then she hoisted a large book bag printed with a picture of a dolphin and took herself off.

Later, just before lunch, another woman stopped by and said that she had—she wasn't sure it was a complaint exactly, more of a question? About her workshop with Mr. Rasz? It seemed that the instructor told them he was going to give them a writing prompt, something they were meant to write about. Then he drew a cross on the blackboard and stood in front of it with his arms extended for ten minutes. Then he had played his harmonica for a while. And her question was, Did this seem, she didn't want to sound old-fashioned, but . . .was he making fun of them?

Tomas Rasz was an experimental writer whose last book had incorporated online links to recorded birdcalls. I said, "Maybe he wants you to have some fun with your writing. Be spontaneous. Try and get the reader's attention."

"The cross part was kind of offensive."

"How was the harmonica?"

"Actually, not bad," the woman said. "Maybe I could write something about harmonicas."

"That's the ticket," I agreed.

The woman left and Gil said, "These people are disturbed. Seriously."

"They're artists. Art is supposed to shake things up. Change your perspective."

"I can do that for them. Take them out for a night on the town. I know a place with a mechanical bull. I know more than one with bullet holes in the walls."

"Okay, but writers, poets especially, use language. They use it in unexpected, fresh, expressive ways."

"Then I know some guys who cuss a lot and they're poets."

I thought that this was entirely possible. "How about this: there's times you feel like singing? But you know you can't carry a tune. And you can't play the piano or guitar or anything else. There's no radio. No nothing. A poet is somebody who can still make music."

Gil considered this. She didn't look exactly convinced. "I guess they just aren't singing my song."

I didn't have any afternoon duties, so I hurried to get some lunch and try to find out how Viridian's morning workshop had been. I saw Barb sitting by herself in the dining hall and writing in a notebook. When I came up to her, she closed it with a snap.

"Jesus, relax, I'm not trying to read over your shoulder."

"Sorry." She did look sorry, at least a little. "This place can be so intense, you have no idea. There are people who run on ego like it's jet fuel. So competitive."

I thought that competition was probably Barb's song. It gave her that battling edge, that intensity of purpose that served her well, even if it didn't exactly make her mellow company. I was trying not to look at her forbidden notebook and I can't say I liked the view of her goofy pink eyeglasses that resembled stoplights on some alien planet. I said, "How was the workshop this morning?"

"Terrific. She was terrific. Calm, careful, kind. No. None of that. There were times she'd be, I guess you could say, indirect, you know, there wouldn't be a straight line from what was on the page to what she started in talking about. But you know what, she'd wrap it all together by the end and you could see what she meant, how one line in a poem can echo through so many different rooms. I guess you had to be there," she finished, giving up on trying to explain it to my inadequate self. She said that Viridian and Sacha and Anders had gone down to the river to swim, and I could find them there.

I ate my lunch of chicken teriyaki, which was to sustain me throughout the week—those cooks had it down cold—and headed for the little swimming beach. Anders was sitting on the deck. He wasn't dressed for swimming, but he had his pants legs rolled up and his big pale feet were submerged in the green water. Sacha and Viridian paddled and floated together nearby. Sacha's curly hair was wet and streaming; her suit, what I could see of it, was cornflower blue. Viridian had a plain black swimsuit and had tied a scarf over her hair.

"Are you coming in?" she called when she saw me.

"I didn't bring a suit." This was to be my answer all week, and it saved me from a lot of embarrassing wet encounters. I went to sit on the deck next to Anders. "How's the water?"

"Cold," Sacha said. "It feels good. As long as you don't overdo it."

Viridian said, "They're here to make sure I don't float away like Ophelia." She was treading water. I couldn't tell how deep the river was. "Why don't you push Anders in, he needs to loosen up."

Anders turned his head to look at me. It was a somber look.

"I wouldn't dare," I said.

"They are not such strong swimmers. Someone should watch over them." You never heard him say that much. He had a deep voice that seemed to come from somewhere slightly off center, as if he was a ventriloquist's dummy. It was unnerving, like most things about him.

"He's such a worrywart," Sacha declared, paddling a little farther out into the water. Anders turned his head sharply to follow her. I wondered if what I'd thought was obsessive love was really obsessive fear, keeping watch against mortality.

Laughter reached us from somewhere farther down the riverbank. Ken Spinner and the two workshop girls were wading in the water, hand in hand, with Ken in the middle. "Count of three!" Ken hollered, and they plunged forward into the river, whooping and screaming.

Viridian said, "Are they naked? I can't tell."

Sacha said, "I must confess, I chose not to look too closely. Talk about swimming at your own risk."

Then she asked me if I was going to be doing the setup for tonight's event. It would be Sacha's turn to read in the auditorium. She was paired with Jane, the young feminist novelist who wrote what were called dystopian futuristic books about the patriarchy run amuck, although they sounded a lot like my high school.

Sacha and I worked out the arrangements for the evening, what they needed in terms of lights and microphones and water bottles. Viridian said she thought she'd had enough of a swim and stroked her way toward shore. Sacha looked over at me and I stood.

"How about I walk up with you? I need to get moving, too."

Viridian said as long as it wasn't out of my way, and I held her terrycloth robe for her while she toweled off. Her body was spare, in the way that an older woman's body can be, but her arms and legs were still strong and shapely. All that yoga, I imagined. She held on to me lightly for balance as she got her feet into plastic sandals. Then we started up the hill, Viridian talking about the other writers, about dinner and breakfast, about the stone-edged swimming pool that she meant to try sometime before she left. When we reached a small seating area halfway to the cabin, she said she'd like to stop and sit in the sun for just a bit.

"I can't get my endurance back. It's maddening."

I said it was probably one of those slow, steady things, and after all she'd just gotten out of the hospital. Trying not to sound too cheery and encouraging. Nobody wanted to hear a lot of ignorant optimism.

"I suppose." She didn't try to pretend she found this convincing, and I didn't try to argue her into it. I think that was one of the things she liked about me. I wasn't very good at shining things up.

We sat without speaking for a time. It was a pleasant place to rest: a couple of bent twig armchairs in a sandy spot that offered a view of the sparkling river below us, and the farther green shore. The air was hot and smelled of pine and dry grass. Last night's darkness had been mysterious and lonesome, but the daylight was pure joy.

"You've gotten to know Boone, haven't you?"

I wasn't expecting the question and it took me a moment to respond. "A little. Not well."

"I worry about him."

"Well, he worries about you."

"I wish he wouldn't. I'm not sure there's much we can do for each other at this point." She turned her head to look at me. "You know the story by now. How I didn't raise him." I ducked my head, meaning yes. "He tells everyone. That's his right."

I wished he hadn't. It would have been simpler if I didn't know. Or maybe if I had known everything, everyone's motives and actions. As if you ever did.

Viridian said, "My son is my unfinished business. It's nagging at me. It's one of the things that burdens me."

I didn't ask what the others were. I thought she only wanted me to listen.

"He doesn't stick with anything. Jobs. People. It's always some new enthusiasm. New idea. Nothing's ever enough. Did I ruin his life? Or would it have been worse if I'd stayed?"

I kept my eyes on the river and the bright water. She sighed and then started up again.

"I left him with a good father. I thought it was the best thing I could do for him. I didn't want him to be around the dreadful mess I'd gotten myself into. The dreadful mess I was back then. I wasn't that much older than you are, and I was so in love. You know what that's like."

I didn't speak. I didn't dare believe myself one bit like her, at any age.

She sighed. "It's a terrible thing to be shackled to someone in that way, yes, shackled. Because when you're in love, that terrible love, you lose yourself, you lose your free will . . ."

She stopped and gave me an unhappy look. "I'm not proud of who I was then, and I hate the idea of disappointing you."

I stammered out that I couldn't imagine ever being disappointed, and that seemed to calm her.

"Such love affairs are awful. It's like a snake lives in your heart."

She was pointing at the jagged rocks a short distance beyond our feet, and my muscles clenched as I saw a thin shape gliding along one edge. Then it vanished, a flicking movement, gone.

Viridian said, "Don't worry. It's going about its own business."

It was as if she'd conjured the snake with her talk or maybe she'd seen it first and, in that instant, made it into words. In either case it shook me.

"We should go," I said, standing.

"All right." She sighed again and stood also. "Even if Boone had those poems? They wouldn't be enough for him either."

I made sure we kept to the path the rest of the way. When we reached Viridian's cabin, she thanked me for my trouble, and said she'd see me later, at the reading.

I had a head full of things to think about as I started back downhill toward the lodge. I suppose I wasn't aware of myself, let alone of anyone around me. And so it was a complete and unwelcome surprise to see Matt coming toward me when I reached the front porch, but I'm afraid I said out loud, "Oh shit."

"Will you read my poems now?" The manila envelope in his hand looked damp and much fondled.

"Why is this so important?"

"I just need you to read them." He was shifting his weight from one foot to the other. He looked nervous, squirrelly.

"Do I get to say no?"

"I guess I'm never going to be good enough for you, am I?"

"Dude, I don't even know you."

"They're the best I've ever written. Go ahead, make fun. 'That guy? The one with the face like a stray dog? He did something worthwhile?'"

"And you don't know me." He actually did look a little like a stray dog, sad and furry.

"So you're not going to read my poems?"

"If you want a different answer, ask a different girl."

Was he nuts? Or maybe this was par for the course in the creative process. You obsessed about somebody and used them as an excuse for all that head-banging and self-involved drama, and then you got shut down and wrote about rejection.

He took a step toward me. I don't know what he had in mind,

or what might have happened next, because just then the air around us *zipped*, a stinging sound. A yellow-feathered fiberglass arrow buried itself in one of the porch timbers, not exactly next to Matt's head, but close enough to make him yelp.

"Jesus Christ!" We stared at each other. "What did you do?"

"Nothing!"

He didn't believe me. He backed away. "That could have killed me!"

"Maybe it was Cupid." But he'd already taken off around a corner of the porch and I don't think he heard me.

I scanned the edge of the forest behind me, the dense tree cover, and although I didn't see anyone, I lifted a hand to wave.

And it was only the first full day.

I checked the conference center, but no one was there. I guess Gil had already cleared away the morning's refreshments. I went back to my room and lay down, thinking I'd catch a nap, but I couldn't fall asleep. I kept hearing the things Viridian had said, going over them without entirely comprehending them. I only knew that I wouldn't be sharing it with anyone else, not even those of us who were intent on helping and protecting her. I felt I'd been told things in confidence, things that might be known but that she never spoke of. Perhaps after a time she'd forgotten I was there, and I had only overheard them. Finally, I gave up on sleeping and went off to see if Tony or Gil needed me for anything.

Tony was in his office at the conference center. He held out his arms. "Look at this, does this look like poison oak?"

There were raised red welts all along the underside of both arms. "Yes."

"Crap. I went on the nature walk yesterday."

"Don't scratch it. Put calamine lotion on it and wash the clothes you had on. It'll start to blister and ooze."

"I don't believe this. How long does it last?"

"If you don't aggravate it? A couple of weeks."

He groaned. "It itches like all get-out. Have you seen Oscar? He said he was taking his workshop out to lunch and they aren't back yet. I have to go, one of the bunkhouses doesn't have hot water. Do you know anything about gas shutoff valves?"

"No, sorry."

"Can you stay and answer the phone if anyone calls? I won't be long. I'm hoping. If anything explodes, call the fire department."

I said that I would, and not to worry. "And don't scratch!"

Tony grabbed a satchel with a couple of wrenches and other tools and left me to sit at his desk.

I'm as nosy as anybody else, I admit, but there wasn't much to look at in the heaps of books and papers. There were some creepy nature specimens: the full jawbone, with teeth, of some medium-to-large-size mammal. And some kind of stuffed hawk suspended above me, molting patches of feathers, a little sawdust escaping.

The phone on the desk rang. I picked it up. "Hello?" I had an awful moment when I realized I couldn't remember the actual name of the conference. "Office."

"Is this the, ah, writers' conference?" Maybe the guy on the phone couldn't remember it either.

"Yes, can I help you?"

"I'm calling for Doug McGregor and *Compass Points*. He's going to be there Wednesday evening and I need to confirm some arrangements."

"Jonathan?"

"Oh my god, Carla, what are you doing there? Oh wait, that's right. You're a camp counselor."

"How are you, how's what's his name, Mr. Scrumptious?"

"Paul. He's such a doll. I've decided to move in with him. You'll have to come to dinner. What's it like up there?"

"Intense. Weird. Good, I think. Why is Doug coming?"

"They bring in a bunch of agents and editors to give talks and solicit, I think that's the right word, for new talent. Didn't they tell you?"

They had, but they hadn't told me who, or when. "What do you need, I'll leave a message."

Doug would arrive in time for Wednesday dinner. He would be bringing a number of copies of *Compass Points*, as well as his own books. He needed a private cabin. He wanted to know if he should bring his own sheets. (Yes.) And so on. I wrote it all down, told Jonathan it was great talking with him, and hung up.

I looked up at the stuffed hawk over my head. A current of air had set it in motion and I moved the chair to get out from under it. I hadn't seen Doug since the night of his party, and the infamous episode with Pancho and Lefty. It didn't bring back pleasant memories. I wondered if Viridian would continue to refuse to give Doug the Mathias poems, especially since Boone was so involved in brokering the deal, or if, as she had always done, she was looking for excuses not to give them to anyone.

I ate a quick dinner and spent some time in the conference building's auditorium with Gil, checking the mikes for feedback and adjusting the stage lights. I took a seat down front while Gil stayed in back to work the lights. The bagel woman sat by herself at the end of the last row. Ken Spinner sat with the two girls. A number of the writers came in with their workshop, like Viridian, who sat serenely next to Barb, surrounded by a half dozen excited students.

Sacha beckoned to me. She was wearing a dress with bright gypsy embroidery. I wanted one just like it. Jane wore a funky black outfit that I also admired. "Have you seen Oscar?"

I said that I hadn't.

"I'm sort of worried. He's been acting so odd," Sacha said, and I was about to say something smart-alecky about how oddness was Oscar's default setting when Tony Presto came to the microphone to introduce the speakers. He wore a long-sleeved shirt, I noticed.

I did wonder about Oscar. It wouldn't be like him to miss Sacha's reading. Scanning the crowd, I didn't see anyone I recognized from his workshop either. But Tony was introducing Jane, and Oscar would have to look after himself for now.

I have to admit, I dozed off during Jane's chapter about the gender-shifting warrior tribe. I was going to have to stop falling asleep during readings, people were going to notice. By the time I woke up, Sacha was already reading. I tried to catch up with her poem. I'd come to the private, disloyal opinion that although I

liked Sacha, her poetry was often enough pretty, like she was, and
not much more. But this part stayed in my ear:

> *Something was eating the roses,*
> *keeping the buds from opening.*
> *Something stopped our mouths*
> *and kept the words of peace and*
> *healing unsaid*

Then the reading was over, and people were standing up,
talking, telling Jane and Sacha how much they had enjoyed etc.
etc. Gil and I waited until the auditorium had emptied out, then
we turned off the lights and Gil headed out, intent on plans of
her own.

Outside, I looked for the arrow in the wall of the lodge, but
it was gone.

That night's party took place around the firepit by the river,
though people went in and out of the lodge to get their drinks. I
wandered from the bonfire to the bar and back again. I wanted
to avoid Matt, though whenever he saw me from his place on the
fringe of one or another crowd, he looked spooked and headed off
in a different direction.

As before, I heard bits and pieces of talk:

". . . meditated on it and decided to change agents."

". . . in the tradition of the murder ballad . . ."

". . . depends on your definition of performance art . . ."

" . . . *New York Times Review of Books*? I don't know whether
to shit or go blind."

There were people to talk to, people who needed flashlight batteries, toilet paper, Pepto Bismol. Literary validation, transactional therapy, emotional support animals. I did what I could, then slipped away to bed.

My phone had been so useless, I'd been leaving it in my room. Now I checked it, and was startled to see a text from Aaron: OK SO DON'T ANSWER MY CALLS I GET IT BUT THIS CAN'T GO ON FOREVER.

Of course I tried to call, of course I couldn't get through. I tried texting and I kept trying, and the messages piled up in a heap. NOT DELIVERED. NOT DELIVERED. NOT DELIVERED.

ANY SLEEP I managed was spotty. In the morning, early, I tried calling again, no luck. I panicked, trying to remember the last time we'd talked, and did Aaron even know I was here and that his calls weren't reaching me? He was right, things couldn't go on forever like this, with the two of us on hold, with me living a separate life from his. I hadn't wanted to jump one way or the other, I still didn't. I kept putting it off and he was tired of it, and I was tired of his resentment.

The sun wasn't quite up yet, the woods were still cold and misty when I left the lodge, being as quiet as I could, and walked along the damp grass to the conference center. It was kept locked but I had keys, and a key to the office as well. I sat down beneath the stuffed hawk and picked up the phone. Thank God there was a dial tone. I punched in Aaron's number and waited while the line clicked and went blank and finally rang through.

I got his voice mail. That figured. He always silenced his phone

while he was asleep, and even if he was awake, which was doubt-
ful, he wouldn't recognize the number. At least I'd gotten this far.
I waited for his familiar prompt: "Let's talk!" And then the beep.

"Hi, Aaron? It's me, I'm sorry, I haven't gotten any calls since
Saturday, I'm in El Dorado National Forest, I thought I told you,
and my phone is crap. Anyway—"

Anyway what? He didn't want to hear any more of me telling
him how I'd been on my voyage of discovery, how I'd met people
he didn't know, talked about things he'd never heard of. "I want
to tell you everything I've been doing, because I want you to be
part of it. And I want to hear what you've been doing, and, I don't
know what happens after that. I'll be back Friday night." I waited
a beat. "I love you," I said, and then I hung up.

I felt a little better, but then I started thinking maybe he
hadn't answered because somebody was there with him, some
other woman, maybe even Pancho or Lefty. Now I was being
paranoid and insecure. Was I going to tell him about Matt? Or
Ken Spinner, for that matter? Oh sure. Way to drive him crazy
with jealousy.

I wasn't going to tell him about Boone, because Boone confused me, and I wouldn't know what to say.

Meanwhile, there was bagel duty. I went to the back door of
the dining hall to load up my cart with the coffee urns and pas-
tries. One of the cooks beckoned me inside the kitchen, pointing:
El señor no se siente bien.

Oscar was sitting at a table in a corner. His head was resting
on his folded arms. A mug of coffee and a plate of toast and eggs
were in front of him.

"Oscar?" He groaned without looking up. "Are you all right? What happened to you?"

"Bad juju." At least that's what I thought he said.

"Look at me." He shook his head. "Do you want me to get Tony?"

That got a response. He raised his head and groaned again. His face was puffy and the lines around his eyes and mouth pointed down, down, down. "God, no. I have to get ready for my workshop. Or wait. I don't think they're back yet."

"Back from where? Where did you guys go yesterday?"

"Tahoe."

"You're kidding." He wasn't. "Why?"

"Wanted to go . . ." he was mumbling now. ". . . casino."

"You took your workshop to a casino."

"I didn't take anybody," he protested. "They wanted to go, a couple of them had cars. It was fun. We played all the . . ." He reached for the coffee mug and drank. ". . . games."

I didn't bother asking if he'd won big. "So where are they? Oscar? Where's your workshop?"

"Ah, it got late, I think they decided to stay at the hotel. I got a ride back. From some . . . lady. She let me off down at the gate. I got lost. I think I saw a bear."

"Did it see you? You look like you slept in a ditch."

"There might have been a ditch involved."

"You better hope those people turn up all right. You missed Sacha's reading. Viridian's fine. Thanks for asking."

Oscar muttered something about me being a hardheaded woman, and how hardheaded women always broke your heart, and in general feeling sorry for himself. Sacha was right, he seemed more distracted than usual, and more genuinely miserable. Usually you could kid him out of it, but this morning, even allowing for the hangover, he seemed lost, in more ways than one. "You know, you might consider taking better care of yourself."

He opened one puffy eye to look at me, then closed it again. "Doesn't matter now. I've had my last spin at the roulette wheel of life."

"Oh listen to you, don't be such a baby. You should eat something. Are your eggs cold? Do you need them heated up?"

He took his coat from the seat beside him and put it over his head like a bag, and that's when I got up and left.

Tony had Gil working with him at the office, so I presided over the bagels and coffee by myself. The bagel woman ate her fill and left. Bettina Cruz was reading that night and she asked if she could play some slides during it illustrating the Puerto Rican diaspora. Somebody else needed a Benadryl, another somebody wanted to know where to find an ATM. I didn't mind; I was kept too busy to worry about Aaron or anything else.

Sacha came looking for me after breakfast. "I don't think Viridian's taking her medicine. She keeps it in our bathroom and I counted the pills."

"She has to take it. Did you tell her?"

"What am I supposed to say? I did ask once, like, did she remember to take it, and she said yes, of course she did. But she hasn't. I checked again."

We looked at each other, stricken. I don't know what I might have suggested, in the way of good ideas, since I had none.

I didn't get the chance anyway. Oscar's workshop students came in then, back from their adventure and looking for coffee and bagels. They didn't seem to have suffered any harm. If anything, they had a swagger to them, having had an authentically wild time, having gotten their money's worth, so to speak. A couple of them seemed to have started in drinking again this morning.

I told Sacha we should talk when I got done slinging bagels.

Oscar's morning workshop session apparently turned out all right. I doubt if any of his students were in fit shape to complain anyway. I saw them all later, sitting together at lunch. Oscar still wasn't talking much or eating. He was attempting to be a wan good sport as the others told their stories. I didn't see Sacha or Viridian.

I looked up to see Gil walking through the dining room distributing a packet of mail. It hadn't occurred to me to give out my address. Who would write to me anyway? Who got mail in a place like this?

Oscar did. Gil handed him a small white envelope. He stared at it, stood up so suddenly that his chair wobbled backward. Then he raised his hands over his head, prize fighter style, and hurried from the hall.

"Poets," Gil said to me, the same way that somebody else might say "kids."

INTO THE WOODS III

By Wednesday it felt like the conference had lasted at least five years. Nervous energy alternated with nervous exhaustion. Things kept happening. Tomas Rasz's workshop rebelled when he told them that the day's session would consist of three hours of silent meditation. Tony was forced to intervene. Someone thought they smelled smoke. It turned out to be a false alarm, but not before we all had to follow the fire drill protocol and assemble in the parking lot in our hard-soled shoes, carrying wet towels. Two of the naturalists formalized their relationship by getting engaged during the evening drum circle. And in between these events, there were writers talking, writers writing, writers talking about writing, a heady mix of brilliance, argument, inspiration, and ego.

Doug McGregor had not yet arrived, but a platoon of other editors and agents had been deployed, and they gave helpful talks and presided over manuscript conferences. Everybody wanted tips from the pros, everybody wanted their first big break. I understood this, even if it was easy to be skeptical of their individual strivings, their talent, their certain unfortunate personal qualities. They wanted soul to clap its hands and sing, no matter how much throat-clearing and croaking was involved in the effort. And they wanted to be heard. They wanted to be loved, as they had loved the great writers, as I loved them myself.

And say the big break came, or say it never did, say you launched yourself full speed into the enterprise of writing. Would it matter, finally, that only some small portion of the earth's people had ever heard of you or your work? No, you told yourself. Because there would still be the singing. There would still be the love.

I DIDN'T GET any more calls from Aaron. After lunch I got in my truck and drove down to Pollock Pines where there was better cell reception. There weren't any messages. I thought about calling him, then I put the phone away and drove back to the conference. Either he missed me or he didn't, either he still wanted me or he didn't, and then there was the whole problematic question of whether I still wanted him. Of course, it was possible that he was being literal-minded, being an annoying man, and since I'd said my phone wasn't working, he wasn't going to bother trying anymore. I'd said I'd be back Friday night. I shouldn't have been upset that he took me at my word and didn't call, but I was.

There was a text from a number I didn't recognize at first. HOW ABOUT DINNER SOME TIME WHEN YOU GET BACK. A New York number. Boone. He must have gotten my number from Doug.

If I was supposed to use this time away to clear my head and decide what I wanted, it just wasn't working. What if you never actually decided? What if you kept going along and going along doing the next thing and the next, then one day you looked around and here was your life, already nailed down, already as good as over.

I drove back, parked, and walked uphill to find Viridian and Sacha on the front porch of their cabin. As we sat, Ken Spinner and his two girls hiked past us, towels in hand. Ken waved. "We're going to check out the hot tub!"

When they'd gone, Sacha said, "How do guys like that keep getting away with it? How does he keep getting invited places when he only does it to get laid? I don't care how many books he sells."

Viridian sighed. "They all used to be like that. The men. Of course, almost all the writers were men. The ones taken seriously. One of the perks of the job was groupies. Please tell me that things have changed."

Sacha said she wasn't sure she could. "Although there are more women writers out there now. Smart, tough women. More awareness. More useless sexual harassment training, at least if you have an academic job."

Same amount of pigs, I thought, and maybe the others felt the same, because we let the dismal topic drop.

Sacha cleared her throat. "We need to talk about your medicine."

"No, we don't."

"I think you forgot to take your pills."

"Then I think she must have been counting them," Viridian said to me. "I think she should be made to admit it." She wasn't going to make things easy.

"We're allowed to worry about you."

Viridian said she had not forgotten her medication; she had chosen not to take it. It made her feel unwell and slow-witted. She could not afford to be less than her best when she was working. She would make a doctor's appointment as soon as she got back home. She felt better today than she had yesterday. She'd felt better yesterday than she had the day before. Everything was moving in the right direction.

Sacha said, "How about if you take your pill in the evening instead of morning. That way if it makes you feel funky, you'll sleep through it. Wake up and be tip-top."

Viridian seemed exasperated, but also aware she wasn't going to win this fight. "All right. If it would make everybody happy."

"If it would keep you from having an adverse health event, then yes, it would make everybody happy."

"I'm an old lady, and I fully expect that there's an adverse health event with my name on it out there."

Sacha turned to me. "You see what we're up against."

"Mortality." Viridian was pleased, as if she'd found the clincher to the argument, and I suppose she had. "How does it go?: 'For the sword outwears its sheath / And the soul wears out the breast / And the heart must pause to breathe / And love itself have rest.'"

"Byron wrote that when he was twenty-nine." Sacha was on her own turf in any discussion of Mary Shelley's circle. "And he died at thirty-six. Take your pills."

I thought it was pretty cool that Byron wrote something two hundred years ago and we were all still talking about it.

Viridian announced that it was time for her nap, though maybe she was just trying to shoo us off. Sacha and I stayed on the front porch while she went inside. Sacha said, "Well, I tried. That's all the nagging I'm willing to do."

"I guess she wants to do things her way."

"Oh, always. She does whatever she wants. And as always, she's completely charming about it."

Never in my life had anyone accused me of being charming. I wondered if it was something I should try for. I fought my fights the same way my mom did, with a hammer in each hand and my heels dug in.

"Sacha? What's she going to do with the poems? The last ones Mathias wrote."

"Oh God. I don't know. Some of them are supposed to be about her. Did you know? It's always been this huge debate. Why should men writing about women be valued more than women writing about themselves? That's the feminist argument and I do understand it. But it's not just about gender squabbling. It's personal. It couldn't be any more personal for her."

I tried to put myself in Viridian's place and understand what kept her from making a decision. Give the poems to someone, or to someone else. Maybe because then it would be over, and no one would care as much.

"Doesn't she need the money?"

Sacha shook her head. "No. I mean yes, of course she needs money. But she doesn't think like that. Which is kind of wonderful, really. Also drives you crazy. She at least needs to dig the poems out from under the back steps, or wherever she has them stashed, and put them in a safe deposit box."

"It must be like when old people don't want to give up the car keys."

"Yes, and then they rear end another car and everybody's sorry."

We heard voices, laughter. At a distance, up the hill, Ken Spinner and the two girls were making use of the hot tub. To judge from the squealing and protests, there was some horseplay, some game of slap and tickle, going on beneath the surface. Flurries of red and yellow leaves were drifting into the water from the tree next to them, or rather, from the vine on its trunk.

I turned to Sacha. "Don't use the hot tub."

She sniffed. "Like I'd get into that same water after them."

"Could you stay here and keep anybody else from getting in? I have to find Tony."

I hurried off downhill. I suppose I could have told them myself, but it was too late anyway. Tony could be the one to tell them they'd been soaking, or rather, stewing, in a broth of poison oak.

KEN AND THE girls were medevacked to Sacramento for emergency cortisone shots and topical ointments, effectively ending their stay at the conference. The hubbub surrounding this made Doug's arrival, half an hour later, just one more in a series of cascading events. Tony came out to greet him. Once word got around, a crowd gathered, and there were plenty of eager volunteers to carry Doug's boxes of books and his suitcases.

Since *Compass Points* was a San Francisco production, because Doug knew so many of the people here, and because he sometimes did publish first-time authors as well as big names, he was an especially exciting guest. I never knew what to expect from Doug, never knew if I was in or out of his good graces. It seemed to depend on circumstances beyond my control, some agenda of his own.

You could believe in the importance of poetry, of art in general, its uplifting and essential qualities, and still disapprove of some of the grubbier behavior associated with it.

"Carla!" Doug spotted me while I was attempting to be an inconspicuous extra in the crowd. He was either delighted to see me or making the most of the moment to pile it on. "How are you, girlfriend? You have to see your beautiful new issue, I just got the copies. It's a knockout!"

"I'm so glad." For everybody watching, I guess my status shot up.

"Couldn't have done it without you."

I said he was giving me way too much credit. (And really, if I had been so valuable, he should have paid me.) As always, I found myself eyeing what Doug wore. His shirt had a print of green palm trees, making it, technically, a Hawaiian shirt, but a discreetly patterned and well-behaved one, in heavy weight linen, and his pants were something resembling khaki, but slim and tailored. Once I figured out who I wanted to be, I was going to have to start spending some serious money on clothes.

"We'll have to sit down and have us a talk and catch up. Promise me."

"Promise," I said, thinking I would avoid it if at all possible. Meanwhile, the assembled conference members were looking at me like they wondered what my superpower was, or if perhaps I was sleeping with, if not Doug, then with someone else of power and influence.

Doug and his helpers headed to his cabin like a procession of native bearers in a jungle movie. Soon I was going to have to think about setting up tonight's reading, which was Oscar's, and which would surely present its own challenges. The remainder of Ken Spinner's workshop students would have to be parceled out among other instructors. Tony needed to be reminded about the sign-up sheet for the student reading. And half a dozen other things, all of them very urgent, which would be of absolutely no importance this time next week.

I was wearing down, losing altitude. There had been too many personalities on display, too much gossip and drama. More than anything, I wanted some time by myself. It was an irony that, in the middle of the great forest, the authentic wilderness, there was so little privacy available.

I started out at the swimming beach, intending to follow the river upstream. But there was no path, only thick scrub growth and ankle-busting gullies I couldn't cross. I turned farther away from the river, aware that I was doing something mildly dangerous, and this was how people got lost, but I couldn't quite convince myself to be worried. Everything sloped down to the river and the conference grounds. If I got too turned around, I knew all I'd have to do was roll myself downhill.

I could still hear the river behind me, at least at first. I found what looked like a trail and followed it uphill for a bit, then came out into an open clearing that looked like it must have been used by other people. A flattened log had been rolled to one side and a couple of tree stumps had been pushed into place to make an outdoor living room. There was even a crumpled beer can and a cellophane wrapper for some kind of snack food. So much for my unspoiled wilderness retreat.

I sat on the log and caught my breath. The day was warm, and I'd worked up a sweat, and of course I'd headed out without water or a compass or a whistle or any of the recommended gear. I was on my stupid own. I don't know how long I was looking straight in front of me, looking without real comprehension, before I saw the hawk staring back at me.

It was perched on a dead stump on the other side of the clearing, not fifteen feet away. A large bird, probably a red-tailed, though I decided that later. Brown above, white and streaked below. It wasn't doing anything else besides regarding me, and whether it was frightened or curious or indifferent or sizing me up for food, I couldn't tell. It only had its one hawk face, fierce and intelligent.

How long did the two of us stay there, staring each other down? A while. I couldn't put a time to it, because I lost track of time, or spaced out, or if you were so inclined you could say it was a transcendental experience, or a visit from my spirit animal. But not everything had to be turned into words. There was only me and then there was the hawk, the two of us, and I understood that here was something that would still be important this time next week, and the week after, and way beyond that.

The hawk was still perched there when I got up to leave. I was glad I didn't scare it away. I was glad it hadn't scared me.

I might have looked for a shortcut back to the conference, but I'd seen *The Blair Witch Project*, and so I retraced my steps along the same path. I got back and found Gil and we headed for the dining hall to grab an early dinner. "How's Rog doing, camping out and all?" I asked.

"He's having a blast. Letting his hair grow and his feet stink. That's just an expression."

I said to tell him he was a good shot, and Gil said she'd pass it on, though she had no idea what I was talking about and that was her story and she was sticking to it. She said she couldn't wait for this gig to be over, she was tired of loony writers.

"Two more days and we're out of here," I said. I both did and didn't want it to be over, though in Gil's company it was easy enough to act as if I did. I was tired, sure, but I'd miss the very craziness of it, the sense that important things had happened or were about to happen, or maybe it was just that whole literary sense of self-importance, now infecting me.

Gil started to speak but caught sight of something behind me and it came out instead as "Sweet Jesus, Mary, and Joseph."

I turned around. It took me a few seconds to sort through what I was seeing. Oscar was standing there, beaming at us. Or rather, Oscar-but-not-Oscar. He was wearing a black fitted jacket with rows of silver buttons along the cuffs, a bit of silver embroidery along the collar, and more silver buttons, connected with chains and tassels, at the jacket's closing. Beneath the jacket was a white shirt, crisp and pleated, with an open collar.

And he'd cut his hair. It was a neat gray fringe just above his ears. He was freshly shaven and his skin was clear and pink. I closed my mouth, then opened it again to say, "My God. What happened to you?"

"What do you think?" He struck a pose, hands on his hips, chin in the air.

"You look like a retired bullfighter."

"But in a good way," Gil added.

"All you need is a rose in your teeth."

"Maybe a sword."

"Who cut your hair?"

"Alverro." Oscar turned and waved to the kitchen entrance, where a few of the cooks had gathered and were nodding and grinning at him. "And he hooked me up with these fine threads for tonight's event. I figure, you can't go wrong with looking good."

Gil let out a wolf whistle. "You'll slay. Totally."

"I had to tell him what I wanted in Portuguese, but it was close enough. This is the new me. I'm making some changes."

"I liked the old you."

"No, come on. This is important. I'm launching a new version. Oscar 2.0. A gentleman and a scholar. Clean living. No more late nights with questionable associates."

I couldn't tell how serious, or not serious, he was. "Okay," I said, going along with it. "You're a brand-new you. Congratulations."

He leaned down close to me. I was afraid he might clasp my hands in his. "I'm going to knock myself out. Live right. Walk the line. I want you to be proud of me."

"What does it matter what I think?"

"Please, Carla."

"Okay," I said, wondering. "I'm proud of you. Go for it."

"It's going to be some reading tonight," he said, then he gave us a bow and a flourish, and headed for the door.

Gil said, "I believe he could be right. About the reading."

I was thinking in terms of bipolar disorder and to this day I don't believe I was wrong, though it's not an explanation for everything.

There were always two readers each night, so there would be Oscar and one of the younger fiction writers. The fiction writer was Robley Calhoun, who wrote historical fiction, novels about the South during the Civil War, except that everyone was gay. He was going to read first, since Oscar's readings were always a tough act to follow, one way or the other. Ken Spinner had been scheduled to read tomorrow, the last night for readings, with Viridian. I guessed that Tony would have to move things around in some way.

People were getting a little tired of going to readings, they couldn't help it. But they all filed into the auditorium at the appointed time. Nobody wanted to be rude. I took my seat in front. Oscar and Robley Calhoun came in together and sat next to each other in the front row, chatting. I was glad to see that Oscar's finery didn't look too out of place. Everybody dressed up a little when it was their turn to read, everybody wore their own kind of costume. Robley Calhoun wore a white suit that invoked some ghost of plantation life. Everything was about irony with these young guys.

I saw that Viridian was sitting with Sacha and Anders, and that Doug had taken a seat in the row in front of her and was turned around engaged in conversation, or rather, he was talking while the others listened. I wished I could find out what he was saying, but there was no way to insert myself into the group and anyway, here was Tony, the master of ceremonies one more time, walking across the stage.

I didn't fall asleep this time, I was too keyed up. Robley read a passage about two guys sharing a tent during the battle of

Fredericksburg that, my opinion here, was perhaps a little too salty. But everyone agreed later that it had been impressively lyrical.

Then it was Oscar's turn. He looked calm enough, but I could tell he was still a pretty live wire. When he stood at the microphone there was a buzz and a murmur from those who hadn't seen his new look. He took a moment to grin in acknowledgement. "I am so very pleased and grateful to be with you tonight." And then he began reading, without more preamble:

> Say I am a tree, a fanciful notion, because
> my love, we are drunk on feeling.
> Say I am an old tree, weather-blasted, full of
> snags and hollows. Say you are a bird. I would
> still hold you with green fingers.
>
> Say I am a bowl of cornflakes and you are milk.
> Now is that strange, imagining yourself as
> something to eat, something you might have a taste
> for. Strange and giddy, how I feel, the two of us,
> what a mouthful.
>
> Say I am dark and you are dawn. Oh say it and
> be true. Make light of my shadows, light of
> my life, lightness in these heavy days, light me up.
> I burn and shine, you are all light and laughter, I
> am all ears.

Voice was everything to me, everything that the snarl of letters on a page was not. Voice was how I fell in love with Viridian's poems. And now when I heard Oscar's voice, something in me quickened and paid attention. It was an ordinary enough man's voice in ordinary circumstances, but tonight it seemed to reach down deeper, into some register of certainty and emotion.

All the poems he read were new ones, as far as I could tell. They were by turns humorous and bereft, full of longing and also the fear of longing, speaking of bravery and of defeat. It took visible effort for him to get through it all, and by the end he was gripping the edges of the podium:

> Let the air in my lungs sound one more chord
> the music of a furious life.

And then he was done. People applauded, and they meant it, I could tell. He'd slayed. I made my way over to him. He was sitting down, he looked a little wild-eyed, depleted. "My God, Oscar," I said. "You've been to the crossroads and sold your soul."

He took a long swig from a water bottle. "You liked it, then?" His forehead was damp, and I was afraid he might sweat through his borrowed clothes.

"Absolutely."

"That's a relief. I was nervous you might not."

"Now you're making fun of me," I said, and he started to protest that he wasn't, and how important my good opinion was, and similar sentiments I didn't buy. But other people were milling around him, around Robley as well, waiting to offer their appreciation, at least that's what they usually did. I went to stand against the wall so the crowd could get past me.

Viridian and Anders and Sacha were slow to get up. Oscar and Robley and almost everyone else had gone out, ready for whatever tonight's party would bring. Gil appeared at the back exit and I gave her a wave, meaning she was free to go and I'd see to closing the room.

I went over to where Viridian and the others sat. I was about to ask how they'd liked the reading, when Sacha said to me, "We need a little time before we get going, if that's all right."

"Oh, sure." I sat down with them. Viridian was quiet and I guessed she was tired, as she often was at the end of the day. Sacha seemed distressed or preoccupied. Anders always looked foreboding, so there were no clues there.

I was wondering if I should ask if everything was all right, when Sacha said, "Oscar was wonderful, wasn't he."

I agreed that he was. Sacha said, "He understands performance. It's a separate skill from writing."

"Sure."

"He looked good, too. Fancy dress suits him."

"And the haircut makes all the difference."

"Oh yes," Viridian said, perking up a little. "He was quite a handsome man, all those years ago. Well. We all looked different back then."

No one wanted to follow up on that. The room had emptied out around us and the last sounds of talk and laughter echoed back to us from the hall. After a moment I said, "Did you have a chance to catch up with Doug? Doug McGregor," I added, because Viridian shook her head: Who? "You know, the *Compass Points* editor."

"Oh yes, of course. We had a very nice conversation. He wants to buy my house."

"No honey." Sacha jumped in then. "He wants to buy some poems."

"Well, he can't have the house. Where would I live?"

"You don't have to worry about it. Not for a minute."

"I simply had to tell him no."

"That's right. It's all taken care of."

"I don't know why everybody keeps pestering me about it."

"Anders? Why don't you help Viridian back to the cabin. Carla and I will be along in a minute."

Anders nodded silently and assisted Viridian to stand. She held his arm, but she didn't seem unsteady. She said, "I haven't forgotten those old pills. When we get back you can watch me take them."

When they'd left the room, Sacha said, "How is she ever going to get through a reading?"

"Can they cancel it?"

"I don't think she'll let anybody do that. She's been talking about it. Looking forward to it."

I thought Sacha was right. Most writers, at least the ones who weren't mortally afraid of public appearances, were like old warhorses. You couldn't hold them back once the bugle sounded. "Maybe it'll be all right. She's not always . . . bad, is she?"

"No, it comes and goes. But I don't want her to be embarrassed. Especially here, in front of this crowd. And I don't want Doug to think she's gone barmy and he can flimflam her."

"What was he saying to her, how did it go?"

"All right, I think. She didn't have to say much, just listen and smile. He had a whole speech worked up. I expect he practiced it in front of a mirror. Her many contributions to American letters. Her enduring and prominent place. My God. You'd think he was speaking at her funeral."

I think both of us would have liked to say something, anything, to smooth over that thought, but instead we sat in silence, and after a moment Sacha said she'd better catch up to the others. I turned off the lights and the sound system and closed up the dark auditorium behind me.

"LAST DAY," TONY said to Gil and me at breakfast the next morning. This wasn't really true; last twenty-four hours was more like it. But today was the last full schedule of workshops and readings. Tomorrow morning the workshops would meet for a quick wrap-up, then disperse. A few people had already made plans to leave early.

You couldn't blame Tony for wanting it to be over. He'd had to referee literary catfights and unclog plumbing. The bagel woman had hoarded food in her dorm room, resulting in an invasion of raccoons. And Tony's poison oak had started to crust over.

When Tony wasn't wrangling conferences, or shooting videos for corporations, or applying for grants, or one of the several other things he did for income, he directed an experimental theater group that performed in public areas like transit terminals and shopping plazas. The group was called Theater in Your Face. He was anxious to get back to it.

Meanwhile. "Never rains but it pours. Guess who's showing up today. Larry Nagel."

Gil and I executed a perfectly synchronized "Who?"

"Barbarians," Tony pronounced us, but without real energy. "He only runs the biggest fine arts foundation on the West Coast. Artists United Institute."

"Holy cats," I said. "Larry the Magnificent."

"I wouldn't go around calling him that. What, you know him?"

"Only in passing." It hadn't been that long ago that I'd sat in the back seat of his extremely comfortable vehicle, waiting for the firemen to clear out of Viridian's driveway. "What's he coming here for?" Although I thought maybe I could guess.

"Who knows. He likes to have his fingers in every pie. At least he's not spending the night. But we need to get ready. Scatter rose petals in his path. Break out the good Scotch."

"I think he brings his own liquor," I said.

Gil said that she hoped Tony was kidding about the rose petals, but that by now she couldn't tell what was supposed to be funny.

I don't know if it was me or Sacha or both of us together who came up with the notion of a panel discussion that night, where Viridian could read her poems, but with others on stage also, to provide backup and nudge her along if necessary. Sacha could be there, along with Doug, and Larry, too. Tony thought it was a great idea, and it also solved the problem of filling the space left by Ken Spinner's departure. "We'll have to make sure the guys are willing to do it. But neither of them is exactly shy around a microphone."

Sacha said she'd explain it to Viridian and go over the poems she'd want to read. I thought that we could pull it off, or rather, that Viridian could, then we'd get her back home and fight the next fight. I thought that with any luck at all, Doug and Larry would provide an entertaining spectacle, two big shots competing to see who was the coolest and most badass, the fastest literary gun in the west.

I was on my way back to the lodge when I saw Oscar down by the river's edge. When I came nearer, I saw that he was scattering bits of bread in the water and watching fish rise to the surface to gobble them down. I said, "Now what, you're St. Francis of Assisi?"

"What? No. He fed birds. Anyway, I'm Jewish." Oscar scattered the last of the bread and dusted his hands together. He wore his usual clothes and he seemed to have lost his air of bravado from yesterday. Maybe he was just tired.

"That was a great reading."

"It was all right."

"It was more than all right, it was bananas."

"It was just the one night. Now it's the rest of my life. You know. Reality." He found another bread crumb in his pocket and shied it into the water.

"What's the matter?" I asked. He didn't seem upset. Serious, maybe.

"Would you do something for me? I'm heading out, I can't stay for Viridian's reading. Tell her I'm sorry."

I didn't understand. "Can't stay? Why, you have jury duty? Oscar!"

"Look, I have to go see about something. It's important. If it works out, well, we'll talk. If it doesn't, never mind."

"Bullshit, what are you saying?" He shrugged. "What about your workshop students, what are they supposed to do?"

"They're cool. Don't worry. I think they're going back to Tahoe. That boyfriend of yours? You think it's gonna work out? Or not?"

I stared at him. "What's that supposed to mean?"

"Life is short."

"Cliché."

"The future is promised to no one."

"Another cliché."

"Sometimes you just gotta go for it."

"Cliché trifecta."

"But all true. Oh, hey." He looked beyond me to where one of the super vans had pulled up in front of the lodge. "I think that's my ride. Adios."

He hurried past me. I watched, from a distance, as Larry Nagel got out of the van's front passenger side at the same time that Oscar grabbed his suitcase from the porch and settled into the rear seats.

Loony writers.

The van pulled away and left Larry Nagel standing by himself, briefcase in hand, looking around him like he'd been shipwrecked. I beat feet over to him.

"Mr. Nagel? Hi, I'm Carla, one of the assistants. Welcome to—" the name of the damn conference once more escaping me. "El Dorado National Forest. Let's get you settled, and I'll go find Tony."

266 JEAN THOMPSON

"Great," he said, making an effort at enthusiasm. He wore a business suit and tie and heavy polished shoes. He couldn't have been more out of place. Most of the conference attendees dressed as if they were at a surfing convention. Larry looked me over, and I wondered if he remembered me, but he probably met fifty different people each day, and he decided he had not. "How's it going up here?"

"Fine. Real good." Awesome, if you could get past the alcohol abuse and raging egos. I led him up the stairs and into the lodge. The hospitality room was empty, and there were still a few bagels. "Could I get you some coffee? We're so excited you're here." Well, somebody was.

"Thanks, I'm good for now." I hadn't seen him before in daylight. He looked older and more weathered than I remembered. He glanced around him at the lodge furnishings, which were both grand and shabby in equal parts. "Nice place. Definitely off the beaten path."

"I imagine that's meant to be part of the charm."

"Yeah, I guess. Blissful solitude. I never understood that. Well. Writers. Excuse me, maybe I'm insulting you."

"I'm not a writer, if that's what you mean. I just clean up after them."

"Me, too," Larry said. "In a manner of speaking. I'm with Artists United." He waited to see if I had any response to that, but I didn't, though maybe you were supposed to fall all over yourself being impressed. He had the most expensive-looking wristwatch I'd ever seen, sleek and heavy at the same time, made of pale gold. What had Oscar called him? An art gangster.

I said, "I've heard of it but I'm a little fuzzy about what it is, exactly, that you guys do."

He lowered himself into one of the leather armchairs, first removing a ball cap wedged in the cushions, and groaned, as if his feet hurt him. "What we do. Sure. We support artists, in different ways. We have a beautiful San Diego campus. Artists come there to teach, or work on projects, or do events. We have a museum and a library, exhibits, you name it."

"Sounds great. Sort of like a big art playground."

For a minute I thought I'd been too flippant, but then he shrugged, laughed. "Sure. It's a big sandbox for very talented children. Because we want a world with art. With paintings, and books, and plays."

"You must make money from it," I said. "I mean you must have figured out a way to make it work."

"What's your name again? Carla? You like to cut to the chase, don't you? Well Carla, you're not wrong. We would like to stay in business."

"Sorry," I muttered. I wasn't being exactly subtle.

"No need to be sorry. Who doesn't think about money? We have some pretty sharp accountants. They know how to cut the chicken into twelve pieces, like my grandmother used to say. We have endowments. We have donors. We have bequests. People like to see their name on museums and plaques. We have an investment portfolio. Most of the time it works out."

"So the art is worth money. It has to be. Some of it."

"Yes, Miss Carla, but the question is which, and how much, and how you maximize its value. Not everybody knows how. We do."

"And does the artist get anything out of it?"

"Of course they do. How much depends on market calculations. Who, how much, when.

Plus, they get a chance at the big prize."

I waited for him to tell me what the big prize was. "Their legacy," Larry said. "A lasting reputation. Immortality, of a sort." He reached into his jacket and took out a card case. "You ask good questions. Here. Call if you ever want to learn a little more about the way we do the things we do."

I took his card without looking at it. "I didn't mean to be nosy." Or maybe I did.

Larry waved a hand at me. "Inquisitive. Not a problem."

"I'll go find Tony for you."

I looked back on my way out and saw him bending over to untie the laces of his shoes.

I DIDN'T TELL anyone about Oscar's leaving. Maybe no one would notice. Anyway, there was already enough going on this last evening. Those who had engaged in romantic liaisons now had to say their farewells. Those who had gotten into blood feuds were busy documenting them on social media. Doug had invited several students to submit to *Compass Points*, among them Barb, who was over the moon, and Matt, who was now giving me silent, spiteful looks. The naturalists were upset because no one had attended their workshop on ferns.

" . . . cultural appropriation . . . "

"Like *Rashomon*, but for a YA audience."

" . . . shot myself in my metaphorical foot."

"Chug! Chug! Chug!"

VIRIDIAN'S PART IN that night's program was all arranged. Both Doug and Larry would give opening remarks. Viridian would read for a time, with Sacha there to manage the pages and anything else she needed. Then there would be some loosely organized discussion. I was looking forward to hearing her read again, holding my breath in hopes that it would go well.

We'd all reached the endurance contest stage of the conference, where we couldn't wait to get out of here, but also couldn't imagine being anywhere else. Only Gil, it seemed, was immune to such mixed feelings. "I'm counting the hours," she said, as we ate our last early dinner in the empty dining hall. "Rog and I can live large on this paycheck. We'll take a week or two off, then I'm thinking we might join one of the fire crews up north. That's some real money. How about you? What do you have going on, back in your real life?"

"Not much." I hadn't wanted to think about my real life. Was that what you called it? "I'll do the laundry. Throw some aluminum cans out the truck window."

"You're so funny."

"No, just tired."

"You're good with these people, you know? You speak their lingo. I guess I can't take them that seriously." Gil had smeared zinc oxide on her nose. I found it distracting to look at.

"Thanks." I thought I both did and did not take them seriously.

I wasn't one of them, although I'd spent so much time among them, although they found me useful, although they might feel affection for me, at least some of them. "Listen, how about, I'll get everything in the auditorium set up ahead of time if you'll handle it afterward."

Gil said we had a deal, and I hurried to finish my food and get going before anyone else came in to eat. All of a sudden, I didn't want to see any of them.

It wasn't anybody's fault. Or at least, it wasn't anybody's fault except mine. It felt like I'd reached the end of something, not just the conference, but of tagging along with people who had actual talent, actual accomplishments. I loved poetry, loved the weight and sound of it. I loved trying to get inside it, the good, the bad, the indifferent. I'd admired and envied those who wrote it. But my brain was still a television brain, a comic book brain. I couldn't read well enough to fool anyone for very long. Even if I attached myself to someone like Doug or Larry and tried to earn a living cleaning up after writers at some higher level, I'd be found out eventually.

I'd been kidding myself, wasting my time. Now I would be going home to a life I'd hollowed out, with nothing left in it to sustain me.

That was the script for my pity party, my last-night meltdown. I guess a lot of things had been building up in me, lonesomeness and yearning and frustration, and at least I chose the empty auditorium to sob and let it all out. When I heard people arriving for the reading, I got myself out of sight backstage behind the heavy curtain.

I stayed there, sniffling quietly and feeling sorry for myself, but embarrassed, too. As the seats filled, I could have come out, but after a time it felt too late for that. Besides, it suited my mood to hide myself away, to feel apart from the rest of them, and if that was childish, so what. The backstage was dusty and dark and populated by cables and scaffolding, equipment trunks, banks of lights. I found a plastic chair and set it to one side of the curtain where I could look out at the stage and the seats beyond, unseen.

The bagel woman took her usual place at the end of a far row. She was one story I'd never know. Tony came in; all day he'd been wearing a pullover cotton shirt that said OUCH, but now he'd put a sports jacket over it. And all the rest of them, a whole gallery of faces, my random fellow travelers for a few hours longer. I don't want to make too much of it, but I think I understood, then, the crazy-making energy that comes from a hive of writers.

I saw Viridian and Sacha enter at the back of the room and make their slow progress to the stage, stopping to talk to people along the way. Viridian wore the green dress I'd seen the first night of the conference. Someone asked her to sign a book, and she bent to do so. She looked relaxed and happy, and even if her face had softened with age, even if you could see the architecture of her collarbone more clearly now, she was still and always would be a great beauty, you would still want to look at her.

Doug and Larry stood in front of the stage talking to each other and keeping an eye on Viridian. Watching them from this angle felt like spying, even though they were out in plain view. I saw how Doug fidgeted, spinning on one heel to monitor Viridian's progress. Larry turned his wrist ever so slightly within his shirt cuff so he could check his expensive watch. I imagine he had some late connection that would take him back to San Diego or his next stop on the never-ending tour of Artists United mergers and acquisitions.

When they all took their seats on the stage, they were only a few feet away from me, though Viridian was seated at the far end and it was more difficult for me to see her. Tony took the microphone and waited for everyone to settle down. He began by saying that Ken Spinner's reading was unfortunately canceled. This made the crowd snigger and buzz. They were in a rowdy mood on this last night.

"But we're really lucky to have two very famous and distinguished guests, as well as tonight's reader, the fabulous Viridian."

Applause. I should have been out there clapping, too. I felt bad about that part. I listened, or half listened, as Tony went on with his introductions. The many accomplishments and notable achievements of the people on stage. It might seem funny, but it actually cheered me up to hear it. You'd think that it would depress me further, you know, how exalted they were, and how miserable and lowly I was by comparison, but no. I understood now how much effort, the work of a lifetime even, went into a poem, or a magazine, or any such enterprise, how much care and doubt and stubbornness and desperation, how they had earned everything. And how I might find something of my own, some achievement or excellence, and so come in time to earn the world's notice on my terms.

There was more applause, and then some whispering, confusion, it seemed, about how to proceed. Viridian said, "Oh don't ask me, what do I know?" loud enough for the audience to hear it and laugh, though it seemed they weren't certain if they were meant to laugh. I leaned a little closer to the curtain's edge and saw Viridian make a shooing motion with her hand, as if Sacha and the rest of them were annoying flies.

Doug spoke into the microphone. "All right, I'll start. Thanks for having me here and letting me be a part of this super-fun and important gathering. I know you've learned a lot from Viridian and the other great writers here. When I'm asked about *Compass Points*, about what we look for when we're putting together an issue, I say we want poems that are of the moment, of the time and place we live in, but which transcend it."

"And what does that mean, exactly?" Viridian said. "Honestly, I never know what that means."

I have to give Doug credit, it didn't throw him off. "Yes, what do we mean? I expect it's the same for everybody. It's how we start each new poem. Hoping to speak to our own experience, to validate it and make it credible and real to others. But also, to stand outside of ourselves, connect with what's universal. What's human and timeless."

He paused, but Viridian didn't speak. "Anyway," Doug said, hurrying a little now, "the magazine has a long and storied history. I'm just the latest in a long line of caretakers. And I've tried to live up to that history. To seek out the best and most distinctive—"

"Honestly," Viridian said.

Dead stop. I saw Larry lean toward Doug, a brief whispered conference. Then Larry took the microphone.

"Who out there is a fan of *Compass Points*?"

Applause, a few whistles and cheers. They were relieved to have something to cheer for, and to keep things on track.

"I'm a fan, too," he said. "When I need to know what's new and exciting, what lovers of literature are going to be paying attention to, *Compass Points* is where I turn."

It was logrolling, but at some expert level. Doing each other favors so that everybody got ahead. These guys were so good at it. I expected that when it was Doug's turn to take the microphone again, he'd say nice things about Larry. Whatever competition there was between them, they'd soft-soap over it, and carry on as if they earned their living playing croquet, instead of trying to clobber each other with giant ego-clubs.

Larry went on. "I've been asked, what is it that you do, exactly, at Artists United?"

I felt my face getting hot. I hoped I wasn't the only one who asked. Maybe I was only the most recent.

"And I always say something along the lines of, 'While magazines like *Compass Points* provide a home for the writing, we provide a home for the artist.'"

Doug had to jump in then. "Not that one's more important than the other."

"Mutually dependent."

"Interdependent, even."

Viridian said, "Which came first, the chicken or the egg? The chicken, I always thought."

Another dead stop. Everyone waited for her to say more, to follow up, but she kept silent.

After a moment Larry said, "You know, who needs to listen

to us natter on about poetry when you can hear a real poet? I bet you're ready for that, right?"

Scattered applause, then more widespread as people realized it was expected of them.

I looked for Tony in the crowd, found him in one of the seats up front. He had a weird expression on his face, like he was watching a foreign-language movie without subtitles and was trying to follow along.

Doug spoke up. "I hope we can get Viridian to talk a little about her place in one of the true golden ages of American poetry. So many now-famous names got their start right then and there. What a grand and exciting time it must have been." He extended his arm, a showman's flourish: Make way.

Edging closer to the curtain's edge, I saw Sacha and Viridian conferring, then Viridian stood and walked to the podium.

"Golden age? Well maybe. So many of them drank too much." Laughter. "A number of them died of it."

The audience went silent. Viridian said, "I'm delighted to be here among you." She took some time rummaging through the pages before her. Then she put them aside. "So many words about words. So much who who who. Does it matter? I don't know. Maybe not for much longer. Who cares who writes what? Who we are or were?"

I wanted to come out from behind the curtain then and take charge, help her somehow, before things went too far wrong, and I imagine everyone else held their breath, too, waiting for something to crystallize. Viridian took a page from the stack and held it at arm's length. She said, "There ought to be a poetry of silence.

There ought to come a point when nothing more need be said. Until then, this is the best I can do."

The body is a house. Who lives within?
The body is a bed. Who has lain there with you?
Does anyone remember? Who has left their bones
behind, their memories tangled in the sheets.
Everyone has claimed you, none of them know the
hard nugget of your nature, the part that can not
be loved. Stubborn, unlovable girl. You went your
own willful way. Now are you happy? And the answer
comes back

SHE STOPPED SPEAKING. A sound like a rush of wind passed through the audience. Even before I pushed the curtain aside, I knew what had happened.

BREATH

At first, we were hopeful. The ambulance came quicker than expected, and Placerville, only twenty minutes away, had a good stroke intervention team. What did I know about strokes? Nothing, really, but I was going to learn. Time was important when it came to treatment. Time seemed to be on Viridian's side. She was given medicine to dissolve the blood clot, as well as a CT scan, glucose monitoring, intubation, more. The whole array of medical weapons.

I didn't know any of this right away. I stayed behind at the conference while Tony, Barb, Sacha, and Anders followed the ambulance to Placerville. Sacha said she'd call the office phone when they knew something. Gil and I were left to try and calm people down. There was some crying, emotions spilling over. We opened the bar, but it wasn't a night for a party.

I didn't cry. I felt numb and shaky. Doug decided to make the drive to Placerville also. Larry trudged down to the lodge to wait for his ride out. He and Doug shook hands and spoke together for a moment. Once they were both gone, I headed to the conference center and sat in the office among the long-dead animals to wait.

I guess I fell asleep. The phone rang and made me come to. I fought the chair for balance as I answered. "Hello?"

"Carla? It's Sacha, I wanted to give you an update, but there's not a lot we know. There was surgery to remove the clot and she hasn't yet woken up, that's what they're waiting for now."

"What are the doctors saying?"

"Nothing definite. They're all very professional. Very nice. I don't know if a larger hospital would have done anything differently."

"But it's serious, right?"

She sighed. "Yes, honey. Any stroke would be." We were quiet, and I imagine both of us were thinking about the damned pills that Viridian wouldn't take, the appointments she wouldn't make, all her stubborn recklessness. Then Sacha said Tony would be coming back that night, he'd make sure we got any news.

I thought about calling Aaron. But I was afraid he might disappoint me without meaning to. His sympathy would fall short somehow, and I'd end up mad. It wasn't that late, not quite ten. I called my mom.

It rang three, then four times. She wouldn't recognize the number and might not pick up. Then she answered. "Hello?"

"Mom? It's Carla."

"Carla? What's wrong?"

"Nothing, I mean, I'm fine." I heard some kind of distant racket, and people talking in the background. "Where are you?"

"Santa Rosa," she said unhelpfully. "Where are you? What's going on?"

"I'm still at the conference. Viridian had a stroke. We don't know how she is yet, or what to expect."

"Oh my god. Why? No, that's not what I meant. Hold on a minute." She put the phone down and I heard some muffled conversation.

"Carla?" A man's voice. "What the hell happened?"

"Who is this?"

"It's Oscar. Tell me about Viridian."

"*Oscar?* What . . ." I couldn't put more than two words together.

"Get a grip, Carla. Where's Viridian, how is she?"

"She . . . Jesus Christ, what are you doing? Let me talk to my mom."

"She stepped away for a minute. Are you going to tell me about Viridian?"

It took me another couple of tries. I was knocked that flat. Oscar said, "Okay, Placerville? We'll get there as soon as we can."

We? "No, don't, I don't know how long she'll be at that hospital, anyway, weren't you just here, or I mean, there? Don't drive all the way back, wait until I find out more. What are you doing with my mom?"

"We're having a drink. And some nachos. Now don't go crazy on us, we need you to focus. We'll talk later. Call back when you know more about Viridian. I have to go now."

And then I was run over by a truck. And then a bear ate me.

VIRIDIAN DIDN'T WAKE up after her surgery. I won't say never woke up, because how long is never, as long as life endures. She had a second stroke the next day that did even more damage, tearing through the webs of nerve cells and tissue. Days and days went by with no change. Expectations were dialed down to the minimum. She could breathe on her own, at least, but they had to insert a stomach tube to feed her, and the nurses bathed and cleaned her and moved her this way and that. She gave no sign that she was aware of anything around her.

I wasn't brave. I didn't go to the hospital. I talked to Sacha and to Barb, and later to Ed.

Boone was involved, of course, but it turned out that Ed had both Viridian's legal and medical powers of attorney. Decisions would have to be made. I was glad I had no part of them. I had enough of my own problems to sort through.

If she had been able, what kind of poem might she have written about the body's failure, unable to either live as it wished, or to die with grace.

I went to see Aaron. I hadn't been gone that long, but I might as well have been an astronaut after a mission to the space station. Everything in the house, everything about Aaron himself, was both familiar and not so. It took me a while to get my bearings, and maybe it was the same for him, seeing me. We hugged, but hugging really wasn't our thing, not unless it was going to lead us straight to bed. And I wasn't going to end up there this time, even though somewhere inside me a familiar slow fuse had been lit.

It was a relief to break the hugging off when Batman came padding into the room. "Batman!" I knelt down and let him kiss my face. "Oh baby, I missed you so much." I looked up at Aaron. "I mean, I missed you both."

"Thanks." He'd put his hands in his pockets and taken a step back. Body language alert.

It was always so much less complicated to love a dog, but I didn't think I should say that. I stood up. "Could we take him for a walk?"

We followed our usual route, past the vacant lots and half-built houses, out to the roadway and the empty spaces where Batman could sniff and pee. It was the first week of September, still warm, still hazy and golden. But the light was receding, day by day. It felt like the end of something. I'd already told Aaron about Viridian's stroke, and now he asked how she was.

"The same. She's in a sort of coma. Or not sort of. I don't think she's going to come out of it." I hadn't said it before. Tears pricked at my eyelashes.

"I'm sorry. That just sucks."

He took my hand then and held it. Sometimes he was the best.

"But she's being taken care of, right?"

"Nobody knows what to do." The doctors had been talking about how, once she had stabilized, meaning, once they could do no more for her, she could be moved to a nursing and rehab place in Marin.

"It doesn't sound like there's much of anything to do."

"But it doesn't feel right. Her life shouldn't just come to this full, stupid stop."

"Carla, that's what life does."

I didn't have any answer to that. After a while we turned back toward home, and Aaron said, "I'm waiting for my passport. Once it comes, I'm all set."

"Set for what?" I said, although I thought I knew.

"Vancouver. I got the job. I can start as soon as my feet hit the ground there."

"Oh wow." He'd told me about the job, this particular job with a software firm, but he'd downplayed it, made it sound like something it was best not to take seriously. Now it was a real thing, churning my stomach like a washing machine. "So I guess—"

"I guess one way or the other, you're going to have to pack up the rest of your stuff."

"That's supposed to be an invitation? Wow, how could I refuse."

"Come on. You know I want you to go with me. You're my girl."

And I guess I did know, though it would have been nice if he'd remind me once in a while. "What would I do in Vancouver anyway?"

"Whatever you want. Go back to school, like you keep talking about. Choose whatever career you want. I'll be making good money."

Maybe he realized he was sounding a little like an army recruiter. He tried again. "I want us to have a life together. I don't want anybody else. You're a total brat sometimes and I even love you for that, because you won't quit on things when they're important to you. Like your crazy poets. But you have to make up your mind and stop putting everything off because of these other people and their problems and ideas and whatever, because, you know what? You were never really a part of it."

I'd told myself pretty much the same thing, when I was feeling sad and hopeless. But I didn't want to give up on everything I'd felt or learned. And I didn't want to just tag along after a man.

Even though I still loved Aaron, had never stopped loving him. I was thinking of Viridian now, even if Aaron was not Mathias or anything like him. Could you ever be in love without being somehow diminished?

Lost in our debate was the fact that I was the injured party, that Aaron had messed around on me and tried to get away with it. It seemed all that had receded, and now it was only me, being exasperating and willful.

He said, "I want things to be the same as they were before. When we were happy. Please."

But I wasn't really the same as I'd been before. Whether he knew it or not.

Aaron was waiting for me to answer. "Well I already have a passport," I said. "So at least that part's easy. The rest might take a little work."

"Don't wait too long," he said. And that's how we left it, with neither of us satisfied.

I HADN'T TOLD Aaron, or anyone, about my mother and Oscar because, for one thing, it was embarrassing, and for another, I wouldn't have known what to say. Here was my practical and no-nonsense mother, wearing one of her usual dolled-up out-fits, this one red and white and featuring a sweetheart neckline, holding Oscar's hand and giggling. No, they were swinging their joined hands back and forth. It was so simpleminded, like something out of a nursery rhyme. As for Oscar, I'd admit that cutting his hair had helped him look less like somebody you might stare at on the street, at least until he started reciting poems.

They tried to be halfway discreet. Oscar didn't spend the night at my mom's, at least for now. I gave them plenty of space, I stayed away as much as I could. But I wasn't going to move back in with Aaron just because my mom was acting like a thirteen-year-old, and anyway, with or without me, Aaron was headed to Vancouver.

They'd gotten to know each other back when Viridian had first been in the hospital. Oscar had sought my mom out and wooed her with his virile charms; I really didn't care to imagine that part. Then there had been an extensive courtship carried on through letters. I'd never known my mom to write a real letter in her life, only cards, and even those were short and unremarkable. *Have a great birthday!* That kind of thing.

I tried talking to her. "Oscar's not exactly reliable. Not a safe bet. I mean, I like the guy, but I'm not sure he's stable. You know, I'm pretty sure he isn't."

"Nobody's ever written a poem about me before. An actual poem."

"That's the kind of thing he does all the time. Mom! He has more old lovers than he has socks. You don't know him the way I do."

"You don't know him the same way I do," said my brazen mother. I covered my ears and begged her to stop. "Besides, everybody has baggage once you get to a certain age."

I tried again. "I don't think you have that much in common."

"And that's a good thing. He needs somebody with sense to take care of him. I know he can be outlandish, but underneath all the carrying-on, he's just a little boy."

"I'm gagging here."

"All of a sudden I'm not allowed to have my own life? You think I haven't been lonesome? You think you know everything?"

"I'm sorry, Mom."

"Denis the First of Portugal was known as the Poet King. He wrote love poems in the troubadour tradition, the *Cantigas de Amigo*. They're amazing."

I hadn't known that either.

I spoke with Boone a couple of times, brief phone conversations to ask how Viridian was doing. There hadn't been much to say, besides sorry. I understood that his position was difficult, as Viridian had been a difficult kind of mother. How much was he meant to be responsible for her, how much was he meant to feel?

And no one could say what might happen to her. While she was not expected to recover, to open her eyes and come back to the world, it could not be entirely ruled out. Nor could anyone say how long she might go on exactly as she was, whether she would die tomorrow or linger for years, or what one might decently wish for her.

"There are money issues," Boone said, during one of our calls. "She'll qualify for Medi-Cal. But her house is an asset, it'll have to be sold. Ed says there's a process for it."

"You're selling it?"

"It'll be a teardown. A buyer's going to want the property, not that barn of a house."

"But she'd hate that." What I meant was, I would hate it.

"I'm not sure that matters anymore."

After we hung up, I tried to think it through. What would be best, what might be possible.

I went round and round and got nowhere.

Of course, different people—Oscar, Boone, Sacha, Ed—had all made a search for the Mathias poems by now. They weren't in any obvious place. They weren't in any nonobvious place. Not in her office files, nor in among the cookbooks, or under the bed. There was no secret drawer, no key to an unknown safe deposit box. At least, none that anyone could find. Maybe she'd destroyed them, some final act of spite toward the poet who had always overshadowed her. We didn't want to think it, but we had to give the idea room.

"No," Oscar said. "She wouldn't. Even if she wanted to. She'd hang on to them like an ace up her sleeve. She'd have some plan in mind. Unfortunately, her plan didn't allow for incapacitation."

We were at Viridian's house. Oscar needed to retrieve more items of his wardrobe. He was still living here, technically, rather than my mom's, and he'd asked if I could drive him to Fairfax and back again. I couldn't think of a reason to say no, except that I didn't want to talk to him. I said I needed to give the garden some attention, he could wait while I did.

He agreed, and we set off for Viridian's. "So what do you think—" he began, almost as soon as we were out of the driveway.

"Honestly, I try not to think about the two of you."

"Come on, Carla. Try and get on the happy train."

"How about, make sure you keep my mom on it."

He muttered something about negative energy, and we rode the rest of the way in silence.

The garden was dry and sad. The rosemary had grown woody and the sunflowers were at an end and I tried not to make a dumb, maudlin poem out of it all, but the big old rambling house, the scene of so much good fellowship, felt bereft. Sometimes life really was dumb and maudlin.

Inside, I found Oscar going through the books on the office shelves. "Have you looked under *M*?"

"Yeah, funny."

"I'm sorry, I don't mean to be a jerk. About you and my mom. It's not such an easy time to be happy about anything."

"Yeah. Love. Inconvenient, isn't it?"

I CALLED BOONE and asked if he wanted to meet for a drink. He'd been in Placerville all this time, and now he was in town to talk with Ed. Viridian was still in the local hospital. The process of not dying was complicated. There were constant phone calls back and forth with insurance companies, with care centers, with Medi-Cal. The doctors weighed in with predictions and cautions, directives and requirements.

I felt sorry for Boone, I knew he was exhausted by it all. And pulled in different directions by duty and resentment and loss. He'd said as much. I guess I had other, less straight-forward reasons for calling him, having to do with my own vanity and curiosity and indecision, and because Boone was flawed as I felt myself to be flawed. We had that much in common. And he was a part of Viridian's world, while Aaron was not. I didn't entirely trust Boone, but even when he'd tried to outmaneuver or flatter me, it meant I might have some purpose or value in that world.

We were meeting in Sausalito, his idea, at one of those restaurants-with-a-view. Again, his suggestion. I didn't want it to be some big expensive deal, didn't want him spending the kind of money such a place would take. But I wasn't going to back out now.

My mom came in while I was drying my hair in the bathroom. "Don't you look nice."

"Thanks." I was making more effort than usual with my hair and makeup. I wore short suede boots, my tightest jeans, and a black top that showed some skin.

"You're going out?"

"Clearly."

"With Aaron?"

"No."

She waited for me to tell her more. She wasn't so love-crazed that she'd quit being my mother. When I didn't speak, she said, "Sweetie, I know you don't want my opinion—"

"But I'm going to get it anyway."

"I had to listen to a lot of your free opinions lately about my personal life, right? Now it's your turn. You aren't happy. I thought you were happy with Aaron. So I was wrong. Try and figure out what's going to make you feel good about yourself. Then maybe you can decide if it involves anybody else. Be careful driving."

BOONE WAS LATE getting to the restaurant, which annoyed me. I sat at the bar, with the drink I'd at least managed to buy myself, watching people chat and laugh and dig into their calamari and polenta and fish tacos. There were places in Marin that could make you believe the whole world was made up of happy people delighting in a night on the town.

"Sorry." Here was Boone, appearing at my elbow. "It took forever to get across the bridge. Let's find a table." He was wearing another of his white-man dress-up outfits.

Every time I saw him, I had to adjust to how much older than me he was, and how unsettling that could be, like maybe we'd met online and one of us had lied about our age. And there was his imperfect resemblance to Viridian as well, so that it seemed I was always looking at his face as if doubting what I saw. He unsettled me for reasons that were really not fair of me to hold against him. The hostess led us to our table, and I wished I'd said I wanted to stay at the bar. The truth behind all those happy-looking restaurant people was that at least some of them weren't sure they wanted to be with each other.

But here we were. "How are you?" he said, then rubbed at his eyes and stifled a yawn.

"Sorry. Jesus, I can't do anything right. Kind of short on sleep lately." He did look tired. All the lines in his face sagging downward. His dark eyes were bloodshot.

I said I was fine. I asked him how Viridian was, and Boone said she was the same, at least as far as he could tell. Maybe the doctors, with their systems for measuring eye movement or pain response, could find something different. She was going to be moved to a care facility in San Rafael maybe as early as a couple of days from now, depending on about a million different crazy-making factors. The money was a nightmare, of course.

"This has to be so hard for you."

"Yes, except for—" The waitress came by then with menus and interrupted him, and Boone said we should get some dinner, which I'd been ready to turn down. But it was easier to give in and order a fancy hamburger.

You could see a portion of the harbor from where they'd seated us, the thicket of masts in the middle distance that marked some moored yachts, and a space of open water, and the expensively undeveloped shorelines of Belvedere and Tiburon. The sun was getting low in the sky behind us and the sky took on shades of gold and pink and, right above the waterline, a deeper blue. "Except for what?" I asked, once the waitress had gone.

"Oh, I guess I meant, I feel like I'm finally doing what I ought to be doing. Taking care of her." He dropped his gaze, maybe embarrassed. Maybe he was one of those men who thought that behaving admirably was a sign of weakness. "Trying to give us a good last chapter."

"It's not like you got to write the first chapter."

"I guess."

"Guess nothing. You were a little kid."

"Yes, but that doesn't keep the irrational voices out of your head."

"What are the voices saying?"

"She had such a complicated relationship with men. Is it all right to use past tense? I don't want to be . . . Anyway. So many men were enthralled by her, and she knew that, and she made use of that. I don't mean calculating, more just, human nature. But then it's a power struggle, because of course they tried to control her, too, and you could argue that a lot of the time they did, or maybe the world did. Her writing. Her career. It wasn't fair and she knew it."

The waitress came with his drink then and he waited for her to set it down and leave again. "I think that love, love affairs, became mortal combat for her, she didn't trust men. She loved them but she didn't trust them. Does that make sense?"

"Absolutely."

"So sometimes I wonder. If I'd been a daughter instead of a son, would she have stayed?"

I felt bad for him then in a way I hadn't before. I said, "Wow, talk about something that isn't your fault."

"Yeah, I know. Irrational."

After a time our food came and we ate and talked a little about other things. He liked California, he thought he might stick around rather than go back to New York. I said I was sort of up in the air about my future, too. Trying to decide what I was good at. Good for.

Boone seemed surprised to hear it. "You? You're pretty good at lots of things."

"Which is the same as being not good enough at any one thing."

"Don't you think you're kind of young to be despairing about the rest of your life?" I gave him an unfriendly look. "Okay, sorry, look, can I ask you something without you jumping down my throat? How come you don't have a boyfriend?"

"Having a boyfriend is not a career plan."

"Granted. I'm just surprised. Is there some respectful way to say you're gorgeous?"

I brushed that last aside. "I do have a boyfriend. Since you ask. Sort of. It's complicated."

"Huh. Well, there's somebody I guess you could call my girl-friend, but it's complicated, too."

We looked at each other solemnly for a minute and then we both started laughing, and that broke some tension that had been between us all along. When we were done eating, we went out to the walkway and looked over the harbor, the water and the reflected lights and the magic, illuminated city across the bay, the million-dollar view free to anyone who wished to see it. I let him kiss me, since we'd both laid down our weapons and nothing would come of it. Then we said good night and I got in the truck and headed north.

Sometimes things come to you, it seems like out of the blue. But your brain's been working on the problem all along, you real-ize later, some underpaid-file-clerk portion of your brain, taking notes and writing reports. Maybe it was Boone telling me that Viridian didn't trust men. Which I already knew, or assumed, knew at least that she resented the power they'd had over her. She'd told me as much. She'd trusted me enough to tell me.

She would have had a plan for the poems. The plan hadn't allowed for incapacitation.

Or maybe it had.

I got off 101 and took Sir Francis Drake up to Fairfax. It was completely dark by now, and I followed my headlights up the hill to Viridian's, hoping a deer wouldn't jump out in front of me, or as often enough happened, three or four deer. The road up to the house was blind dark, as was the house itself, nobody home.

Oscar must have been back at my mom's, trying to come up with more rhymes for *Dawn*: *Lawn. Fawn. Brawn.*

I parked the truck in the courtyard and found my heavy-duty flashlight beneath the seat. I played it over the house, startling a bird out of sleep. It squawked and flapped into the woods. I didn't try the front door, but I went around to the back, betting that Oscar wouldn't have thought to lock it. He'd go out the front and close up behind himself and think it done.

I was right. I let myself into the dark kitchen, calling "Hello? Hello?" Not expecting an answer, and there was none.

I didn't want to turn on any more lights than I had to. I let the flashlight lead me through the tidy kitchen. Either Oscar wasn't doing any cooking these days, or else he was being good about cleaning. Here was the familiar, almost muddy smell of the herbal teas and supplements, the green matcha powder, the canisters and jars of beans and whole grains and other healthy ingredients that had failed to keep her healthy.

I passed on to the office and here I did turn on a light, blinking at the sudden brightness. The room had been gone over and then gone over again, the site of many rummagings and searches. The books were out of order in stacks on the floor and on the desktop, and file folders labeled in Viridian's small, distinctive script were also set aside in piles. I looked for what seemed like a long time, keeping my ears open in case a car pulled up out front, or worse, some creepy sound came from within the house itself.

When I found it, finally, I saw that I'd mistaken it for something else. I hadn't expected it to be this large volume bound in dark blue leather with a gold-embossed spine, like something you might give as a gift in the last century, or the one before:

A Defence of Poetry
and other works
of Percy Bysshe Shelley

One corner of the heavy leather cover had been loosened, then glued back. You might not notice it if you weren't looking for it. I pried it apart with care and extracted a thick bundle of printed pages. There were also many plain lined notebook pages covered in handwriting. All of it slightly crumbly with age, smelling stale and airless.

I spread it all in front of me on the desktop and began to read. A buzzing noise started up in my head, blotting out any other sounds.

After a few minutes? An hour? I finished reading and stood, blinking and wobbly. I got out my phone and took close-up pictures of each page, both printed and handwritten, like a spy or a secret agent. When I had them all, I put the pages back in order and set them in their hiding place in the book's cover. I resealed the cover, moistening the old glue with water from the kitchen tap so it would hold. Then I returned the book to where I'd found it on the shelves. After a moment I took my phone back out and took a picture of that also.

I still had the business card Larry Nagel had given me, and the next morning he was the first call I made.

It took three days to set everything up. We were meeting at Ed's law firm in the city. I hadn't said anything to Oscar or my mother, in case nothing came of it. And maybe because they'd kept a few secrets of their own from me lately.

I picked up Sacha on the way. She asked me if I was nervous about the meeting and I said, Not so much about that, but . . . She reached across the front seat and squeezed my hand.

The care center was sunny and institutionally pleasant, meaning that attention had been given to making the public spaces welcoming, with plants and cheerful wall art and good furniture. Once you reached the patient rooms, there was a more mechanical look to everything. Carts and wheelchairs and electrically powered beds. Machines for assisting with movement, for providing treatments, for measuring medical deficits. I guess I'd thought Viridian would have her own room, perhaps a window with a view. Things that wouldn't matter much if you needed to be here in the first place.

Viridian was in the bed closest to the door, and a curtain was drawn around the other bed, the unseen one next to the window. The blinds were closed and the light in the room was dim. Sacha reached for Viridian's hand. The hand appeared to be weightless, curled in on itself, a bundle of twigs.

"Hi Virdie. It's Sacha. Carla's here to see you, too."

It was my turn. I came closer. Her face had already changed so much. I concentrated instead on the rise and fall of her breathing, thin and regular.

What if the body is a house? Who lives within?

"I'm going to tell them. I'm thinking you'd want me to."

I'd imagined I'd have more to say, but that was it. We only stayed for a little while. When we were in the truck again on the way to the city, Sacha said, "They say people can still hear. I don't know how they know that."

"How's Anders?" I asked, for the sake of making conversation.

"He's fine. He's in Japan doing research on animistic folk tales. He's trying to branch out a little." She saw me looking at her. "Anyway, it's good to take a break now and then."

Ed's law office was in a converted warehouse in China Basin. "Artsy but inconvenient," as Sacha said. It took us forever to find it, long enough at least for my hands to start sweating and my stomach to get seasick. "Now I am nervous," I announced. "Is this even going to work?"

"All we can do is try." Sacha didn't look super confident either. I was glad she was with me, an actual grownup, with her perfume and smart handbag and nice shoes, all the things it never occurred to me to acquire. I was thinking, who was I for anyone to listen to me? A kid, a nobody.

And once we got inside and were shown into the conference room, none of them—Larry, Doug, Ed, Boone—looked anything but peeved to be there, wondering what I was trying to pull.

"Come on in," Ed said. "Please. Coffee?"

"Sorry, I hope we're not too late. Parking. Oh, nice view," I said, indicating a patch of the bay visible in one window. No one said anything. I took a seat next to Boone and across from Doug, who seemed especially annoyed that his unpaid intern was now calling meetings. I hadn't seen him and Ed side by side for some time, and I was struck again by their resemblance, both of them fair, slim, and well turned out. Although today Ed wore a business suit, while Doug had selected some leather items from his closet.

No one spoke to us, not even to say hello. Larry was at the far end of the table, going through his phone, improving every shining hour. I was aware of his cologne, a subtle, heady scent that was probably called something like Potentate or War Lord. He turned the phone off and put it away, waiting, Boone was leaning back in his chair, not looking at me.

"Well," Ed said. "Let's get started. Carla, you wanted to share some information about the Mathias poems."

"I want to discuss them, yes."

"Do you have them?" Doug asked.

"No." I heard a muttering start up. "But I know where they are."

"Perhaps you'd like to tell us." Doug again. He really didn't have the most winning ways.

I tried to get a breath all the way in me. "I know where they are. I've seen them. I have not removed or in any way disturbed them."

"That's great, but—"

"They're still where Viridian put them. I think she wanted me to find them."

Larry said, "Excuse me, that's a nice sentiment, but they aren't yours to make decisions about. If they're the real thing, like you say. If you have them, you should turn them over. They're part of Viridian's estate, they belong to Boone."

Now it was my turn not to look at Boone. "They aren't his yet," I said. "Technically. Not as long as she's alive." I hated to hear myself saying it. "I just meant, it's so sad, and nobody knows anything for sure."

"What's your point," Ed said.

"I'm not a lawyer. I guess you can go to court, right, and be granted possession, but maybe that takes time, or, who knows how stuff might fall through the cracks, and wouldn't it be better to know where they are now?"

Boone spoke up then. "Has anyone else seen them? Sacha?"

"I have seen pictures of them."

"And?"

"They appear to be genuine."

Boone turned to me, stone-faced. "Why don't you tell us what you want."

"I don't want you to sell her house."

More of the muttering. "I want to keep her . . . spirit alive. Make sure the world remembers her and her poems."

"We all want that," Doug said. "You don't have to give speeches."

I ignored him. "There's something else, too. The Mathias poems? Mathias didn't write them."

That whole room full of men were all talking at once, roaring back at me. I nodded to Sacha and she stood up and began passing out the printed copies from my phone photos. One page showed a Mathias poem in typescript, then there were several pages of the handwritten notes. "What are we looking at?" Larry asked, once everyone had settled down.

"Drafts of a Mathias poem in Viridian's handwriting. You can see her whole process, how she crossed out a line or a word and came up with a variant, how the poem changed and evolved. They're very detailed."

Sacha said, "I certainly found them convincing. There are a lot more. They cover some of his known poems, and the last, unpublished ones, the ones he burned. Remember, those were submitted in the court case, they can be verified."

"She wrote them all," I said. "But she kept it secret."

Boone said, "That's nuts. She wrote love poems to herself?"

"Like, a ventriloquist act. Why not."

"But why write them in the first place?"

"Pick your own reason," I said. "Because she loved him and wanted to help him? He wasn't writing any more, he was too far gone. Because he made her do it? Anyway, it wouldn't be the first time a man took credit for a woman's work."

None of them wanted to explore that last one. Doug said, "He burned them. He didn't mean them to survive."

"Maybe because he was ashamed of himself. Maybe he wanted to hurt her. Again, pick your own reason."

"She could have told everybody after he died, it's nuts that she didn't."

"No, it's not. Maybe she was embarrassed. Maybe she didn't want to undermine him, she felt guilty. Or, like you're doing right now, people would think the poems weren't as important because they were hers."

Nobody said anything to that.

I said, "Anyway, she's telling us now. She saved them. She was proud of them. She knew they were extraordinary."

Sacha cleared her throat. "She loved him. She felt sorry for

him. I expect he bullied her. I expect she allowed herself to be
bullied. Love is complicated."

Or sometimes, I thought, it wasn't even love. Viridian had
called herself foolish and weak, and I hadn't understood her
then, but I thought I did now. She'd given a part of herself up
for love, and the whole long rest of her life was an effort to get it
back.

Doug put his head in his hands. "So there really aren't any
Mathias poems. Congratulations, you just knocked the bottom
out of the market."

I said, "I don't think so." I turned to Ed. I trusted him more
than the others. If I could get him on my side, there was hope. "I
think the truth makes for a better story."

It took time to bring everybody around to an agreement. They
finally realized how much attention, how much uproar and pub-
licity there would be, as people argued for their own interpreta-
tions of the poems and how they came to be. It was a full month
of negotiations, phone calls, all while Viridian just breathed,
while everyone wrestled for a part of what she left, good inten-
tions or not. Here's what was worked out, finally: Larry Nagel
would purchase the poems from Boone, once Boone had legal
possession. He would house them in his museum and sponsor
exhibitions and allow scholars access to them. Doug and *Compass
Points* would have first publication rights. Of course, there would
be a book somewhere down the line. Sacha still had her television
contacts from appearances about her Frankenstein project. Who
knew what might be possible?

It wasn't all sweet harmony, of course, people being people and writers being writers. There was a lot of squabbling about the valuation of the poems, and even when that was settled, Larry dragged his feet on the payouts. Ed and Doug eventually split up. A month later, when the poems went on display, and they went out into the world, some critics, the professional doubters, were unconvinced that Viridian had any hand in Mathias's work. The second-wave feminists argued with the third-wave feminists over whether adopting a male persona was a betrayal of self, or no big deal.

Whenever you could see the personalities behind literature, there was a lot more interest in it. Weren't people still arguing about who Emily Dickinson wrote her love poems for?

When Viridian slipped away the following summer, there was already a lively public conversation in progress. And it was possible that, somewhere out there, people who had never given a thought to poetry might now consider it worth their attention. So that a life spent in the service of art continued to nourish it after death.

That next year, Viridian's house was given some careful upgrades, and Barb was put in charge of its management. It provided subsidized stays for writers who needed a month or two to work on book projects. There were tax regulations that made such high-minded, money-losing arrangements possible. Ed knew all about them.

Boone wasn't inclined to forgive me at first. I had to convince him I didn't want any money. Before we had signed off on anything, I figured he'd make one last pass at finding the poems, and I figured he'd fail. I was right on both counts. Only when we had our memorandum of understanding filed away did I tell him where the poems were, and how talking with him that night had led me to them.

"You are too much," he told me. "The girl detective."

"I couldn't have done it without you. You were sort of the last piece of the puzzle."

"Right. In the movies, I'd be the guy who's been using the priceless Ming vase as an ashtray."

"Well, everybody's happy now, aren't they?"

"Sure. It's a triumph of Capital *A* Art."

I'd come into the city to meet him for coffee. I figured I owed him that much, after all the aggravation I'd put him through. And he would always be Viridian's son, and I would always love that part of him. In spite of his complaints, I knew he thought well of me, too, and we'd be content to leave it at that. A kind of mutual fondness and mutual wariness.

Now he brought a shopping bag out from underneath the table. "Here. I didn't have time to wrap it."

"What's this?" I reached inside, past layers of tissue, and drew out a heavy book. *A Defence of Poetry* was printed on the cover in modern block letters. Same book, different look.

"Your own copy," Boone said. "Use it wisely."

It would be pure murder to get through it, and I ended up needing an audiobook and a study guide, but I did eventually. I made myself do it. It was a point of pride.

"Thanks," I said. "Really. It's like, you think I might have some future in poetry. Very reassuring."

"You are scary," Boone told me. "I'm not worried about your future. I'm worried about Canada."

Because I was going to Vancouver with Aaron. All along, the problem had not been him, but me, and who would have thought it, my mother's advice: "Try and figure out what makes you feel good about yourself, then you can decide if it involves anyone else."

I had finally done something that made me feel good about myself. Now I was going to go back to school, but this time to try and understand how reading-allergic brains like mine worked. And then I wanted to find kids like me and read poems to them so that they wouldn't miss out on poetry, so they wouldn't feel so bad or shamed or left out. Or maybe play them music or take them to art museums. Whatever it took to make them feel good about themselves.

I STOOD WITH Aaron in my mom's driveway, saying good-bye to her and Oscar. I was leaving my truck with my mom. She was going to teach Oscar how to drive. It was early and the sky was still gray, and my mom was still in her robe. Oscar had a thermos of his special espresso for us. Batman kept looking through the rear window, waiting for us to get back in the car.

My mom was giving me another five pounds of advice for the road. "Did you make a copy of your passport? Keep it in a different place. Is your phone going to work up there? I don't think you need voltage converters, or do you?"

"No, Mom. Pith helmets, mosquito netting, but no voltage converters."

"Watch your smart mouth at the border crossing. Those people have no sense of humor."

"Mom, we need to get going."

"Aaron, honey, good luck with the new job. I know you'll shine."

"Thanks, I appreciate that," Aaron said, a good sport as always.

My mom hugged me, then she hugged Aaron. Aaron and Oscar shook hands. Oscar tried to give me a kiss on the cheek, but I dodged him. Once we were in the car, I put the window down to wave. I heard my mom yell that I should call her. Oscar cupped his hands to his mouth and hollered after us: "Let me not to the marriage of true minds admit impediments!"

We reached the end of the street and headed for the freeway. We exhaled and smiled at each other. Finally underway, and on our own. "What was he saying?" Aaron asked. "About marriage, what?"

"Don't worry about it. It's just Oscar, and he's just happy."

The body is a house. Who lives within?

ACKNOWLEDGMENTS

My thanks, as always, to the wise and indefatigable Henry Dunow. My gratitude to Arielle Datz for assistance above and beyond the ordinary. Thanks to Kathy Pories for her enthusiasm and guidance. To Chris Stamey for his careful reading of the manuscript, and to everyone at Algonquin, who bring experience and skill to the production of quality books.

Fond greetings to my California friends, Laurel Ladevich, Karen Serlin, and Fran Koenig, who help me get the details right and make me want to move back there. Thanks to Jim Tushinski, who has been on this writing journey with me for a long time now, and to Glen Worthey for his research skills, patience, and encouragement.

Above all this is a book for poets and fellow writers, the great and the small, the just starting out and the much acclaimed. Comrades in the struggle, wooers and sometimes stalkers of the muse: we are hopeful and despairing, ridiculous and sublime, often within the course of a single day. Let us continue.

the
POET'S
HOUSE

An Essay by Jean Thompson

Questions for Discussion

AN ESSAY BY JEAN THOMPSON

In James Conrad's great comic novel, *Making Love to the Minor Poets of Chicago*, the poetry is sublime, but the poets are all too human. They scheme and gossip, compete for jobs, fellowships, and awards. They form strategic alliances, envy each other's publications and even each other's apartments. And the biggest prize is the chance to write a poem that will be engraved on the doors of the Yucca Mountain Nuclear Waste Repository. It will be a peculiar kind of literary immortality, measured by the half-life of plutonium. It serves as a fitting device for the absurdities, seductions, betrayals, and high jinks that follow. It's all good fun, because who among us doesn't enjoy seeing the very serious practitioners of literary truth and beauty brought down a peg or two? I'm also remembering very early television, and Ernie Kovacs's sketch comedy character Percy Dovetonsils, who lisped poems while wearing a smoking jacket and fake eyeballs.

If you write, as I have my entire adult life (fiction for me, not poetry), you can find yourself meditating, or brooding, on the disjunctions and contradictions of the writing life. How literature is both central to our culture and marginalized. How much bloody work can go into even a mediocre or downright bad book, how fickle is fame or recognition of any kind. And how mismatched a great achievement and its ordinary, fallible author can be. Or, as I wrote once in a short story, "There was for every artist the awful moment when they stepped out from behind their splendid creation and revealed the meager, human-sized self that was bound to disappoint by comparison." Except the artist in the story is a baker, and her creations are pies. A much more transitory medium than that nuclear mountain.

Why write? Why even try? Why put yourself through the exasperation, the effort, often enough thankless, invisible, unrewarded? Forget, for the moment, questions of vanity, fame, money. We have a human need to make words sing. If a piece of writing has ever made you giddy, made you burn or soar, made you think or feel, then you know the urge to take up the sword yourself. And just beyond your hearing, teasing you, leading you on, is the ideal of what you wish to say, and how wonderful it will be once you get it exactly right.

There are those who get it right and those who never do, those whose job it is to sit in judgment, and those whose job it is to resist the judgments. As it was in the beginning, is now and ever shall be.

How did my novel come about? I began to tell myself a story about a group of poets. I chose poets rather than fiction writers, both because poetry is the purer literary art form, and, more important, because I don't write it myself and could hope to approach it with more objectivity. I wanted to poke fun at my poets, while at the same time taking them absolutely seriously. I wanted to show that even the most difficult and ungainly personalities can produce poems of merit, of genius. (And unpleasant people can produce unpleasant writing; we know this to be true.) A few years back, I took a trip to see migrating sandhill cranes at one of their flyway resting stops in Indiana. After a day spent foraging in farm fields, the cranes, which are huge, prehistoric-looking creatures, gather by the hundreds in an open field, strutting and preening, calling and squawking and flapping their wings in courtship rituals. They resemble nothing so much as a literary cocktail party. Yet once they take flight, cranes can glide for hours.

The characters in my novel's literary flock are all pure inventions, although most of their quirks and traits are borrowed from life. I knew from the outset that there would be a woman poet, accomplished, queenly, with a mystery somewhere in her past. That mystery only took shape as I wrote. It had to do with the sacrifices one makes for love, and for art, and the particular difficulties faced by women artists. I knew I wanted a group of other poets, friends and acolytes, who would gather round her and fill in parts of her story.

I wanted this group to be introduced and observed by someone who was a newcomer and an outsider. Somebody watching the flock of cranes with binoculars and a notebook. My narrator is a young woman with challenges and issues of her own, who falls in love with the poets and with poetry itself. She is, in James Conrad's apt phrase, "the empty vessel politely asking to be filled."

Comedy, like virtue, is its own reward. If my reader laughs half as hard as I do at my own jokes, I will be content. But comedy also implies its opposite, the tragic mask. Writers are censored, silenced, exiled, jailed, and executed because they have power, and because that power can threaten. Anna Akhmatova memorized her poems and burned the scraps of paper to hide them from the secret police. The dictator of Chile forbade a public funeral for Pablo Neruda; thousands lined the streets in defiance. Amanda Gorman gave us an inaugural poem that rang out like a bell.

Finally, *The Poet's House* is my love letter to Northern California, a place I think of fondly when the Midwest is at its most severe, when we have snow one week and tornadoes the next. Here is my vision: a comfortable old house, and a beautiful garden in lingering afternoon light. Someone is pouring wine, someone is preparing food. Someone is quoting Yeats, someone else, *Alice in Wonderland*. All of us here are writers, by the grace of God. And God is merciful, God is wise. He knows exactly what it is we keep trying to say.

QUESTIONS FOR DISCUSSION

1. What factors do you think contribute to Carla feeling stuck and unhappy? How much do you think is coming from herself, and how much is due to the people around her? How are the two intertwined? If you have had a phase in your life when you felt stuck, how did you overcome it?

2. What is it about Viridian that speaks so much to Carla?

3. To what extent does social class, or perceived social class, play a role in how Carla is treated by others?

4. What do you think of Viridian's decision(s) in relation to Mathias's work?

5. In what ways does Mathias's relationship with Viridian circumscribe her career and reputation as a poet? Can you think of other relationships between famous artists that influenced the trajectory and reputation of the woman?

6. What do you think of Viridian's characterization of poetry and talent in this exchange with Carla:

"You think writing poems has something to do with talent? Not much at all. It has to do with pure, stubborn determination to keep doing it, to not be discouraged by the thousand thousand things that are meant to discourage you. Nobody cares if you do it or not. No guarantees that anybody is going to read any of it."

"But that hasn't stopped you."

"Because I have been absolutely selfish about my art. Do you know how hard it is for a woman to be selfish?"

7. Have you ever been to a writers' retreat? If so, did this portrayal match your experience, and in what ways? If not, were you surprised by how Thompson describes it?

8. Carla says she feels "the ache and hunger that can both be awakened and soothed by a poem." How would you describe her ache and hunger? When have you felt this, and with what poem? Was it related to a moment in your life that you can remember?

9. Oscar Blanco says, quoting William Carlos Williams, "It is difficult to get the news from poems, yet men die miserably every day for lack of what is found there" (p. 24). What does he mean for Carla and Aaron to take away from this?

10. What do you think of Carla and Aaron's relationship? Do you sense a power imbalance, and if so, why?

11. Carla's mother tells her, "Women can't get away with things the way men can" (p. 20). Why does she say this to her—what is she hoping to teach her daughter?

12. What did you think of the book's ending? How has Carla changed? What has she discovered about herself? How has Aaron changed?

© MARION ETTLINGER

Jean Thompson is the author of fourteen books of fiction, including the National Book Award finalist *Who Do You Love*, the *New York Times* bestseller *The Year We Left Home*, and the *New York Times* Notable Book *Wide Blue Yonder*. Her work has been published in the *New Yorker*, as well as dozens of other magazines, and anthologized in *The Best American Short Stories* and the *Pushcart Prize*. She has been the recipient of Guggenheim and National Endowment for the Arts fellowships, among other accolades, and has taught creative writing at the University of Illinois, Reed College, Northwestern University, and many other colleges and universities. Visit her at jeanthompsononline.com.